The OUTLAW'S DAUGHTER

ANNA ROMER

For my dad, Bernie

1

SOLAINE

1866

GOLDEN SUNLIGHT FILTERED through the stable doors, casting long shadows across the hay-strewn floor. Magpies warbled outside, and the morning air was fresh with the mingling scent of horses and leather.

I watched my daughter's small hands patting the grooming brush over the pony's neck, her little teeth nipping her lip in concentration.

"Don't be shy, love," I said, guiding her hand. "She trusts you, see how she leans into your touch?"

"Like this, Mama?" Charlotte smoothed the brush across Sparkle's chestnut coat slowly and with more pressure, her brown gaze darting to mine.

"Exactly. You're good with her, you know." I smiled, tucking a loose strand of dark hair behind her ear. "Your grandmother was wonderful with horses. Her name was Charlotte, too, though everyone called her Lottie. You remind me of her."

"I do?"

"Hmm, she was brave and beautiful, just like you. She loved horses and rode every—"

I tensed, cutting my gaze to the stable door. The faint thunder of hoofbeats broke into the quiet, getting louder.

"Someone's here," I murmured, my pulse fluttering in my throat. Dust churned out in the yard, and the pounding became a roar as four armed men on horseback approached the house.

A shiver went through me.

The stable vanished. Years stripped away. I was twelve again, watching from the window as mounted troopers surrounded our family farm. My father's resigned face as they dragged him out, cuffing his wrists. His eyes finding mine: "Be brave, little sparrow."

Charlotte tugged my skirt. "Who are they, Mama?"

I blinked in the golden light, forcing my lips into a smile. Taking the brush from her, I set it aside, my fingers trembling slightly as I drew her protectively to my side.

"They've probably just come to see Uncle," I told her, moving closer to the doorway, keeping to the shadows. "Let's stay in here with Sparkle, out of their way."

Through the stable door, I watched the dust-covered hunting party dismount in the yard. The leader, his sunburned face creased in a frown, held something in his hand that made my stomach knot—a sheet of rumpled paper.

Uncle Niall emerged from the house to greet the men.

"Morning, Commissioner," the trooper called, removing his hat as he approached my uncle. "I've news of a convict who escaped from Cockatoo Island a month back. We've had reports of robberies south of Tamworth. It could be him heading this way." He brandished the paper. "Here's a likeness, in case you see him around."

Uncle Niall took the paper, squinting at it in the morning light, the breeze catching his sparse gingery hair, a frown carving his bony face.

"Cockatoo Island, you say? Thought it was inescapable?"

The trooper spat into the dust. "Turns out he knew how to swim. Most don't."

"He's a long way from Sydney." My uncle's voice was carefully neutral, but his jaw ticked. "Reward?"

"Government's offering a thousand pounds for his capture," the trooper said. "Dead or alive."

I inhaled sharply, and Uncle Niall glanced over to where we stood in the shadows of the stable doorway. His eyes locked with mine, a silent warning, before turning back to the trooper.

"A thousand pounds?" He huffed, handing back the drawing. "A hefty sum. The bounty hunters will be out in force. What's this fellow's name?"

"Henry Hawke." The trooper tucked the paper inside his jacket. "Been in chains for ten years, escaped with another inmate who was shot and killed in the water. One of them murdered a guard before they jumped. It was likely Hawke, he's a vicious mongrel. Deadly as they come."

As they described the convict—tall, dark-haired, with some kind of bird tattooed on his forearm—I touched my throat. A phantom noose tightened, cutting off my breath. My father used to have a bird tattoo, a sparrow. He used to flex his arm so the muscles bunched, making its wings appear to move. *My work takes me far and wide, Solaine,* he used to say, his eyes crinkling. *But my little sparrow always guides me safely home.*

"Oh, Papa."

I shuddered, closing my eyes, flashing back in time. Twelve years old again, standing in the courthouse yard with Uncle Niall's hand clamped on my shoulder, drowning in the smells of wet hemp rope and tears as I watched the noose slip over my father's head—

"Mama?" Charlotte whispered.

I blinked, willing my racing heart to slow as the sound of retreating horses pounded along the road.

The stables smelled of horses and leather, not hemp rope and fear. Charlotte was safe beside me, her dark hair catching the morning light that streamed through the open doorway. Not Papa. Not the gallows.

Uncle Niall entered the stables, his footsteps heavy on the packed earth floor. Charlotte peered up at him with enormous eyes, but he barely glanced at her as he strode to the stall where his big horse Caesar waited.

I'd saddled the bay gelding earlier that morning, knowing Uncle had a long day inspecting the new goldmine north of Elliotville. He took his role as Gold Commissioner seriously, and news of the convict would now occupy him until the man was caught.

He led his horse through the doors and outside, swinging up into the saddle, glancing back at Charlotte and me as we trailed after him into the sunlight. He sent me a look—stark and disapproving, as though blaming me for the criminal's escape. Blaming me for all the heartbreak he still carried inside him.

Charlotte waved to her uncle, her small hand fluttering happily. He tipped his hat at her, his angular face grim.

"Take the child inside, Solaine," he called over his shoulder, gathering the reins. "Lock the doors while I'm gone."

I nodded, my arm tightening around Charlotte's shoulders as the morning sun beat down on us. We watched Uncle Niall ride away, his back straight, disappearing in a cloud of dust down the long drive.

"Is Uncle cross, Mama?" Charlotte's dark gaze followed until the swirling dust hid him from view. "Did we do something wrong?"

I sighed, steering her back towards the house. "He's not cross, love. He's worried, that's all."

"About the bad man?"

A chill ran through me, chasing the morning's warmth. "He's got a lot on his mind. He's an important man, and clever too. He'll make sure they catch the convict and lock him up again. You can count on it."

2

HENRY

A MONTH of running had worn me down to the bone.

My stolen clothes hung in tatters, stained with sweat and dirt and dried blood, my bare feet cut and bleeding. I'd tramped through the roughest bushland to avoid the roads, slamming between trees at the slightest noise, walking nights, sleeping days in hollows, putting as much distance between myself and Sydney as fast as I could.

The landscape grew more familiar. The granite outcrops and tall ribbon gums, the sharp blossom-scented air I'd known since childhood. Moonlight filtered through the eucalyptus leaves, casting dappled shadows that played tricks on my exhausted mind. Was someone following unseen? A native tracker reading my trail in the dirt?

I stopped to listen.

The night was thick with sounds—crickets chirping, the rustle of creatures in the long grass, the distant hoot of a boobook owl. At least there were no hoofbeats. No men giving chase. Not yet.

I walked on, letting the moonlight guide me, cursing when a stone jabbed my bare heel.

No shoes. No proper clothes. No horse. No papers. Nothing but the rags I wore and a desperate plan that had fallen to pieces before I'd even left Cockatoo Island.

"Trust me, Hawke," Barclay had said, his voice low as we huddled in the shadows of the stone yard. "I've got a boat waiting, a man with papers, the whole shebang. You just follow my lead."

I'd been a fool to believe him. Fred Barclay, confidence man, murderer, liar. I had known what he was and trusted him anyway, because after ten years, desperation made even the most transparent lies seem plausible.

The sound of running water drew me forward. I knelt by a creek, cupping the cool liquid to my cracked lips, splashing it over my face. In the moonlit surface, I caught a glimpse of myself—gaunt cheeks, wild eyes, ragged beard.

The face of a hunted animal.

Barclay's plan had gone wrong from the start. No boat waiting. No accomplice with fresh clothes and papers. Just the two of us, diving into the harbour as shots rang out, swimming for our lives towards the far shore. Barclay had sworn he could swim.

Another lie.

His panicked thrashing had drawn the guards' attention. I had watched from further out as Barclay's body was dragged from the harbour, full of bullet holes. Worse, one of the guards lay dead on the dock, Barclay's shiv buried in his throat.

Murder of a prison guard. The noose was already tightening around my neck for that, never mind my original crimes.

I pushed on through the bush, each step battling the deep bone weariness that threatened to overcome me. I must be fifty miles south of Elliotville, a fraction of the distance I'd already come. But it seemed never-ending.

A month without proper food, snatching fitful moments of sleep hidden in hollow logs or dense thickets. The hunger was a living thing now, clawing at my insides. Making me stumble. Clouding my instincts.

A faint light flickered through the trees ahead. I froze, suddenly alert. Slowly, I crept forward, staying low to the ground.

A small farmhouse came into view, a single lantern burning in the yard. A man stood swaying beside a hitching post, the stench of cheap rum carrying on the night air. Before him, a saddled black mare shifted nervously, head lowered, hip bones visible even in the dim light.

As the man approached, bridle in one hand, whip in the other, the mare's eyes rolled white with terror. She reared backwards, tossing her long mane as the man raised a whip and lashed it hard across her flank.

"Worthless nag!" His slurred voice carried in the still night. "Cost me more'n you're worth in feed!"

The crack of leather on flesh made my jaw clench.

I knew that sound too well, had felt it across my own back more times than I cared to count. Something stirred in my chest, an emotion I'd thought dead after ten years in chains. Anger, yes, but not the cold, calculated kind that had kept me alive in prison. This was hot and immediate, directed at the drunken fool beating an animal too loyal or too tired to fight back.

The whip cracked again, and the mare's scream of pain drew me from the cover of trees. I moved closer to the yard, keeping low.

"Easy, girl," I murmured under my breath. "Easy now."

The mare's ears flicked towards my voice, and for a moment she stilled. The drunk, thinking he'd finally broken her spirit, stepped forward with the bridle.

I stalked silently up behind him, one arm snaking around his throat in a chokehold that cut off both air and sound. The man struggled for maybe ten seconds before going limp. I lowered him to the ground—unconscious but breathing. He'd wake up with a headache and some bruised pride, nothing more.

I stripped the man quickly, donning his rough work clothes. They stank of sweat and rum, but they were better than the rags I'd stolen back in Sydney. I took his boots too and then turned to the horse.

She watched me with dark eyes, and when I approached her slowly, hands open and voice soft, she didn't shy away. She was even more beautiful up close. Probably three or four years old, with lean legs and a proud arching neck.

I extended my hand slowly, palm down. The mare sniffed cautiously, then nudged my fingers with her velvety muzzle. A good sign. I stroked her neck, feeling the warmth beneath her coat, the steady pulse of life.

"What do you say, beauty?" I smiled as she nuzzled my palm. "Fancy a ride north? I promise I'll treat you better than this bastard."

The mare whickered softly, as if understanding. When I

gently bridled her and swung up into the saddle, she stood steady as a rock beneath me. No bucking, no fighting—just a gradual tensing of muscles as if she couldn't wait to get going.

She moved like liquid shadow beneath me, her hooves barely whispering against the thin soil of the yard. By the time we reached the main road, she was running with the hectic joy of an animal finally free.

I felt it too.

The giddy sense of answering to no one. The promise of what lay ahead. Seeing my old friend again. A hot meal. A warm stable and fresh hay for my horse.

If anyone could help me disappear, it was Old Cap. False papers, maybe a job in his saddlery or stables until the hunt died down. A chance to become someone else, someone without the stain of Cockatoo Island on my soul.

Thinking of Old Cap, I smiled, leaning down to smooth my palm along my steed's sleek neck. "Cap's wife had a black mare just like you. Called her Shadowlark. What do you think of that for a name, eh?"

The mare whinnied, tossing her head.

I laughed. "My thoughts exactly."

Her stride lengthened as we reached a proper road, her hooves quiet on the packed earth. Above, the stars glittered brightly in the velvet sky, the same stars I'd watched through the barred windows of the convict barracks, dreaming of this moment night after night for ten years.

Freedom had a taste, I realised. Salt from the harbour, eucalyptus on the night air, the metallic tang of fear at the back of my throat. And beneath it all, the bitter knowledge that no matter how far or fast I rode, the shadow of the noose would always follow.

I urged Shadowlark into a canter, leaning low over her neck as the miles fell away behind us. Towards Elliotville. Towards Old Cap. Towards my chance at a life beyond chains. A life that hung by the thinnest of threads.

3

SOLAINE

"STORY, STORY!" Chubby fingers gripped my hand and drew me closer to the bedside. A little round face beamed up at me, cheeks flushed pink, eyes dark as chocolate, hair fraying from its plaits in black wisps. "Tell me a story, Mama!"

I flopped into the chair, settling my skirts.

It was late. She should have been asleep an hour ago. But how could I be cross? Tomorrow was her birthday. Five! It seemed only yesterday I was rocking her to sleep in my arms, a tiny bug in a rug I couldn't stop kissing.

You indulge the girl, my uncle complained. *If she asked for the moon, you'd be rushing around in search of a long enough ladder.* He was wrong, as usual. Proving once again how little he knew me. If sweet Charlotte wanted the moon, I'd sprout wings out of my back and fly her straight to it.

"What would you hear tonight, my sweet?"

"The escape conbict!"

"Oh." The convict, really? "Oh no, love."

Her eyes were wide, a little fearful. "Please, Mama?"

"But Charlotte, he's a wicked man. We don't want to know his story."

"Yes!"

The room felt snug and safe. Our own little haven tucked away at the top of my uncle's huge stately house. Lantern light cast a quivering glow over the patchwork quilt, the cast-iron bed ends, the yellow velveteen curtains. Warm January air wafted in, bringing the scent of jasmine.

"What about the dancing princesses? Or Red Riding Hood?"

"The conbict!"

Her eyes gleamed, her teeth white pearls behind cherry lips. Such a pretty child. Spoiled, according to Uncle Niall. Headstrong and wilful. Like her mother, he didn't say. He didn't have to. The way he looked at me, one eye narrowed, the other intent on my face as though trying to solve a mystery. He would shake his gingery head, his pale eyes boring into me. *She has the look of a gypsy, Solaine. That black hair, those heavy lashes. They didn't come from our side of the family, to be sure.* Oh Uncle, I would say, averting my eyes lest he see the anger in them. She adores you completely, isn't that enough?

"Mama?" Little fingers waved at me. "Story?"

Reaching over, I tugged her out from under the covers and pulled her onto my lap.

"There was once an escaped convict."

She shivered happily, melting against my warmth. "Henry Hawke."

Lord. Little ears. I grimaced against her hair. This was a

bad idea. I'd much rather have sprouted wings and given her the moon than a tale about that dreadful man. But ... oh well.

"He ran through the night, limping and hungry. His feet were bare and bruised, and he would have loved to stop and soak them in the creek. But on he ran because the brave lawmen were close behind him. Soon, he found a cave and made his home there, but the wicked thing could not find peace. He stalked through the bush, searching, until he found—"

"The princess."

Ah, the princess. Of course she'd pop up. She was Charlotte's favourite. Maybe there was hope for my convict tale, after all?

"Yes, Princess Marigold. She lived in a grand house by the woods with her noble parents. Marigold was special. Some said she came from the fairy fey. She could tie a bow with a flutter of her fingers. Whistle bush wrens from the trees. Heal puppy dog tears with a kiss."

"Could she fly?"

"No, but she could ride like the wind. She loved to ride! Climbing onto her mother's ink-black mare, she'd ride out to a beautiful meadow to pick wildflowers. Paper daisies and rock ferns, nodding orchids and shivery grass. Then she'd sit for hours sketching them all into her book."

"And then the conbict came!"

I cuddled her to me. "One day, a shadow slipped between the trees. A big, fearsome shadow. The birds stopped singing. The butterflies flew away. Silence descended on the meadow and Marigold sensed that all was not well. When she saw the ugly convict, she dropped her flowers and ran."

"But he catched her."

"In his big, strong hands—"

Behind us in the doorway, a floorboard creaked. My shoulders tightened. *It's only Daisy come to light the lamps, she'll see I'm still in here and not linger.* But there was no retreating footfall. Just the silent presence, watching. Waiting. Small hairs stood on the back of my neck. I cuddled Charlotte closer.

"Marigold began to pound the convict with her fists. But her blows did not put him off. Rather, they seemed to delight him. He bared his terrible teeth and carried her back to his cave, where she became his prisoner."

Charlotte's dark eyes peered up at me. "She didn't like the cave, did she, Mama?"

I gave her a squeeze. "It was dank."

"And dark!"

"Deep underground."

"No sun."

"Nor windows. The convict had barred the entryway, too. And in that horrible place, Marigold's fairy spark shrivelled up. Worst of all, the convict kept her awake at night scratching his fleas!"

Charlotte's little hands clamped over her mouth. She peered up at me, eyes sparkling as giggles rippled through her body.

"Fleas?"

I made a shocked face. "Don't you know? All convicts have fleas."

A soft grunt from the doorway. The boards creaked disapprovingly, and footsteps trod away. I frowned. *If Uncle Niall doesn't like my stories, then why does he listen at the door?* Trying to catch me out, hoping to overhear something incriminating? A slip-up? A lie? Or maybe something even more shocking … like the truth.

I bent my head and whispered. "Dirty smelly fleas and bad breath!"

Charlotte giggled into me, pressing herself against my chest, her fingers slipping up to cover her lips. She always laughed this way—silently, hiding her face—as though mirth was something to be ashamed of, to be hidden. I cocooned her in my arms, resting my chin on her warm head.

"Marigold dreamed of escape. She longed to return to the forest and collect flowers and talk to the birds. See her beloved parents. Night and day, she plotted and planned, but the convict blocked her every move."

"She got all worned out."

"As the months passed, she began to fade. The dankness of the cave seeped under her skin. She grew pale, refusing to get out of bed. She wouldn't even brush her hair."

Charlotte fought back a yawn. "So she … painting lessons."

"The convict thought it would do her good. And he was right. But it wasn't just the lessons. The moment Marigold saw the handsome young artist with his raven locks and kind brown eyes, her spirits lifted. As the weeks passed and colour and purpose and light filled her days, she came back to life."

Charlotte yawned contentedly, a heavyweight in my arms. I gathered her up and tucked her back under the covers. Kissed her brow and murmured against her skin.

"Soon, Marigold and the artist fell in love."

I glanced back. The doorway was empty. We were alone

with the shadows. I bent closer to Charlotte and stroked her brow, trying to ease away the tiny frown. No five-year-old should frown in her sleep.

"Their love was so great that it cracked the cave walls. Stones rained down and buried the wicked convict under the earth, where he couldn't hurt them anymore. Marigold and her true love returned to the forest where they built a home of their own. Soon, a little daughter was born to them."

Charlotte's eyelashes cast dark half-moons on her cheeks, and I couldn't resist pressing a kiss to one of them.

"A perfect little daughter who they loved with all their hearts."

4

SOLAINE

Downstairs, the parlour was dim, lit only by the dying embers in the grate and a single oil lamp on the side table. Uncle Niall sat in his leather armchair, staring into the flames as though searching for something in the glowing coals.

I poured him a sherry from the crystal decanter and carried it to him, the glass cool against my fingertips.

"Thank you, Solaine," he murmured, taking the glass without looking at me. Dark shadows hollowed his eyes, and he'd raked his gingery hair into unruly tufts.

He'd been working tirelessly for months, juggling the increasing responsibilities that came with the tidal wave of people drawn here by the gold boom.

The new Elliotville mine was ten miles north-east of town, and Niall spent much of his time sorting disputes between miners. *When a man is driven by greed*, he liked to say, *his conscience takes a back seat.* Knife fights were frequent, and deaths occasional. He had acted as magistrate, even coroner. But his duties didn't stop there. Gold had to be weighed and transported in heavily guarded coaches to Sydney. Hundreds of new prospectors had to be licensed and added to the electoral roll. Construction at the mine needed overseeing.

Once, I asked him why it mattered so much. Why he worked so hard. The long hours, the worry of the gold, the threat of bushrangers and knife fights and mine shaft collapse. He needn't have worked at all. His family was wealthy, and—at least for now—he also had my vast inheritance to draw from.

But he'd looked at me, surprised. *You ask about things you can never hope to comprehend, Solaine. Politics and business are a man's domain. Now, fetch my reading glasses, there's a girl. And go on back to your stitching.*

He sipped his sherry, eyeing me over the rim.

"I heard your story."

I settled into the chair opposite him, smoothing my skirts. Daisy had laid out a teapot and a cup for me, but the tea had gone cold. I poured a cup anyway and topped it with milk, gulping it down.

"News of the escaped convict spooked her, Uncle. It's all she's talked about all day."

"But your stories." Another sip. "Must you fill her head with rot?"

"She was frightened," I said, my voice cooling. "What else should I tell her?"

"The truth." His voice hardened. "That outlaws like Hawke are dangerous men who prey on decent folk.

Conmen, thieves. Murderers. Men of low class, and even lower morals. Charlotte's father was no better."

I gasped softly, my knuckles whitening around my teacup.

"How can you say that, Uncle? Billy was a good man. The best."

"He was weak." He scoffed, swirling the amber liquid in his glass. "A dreamer with no idea how to care for a family."

"Unlike you, I suppose, Uncle? An exemplary family man?" I bit my tongue, but it was too late to take back my scornful words. I shrank inside, gripping my teacup, my attention fixed on the leaf dregs that swirled at the bottom.

I could feel him glaring at me, his rage burning like a furnace in the cold room. He had gone still, his head turned towards me like a vulture spying a carcass.

"Haven't I given you everything?" he said in a low, hard voice. "Everything you ever needed—a home, provisions, fine clothes? A secure future for your child—all at my own expense? Aren't you happy here at Elliot House with me?"

I set down my cup with a sharp clink. "Of course, Uncle. Very happy. But as you know, next year I'll come into my inheritance. I plan to buy a small farm."

Uncle Niall looked at me sharply, his shoulders suddenly rigid.

"Farm?"

"Yes, it's always been my dream. To breed horses, like Mama wanted. There'll be livery yards, and pastureland for horses too old to work."

"Breed … dear God, Solaine. How can you even think such a thing? Especially now, with a murderer on the loose?"

"They'll catch him long before my inheritance comes through."

Uncle Niall sighed, massaging the groove between his eyes. "Money has a language of its own, Solaine. One that women don't understand."

"I'm sure I'll—"

"What, muddle through?"

"Whatever I don't know, I'm willing to learn."

He sighed deeply, a shudder running through him as though his well of patience was moments from running dry. "So typical of you, Solaine. Waiting for a knight in shining armour to ride up and save you. You're so like your wretched mother." He gave a low snarl. "Lottie was wilful and strong on the surface, too. But you lack her conviction. The moment life gets tough, you crumble. You need a lesson in gratitude, my girl. So you understand how harsh life can be in the real world. Maybe then you'd truly appreciate what you have here with me."

"But, Uncle—"

"But nothing." He cut me off, setting his glass down with such force that sherry sloshed over the rim. "Your plans are foolish at best. Whoever heard of pasturing worn-out old nags? Besides, plans have a way of turning sour, Solaine. You of all people should know—"

"Mama?" Charlotte's small voice interrupted from the stairway. She stood on the bottom step in her white night-gown, her wispy dark hair tumbling loose around her shoulders, eyes wide and troubled. Her tiny fingers plucking at her lip.

"I dreamed the conbict took Sparkle."

"Oh, darling!" I crossed the room quickly, taking her small hand in mine. "Come on back to bed."

Uncle Niall rose to his feet and stalked over, looming

above Charlotte. His face softened as he looked down at her, but there was something cold in his eyes that made me pull her closer to my side.

"You're right to be frightened, Charlotte," he said. "That man they were hunting today is a very bad criminal. The worst. Men like him destroy families. Corrupt good men." His stare flicked to me, sharp as a blade. "Lead them to the gallows."

I stiffened. "Charlotte's already frightened. She doesn't need to hear this."

"On the contrary." Uncle Niall's voice was silk over steel. "She needs to understand the consequences of keeping dangerous company. Consequences that her grandfather learned the hard way."

The tension between us crackled like the dying fire. Charlotte looked from one to the other, confusion clouding her small face as she sensed the undercurrents.

"Was my grandfather a bad man, Uncle Niall?" she asked in a small voice.

I squeezed her hand. "Your grandfather was a good man who made one mistake—trusting the wrong people."

Uncle Niall's eyes narrowed at me. "A mistake that cost him his life. And nearly cost us everything."

He reached out, touching my shoulder, his fingers pressing too firmly into my flesh.

"I couldn't save your sweet mother from ruin, Solaine," he said. "I warned her about marrying your father, but her infatuation with anything wild and untamed addled her mind. Thank God I was there to save you. And now your child." His grip tightened momentarily. "My methods may seem harsh, but I'm only trying to protect you both."

I moved away from his touch, keeping my expression neutral even as my heart hammered against my ribs. "And we're very grateful. Aren't we, Charlotte?"

The child nodded obediently, but her eyes remained troubled, darting between us.

"Come on, sweetheart," I said, steering her towards the stairs. "Let's get you back to bed."

As we climbed the stairs, I could feel Uncle Niall's eyes following us, watching with that peculiar intensity that had always unsettled me, even as a child. Charlotte's hand was warm in mine, trusting, and I felt a surge of protectiveness. I would not let her grow up caged as I had been, bound by fear and obligation. One day, we'd both be free.

IN HER BEDROOM, I tucked her under the quilt and smoothed the hair from her forehead. "Close your eyes now, little wisp. Think of happy things—riding Sparkle through the wild meadow, picking blackberries by the creek."

"Will you stay till I'm asleep?"

"Of course." I settled beside her on the bed, humming softly until her breathing deepened and her small face relaxed in slumber.

While she slept, I took out my sketchbook and began to draw her—the curve of her cheek, the fan of her eyelashes, the wild tumble of dark hair against the pillow.

Uncle Niall was wrong. About Charlotte's father, Billy. Billy had been a gentle soul, a free spirit who marched to no one's beat but his own. He cared nothing for the power and influence that motivated my uncle and his rich landowner friends. What mattered most to Billy was family and love. Yes, he was an artist and a dreamer, but he had loved me and baby Charlotte, and he'd been mine.

My Billy.

I shut my eyes. How easily it came back to me, that long-ago day. Me and Billy, our faces flushed from the sun. I was sixteen and he was twenty-one—a thin, bespectacled young man with a chesty cough and watery eyes. Beautiful eyes. Brown as warm chocolate, endlessly deep as they gazed into my soul and promised me the world. *We'll have lots of children, Solaine. And a cottage on the edge of a pretty valley, with geese and a garden, and horses—*

Anyone would think he'd been the one to lead me astray. But I had eagerly led him, begging and pleading until he'd given in and we slipped from the house one twilight, hand in hand. Racing each other to the edge of the forest, the same forest I'd explored as a child.

We lay in the long grass and told tales of our lives. His brothers, all so different to him, his family of woodcutters big and burly as the trees they hewed. While Billy—my sweet Billy Fernley—had blinked and coughed his way through adolescence and then into adulthood with a paintbrush in one hand and an inkpot in the other.

"Oh, love," I murmured. "You were the best of men."

It had broken my heart when Uncle Niall insisted I return to my maiden name. *If something happens to me, Solaine, you'll inherit the Granger fortune. And think of Charlotte, my dear. If tragedy left her motherless, your legacy would secure her future—*

I looked down at my drawing and sighed.

I'd captured my daughter's features but missed her essence, the spark of life that made her uniquely Charlotte. There was just the hint of her father—Billy's earnestness in her brow, his warmth in the gentle curve of her lips.

Setting aside the drawing, I wandered to the window and stared out at the moonlit road where the hunting party had appeared this morning. The night was quiet, the landscape bathed in silver, beautiful and wild.

Somewhere out in that darkness, a man named Henry Hawke was running for his life. And somewhere beyond that lay the freedom I craved.

I pressed my palm against the cool glass, my breath fogging the pane. In less than a year, I would have the means to leave this gilded cage. To build a life where Charlotte could grow up free from Uncle Niall's suffocating protection, his warnings, his control.

But freedom came with risks. I had seen firsthand the price of defiance. My mother had fled her wealthy family to marry a humble saddler with big dreams and limited prospects. A man she loved and adored with all her heart.

A man with secrets.

Deadly secrets.

A man Uncle Niall had bitterly blamed for her death.

Behind me, Charlotte stirred in her sleep. I turned from the window, watching the gentle rise and fall of her chest. Tomorrow was her birthday, and I'd planned something special. A surprise picnic. Uncle would not approve, but I didn't care. For Charlotte's happiness, I would risk anything. For her, I'd find the courage that had deserted me for so long.

No more fairytales. No more dreams deferred. When my inheritance came, we would go—Uncle Niall's warning be damned. I would not let fear rule us any longer. I'd not let my uncle scare away my plans.

Yet even as I pressed a kiss to my daughter's forehead and slipped from the room, his words followed me. *Plans have a way of turning sour, Solaine. You of all people should know that.*

5

HENRY

Elliotville had changed in ten years.

Once a sleepy locale with barely more than a general store and public bar, its wide streets now bustled with people.

Most had come because of the gold. Finding work in the mines or plying trades that served the miners. There was an ironmonger selling everything from shovels and sluiceboxes, to spoons, billycans and rope. Bakery, butcher shop, blacksmith. Even a haberdasher with bolts of fine cloth in the window.

I lingered on the street corner, hands deep in my pockets, hat pulled low over my face, getting my bearings.

It felt good to be back. Good to have decent clothes and boots that actually fit.

I'd traded some stolen goods for cash on my arrival last night and wrangled some supplies. A package of tea. Flour and sugar. Matches. Soap. A generous sack of oats for Shadowlark. A length of rope and a sharp knife, some snaring twine, and saddlebags to stow them in.

All I needed now was to see Old Cap and get those false papers. See where I stood on finding employment until the hunt for me died down.

Last night, I went to Old Cap's cottage outside town, my heart aching hard as memories punched through me, but the place was abandoned. I'd stalked around for a bit, my spirits plunging when I saw the stables run down and the horse yards in disrepair, the verandah—where I spent some of my happiest times—collapsing under neglect. The family, who I always thought of as *mine*, were long gone. Old Cap's saddlery in Hay Street was the only other place I knew to try.

I turned along the main street, then stopped.

A tall woman stood on the verge of the thoroughfare, a child tucked beside her. They wore expensive clothes, looking totally out of place among the dust and scattered horse dung littering the dirt road.

I stared at the woman.

Her silk skirt gleamed like copper, her fitted blouse a pale translucent material that moulded to her curves, the garment seeming too fragile for anyone to wear at all, least of all into the rough streets of a place like Elliotville. Maybe an elegant parlour, not that I'd ever seen inside one of those.

The only places I knew were made of hewn timber with dirt floors. Or stone walls with barred windows. Which I'd be returning to in a flash if I lingered here in open view much longer.

The woman glanced along the street in my direction.

She was frowning, her dark hair restrained, a single rebellious tendril fluttering on her cheekbone as if trying to get her attention.

It had my attention.

Fully. Completely.

Lord. Blame it on my years in lockup, but the sight of her soothed my soul. Like sinking into steaming bathwater, up to my neck in fragrant comfort. Wrapped in something soft and gentle that made my stony heart ache as if mortally wounded—

The little girl at her side chirped, and the woman smiled down.

I froze.

Struck by her raw beauty … and her smile. Like a ripple of something forgotten reaching me from years past. Had we met before? Ha, not likely. But her face. Her goddamn beautiful face. The way her smile lit her up.

In all my long years in lockup, the cold, heartbroken nights I'd pictured myself curled in a woman's arms to escape the pain of another brutal beating or humiliation— even my wild imagination could never have conjured a beauty like hers.

"Jeez, Hawke. Get a grip."

The woman frowned, glancing in my direction.

I took a step back, lowering my eyes.

Leave, man. While you still can.

I tipped my hat to her—*why, you fool? She's not even looking* —and turned away, but the little bird at the woman's side chirped again. Her tinkling voice made me glance back. She was a tiny version of her mama with a mop of dark hair and rosy apples in her cheeks, her eyes quick and bright.

She made me think of another child from long ago.

That little one had been a chatterer too, always chirping and squawking. Little Sparrow, I'd called her. It started as a joke, but stuck. Even Old Cap had started calling her that.

"Which reminds me," I murmured, shaking off the memory and moving along the main street towards a narrow alleyway. I needed to see my old friend … and then get the heck out of town.

6

SOLAINE

THE STREETS of Elliotville buzzed with the energy of a town on the rise.

The new gold mine was booming, and miners and their families flocked into Elliotville from across the colony, bringing high expectations. The main thoroughfare teemed with loaded wagons, packhorses, and crowds of hopeful prospectors.

Charlotte gripped my hand tightly as we navigated the chaos, her wide eyes taking in everything.

"Look." I pointed to a shop on the other side of the road with brightly coloured fabric draped in the window. "Guess what we're getting today."

"A new dress?" She looked up at me with wide eyes.

"Of course, my pretty wisp. It's your birthday." I squeezed her fingers gently. "And then I have another surprise for you."

"What surprise?"

I laughed softly. "You'll have to wait and—"

The thunder of hooves and wheels made me look up.

A loaded dray was careening down the street at a dangerous speed, the ruddy-faced driver swigging from a bottle, the reins slack in his hand. The horses—startled by something in the crowd—were fighting the bit, their eyes rolling white with panic.

"Charlotte!" I pulled her back towards the walkway, but the dray lurched sideways as one horse faltered, swinging in our direction. The driver jerked to attention with a curse, hauling on the reins and sending his team into a panic. They reared and plunged, the heavy wagon swaying behind them like a ship in a storm.

I scurried further backwards, but my heel caught on the uneven ground and I lost my footing, Charlotte's hand slipping from mine as she stumbled forward in panic, tripping directly into the path of the maddened horses.

Time slowed to a nightmare crawl.

I scrambled across the ground for her, fearing we'd both get crushed. I saw her small figure sprawled in the dirt, saw the iron-shod hooves descending towards her like hammers, heard my scream tearing from my throat—

A man exploded from the crowd like a bolt of lightning.

He moved with the grace of a wildcat, scooping Charlotte from the ground and rolling them both clear of the stamping hooves. The lead horse's shoe struck sparks from the stony earth exactly where she'd been lying.

For a heartbeat, everything was in an uproar—the driver shouting, the horses screaming, dust filling the air. Then strong hands were setting Charlotte on her feet beside me, the man towering over us like an avenging angel.

He reached for me, and I gripped his calloused fingers as he hauled me to my feet, and then Charlotte was in my arms, safe and wriggling warm. Her little heart raced, while mine thumped low and hard, a fist punching the breath out of me. My hands trembled as I checked her for injuries, my pulse so wild I could barely breathe.

My daughter elbowed away from me and stood gaping up at the man who'd just saved her life.

He crouched in front of her.

"All right there, little ladybird?" His voice was deep and rough, with the drawl of someone raised in the bush. "All in one piece?"

She nodded, blinking at him with round eyes.

"Thank you," I gasped, gathering her to me and pressing my lips against her hair. Dashing the wetness off my face as I finally looked at our rescuer. "Dear God, thank you—"

Storm-blue eyes met mine, and the world tilted sideways.

His face was rugged, unshaven. Framed by black hair in need of a cut. A scar marked the skin above his lip, a whitish notch, and a bloody graze darkened one swooping eyebrow. But those eyes. Blue and deep as the ocean, and just as fathomless. Just as cool.

Just as dangerous.

I stepped back, pulling Charlotte against me.

"I ..." The word came out as barely a whisper. I cleared my throat and tried again. "I'm grateful, sir. Truly."

Charlotte wriggled free again, peering at the man. Her smile was luminous. No fingers to her lips, no hiding behind her hand. Just a big, open sunbeam of a smile.

"My name's Charlotte," she announced, as if they were

meeting at a tea party rather than in the aftermath of near disaster. "Today's my birthday. I'm five."

"Is that so?" A smile ghosted across his features, and he leaned in as if with a secret just for her. "I think five's gonna be your lucky number, Miss Charlotte."

He glanced at me and then reached near my foot to pluck something off the ground. A yellow ribbon, fallen from my daughter's braided hair.

"Best not lose this," he said softly and passed it up to me. His large fingers brushed mine as I took it, his shirt cuff riding up. A bloody welt scarred his wrist, and a tattoo peeped from under the cuff, an inky wing that quickly vanished as he stood.

"Oh," I blurted, meeting his stormy blue gaze. "We should go."

"Probably wise," he agreed, but neither of us moved.

The crowd was already dispersing, the excitement over. The drunk driver had wrestled his team back under control and disappeared down a side street, leaving only the lingering smell of horse sweat and spilled rum. But I remained frozen in place, manners forgotten, staring at the man who seemed as lost as I felt.

I took Charlotte's hand, gathering her to my side. "I am much obliged, sir. Good day to you."

With his gaze still locked to mine, he touched the brim of his hat, leaning in a fraction, a gesture somehow so intimate that a scorching flush pulsed over my skin. Then he melted away back into the crowd as suddenly as he'd appeared.

I stood there for a long moment, Charlotte's small hand in mine, watching the spot where he'd vanished. My heart was still racing, but not from fear. Something far more dangerous had taken its place.

Curiosity. Yearning for something I had no name for.

An ache in my bones that made me feel restless. Uneasy. A tiny bit wild.

"Mama?" Charlotte tugged at my skirt, her small face tilted up, worry creasing her brow. "Was that my pa?"

I stared at her in horror. What a thing to say. I took her hand and forced my feet to move, leading her towards the haberdashery.

"Of course not, Charlotte. You know your papa's in heaven. That man was—" I glanced along the thoroughfare, frowning. He was dangerous. A feral thing who'd probably acted from instinct, that was all. "Just a stranger, love."

"Will we see him again?"

Lord, I hope not. "I doubt it. Come along now. Let's visit Mrs Simmons for your new dress."

I hurried her across the road, my fingers damp around her small hand. She seemed unbothered by her near escape. Kept craning around, looking over her shoulder. Trying to tug her fingers from my grip.

As we reached the haberdashery, she finally twisted free and took a step back.

The street bustled with people, darting between horses and drays and market carts, or congregating in tight-knit huddles at the curbside. But the man who had just saved my daughter's life had vanished among them as though into thin air.

I took Charlotte's hand again, holding it tightly.

Trying not to think of him.

His tattoo. The wings peeping from his frayed cuff. The brutal scars circling his wrist.

I shivered, remembering the trooper's description. *Henry Hawke is tall and dark-haired, with a bird tattoo on his forearm.*

But it wasn't just that. I'd sensed something about him, something vaguely familiar. The jaunty angle of his hat, the snug-fitting waistcoat, the belt buckle. He was just like my father, I realised. Not in looks, but ... in his style. His manner. A ghost from the past, returning to haunt me.

I huffed a sigh.

Uncle Niall was right about my tendency to crumble under pressure. I was blowing a molehill into a mountain. Yet my mind was buzzing. I couldn't let it be.

Many men had birds inked on their skin. Alone, it meant nothing. But the ill-fitting clothes, the fresh graze and shadowy bruise. The air of danger, as though he was keeping himself on a tight rein.

He's a vicious mongrel, deadly as they come.

Should I report the encounter? Make a detour to the police station, describe the man who had ... just saved Charlotte's life.

It seemed wrong.

Repaying a man's kindness by placing him under suspicion. Besides, he was probably just some harmless drifter come to find work in the mine.

We turned away and entered the haberdasher's shop, but I couldn't shake the memory of his direct blue stare, or the way my pulse had stumbled when he smiled. The way he made me think of someone long ago. Someone torn away, now lost to me.

Whoever he was, he was also the reason my daughter was still breathing.

And God help me, I knew exactly which mattered more.

7

HENRY

I DUCKED INTO A LANEWAY, glancing over my shoulder.

I'd been a fool to stop in the street back there.

Of course, I'd never have let the little girl get trampled. But what possessed me to linger, chatting with her? All the while, the mother's eyes were raking over me, a stranger in town, wondering who I might be.

A right fool, that's who.

The only reason I risked showing my face in Elliotville was to see Old Cap. To ask him to write me up a letter of introduction with a false name. It would set me up as a free man, effectively wiping out the past. Wiping out a lifetime of bad choices, wrong steps. Wrongdoing. Give me what I'd always dreamed of—the chance at a new life.

I looked over my shoulder.

The lane was empty, but beyond it, the main street was full of people. Carts and drays, horses. Somewhere, a barking dog. I'd seen no sign of the traps, but that didn't mean I could relax. Maybe the woman was making her way to the police station right this minute, my name ready on her lips to turn me in.

I hunched into my coat, walking faster.

Lord, what a fool.

At least I wasn't a drunken fool, like the idiot in the dray who'd almost run over the child. I might be a wretched convict, but my heart wasn't entirely cold. Any man worth his salt would have done the same. She'd been a real sweetie, too. Eyes big as moonstones. Hair almost as black as my own, framing the heart-shaped face of an angel.

But that wasn't what made me stop and help.

I'd seen something in her little face. Wide-eyed panic. Fear. It had wrenched something loose in me. Something I thought buried. A memory locked deep in the vault of my mind, dredged from my own short childhood.

I was eleven again, stumbling along the riverbank, mud slipping and sliding under me. The echo of screams ringing loud in my ears. Blood trickled down my face, my father's blood, gumming my hair, burning bright hot holes across the front of my shirt, the stench of death clinging to my skin. My eyes pulled so wide they hurt, breath scorching my throat as I stumbled away, away from the bodies cooling somewhere in the dark behind me ...

I grunted softly, shrugging off the memory.

Fool.

Long ago, I'd mastered the art of banishing my demons down into the murky depths of my soul, where even I feared to venture. I kept them chained there like wild animals, padlocked in the dark. But from time to time, something— the sun glinting off a knife, the smell of blood at night, the violent gurgle of the river—would loosen the chains and the beasts would escape, forcing me to battle them back into their shackles all over again.

I kicked a stone out of my path.

It wasn't just the girl, though. Somehow, in the span of moments, the child's mother—with her wary eyes and lush unsmiling mouth—had unlaced me, gotten under my skin. Made me angry, somehow. Yet also warmed me, made my pulse race and my limbs grow hot.

I'd been invisible for so long, a lowly inmate, an animal— but she had seen me. She had looked at my face and seen me. Beyond the scars. Beyond the stubble and frayed clothes. Deep inside me, everything, even the wild things caged in the dark. And still, despite all that, she'd thanked me politely and let me shake her little girl's hand.

Lord, the way she'd almost smiled at me, the rush of hot thanks, as if I'd stepped forth with all guns blazing—heck, in that moment I'd have given her anything.

My blood quickened.

She'd cast a spell on me. Her dark hair fraying from its pins, her angry eyes. Her protective stance over her child, less the mother hen and more the lioness. The way she moved, carefully, as though using all her strength to rein in some raw force within her. Some fury. I had sensed a kindred soul, but it was the dark side of myself she spoke to. The secret side.

Fool. She copped a good look at your face. What are you, crazy? She's no kindred, and you sure as heck are nothing to her. She's probably talking to the traps this red-hot minute. She could get you caught. Hanged.

I huffed, not quite a laugh. "It's just a matter of time

before you swing, boyo. And if those sweet lips of hers hurry things along, then so be it."

That was a lie. I was all brim and bluster, as Old Cap liked to say.

I didn't want to swing. Not now. Not yet.

Not with freedom so close.

I turned down a side street, my shadow slithering along the stone walls. I scanned the rows of shops on either side.

These were alleyway stalls with none of the glamour of the bigger establishments that lined the main street. Their doors thrown wide, the busy darkness beckoning within. Bootmaker, blacksmith. The produce store where farmers congregated to buy their whetstones and scythes, their bags of feed in lean times. The imposing flour mill, and the forgery that plumed its hot metallic gases into the cool morning air.

Past all this, I came to a stone building with a weather-beaten sign swinging over the door. Beaumont's Saddlery. The door was bolted shut, so I rounded the building and pounded on a side door. A tremor shot up my arm, acid pooling in my gut. Bloody nerves.

Twelve years had passed since I last saw Old Cap.

Since I crept away in the night like a thief.

He'd given me a home and decent work and made me one of his family. But I'd been so broken, so twisted up with fear that I'd fled with a curse on my tongue and the burn of deep regret in my heart, leaving behind the man who'd been my truest friend. More than that, a saviour. A father, even.

"Beaumont?" I banged the door again. "You in there?"

Twelve years. Had it really been that long? I'd spent most of it under lock and key. Nights in chains, days of hard labour. Facing my night horrors with a belly full of maggoty meat and a guilty conscience. Cockatoo Island was an unforgiving place for the guilty. I'd taken a chance, knowing I wouldn't survive another day inside its punishing stone walls.

I leaned back, breathing in the sky.

The sun soared overhead, drawing ghostly veils of mist from the timber rooftop shingles. The sharp tang of eucalyptus and fresh hay filled every breath. How sweet it was, the taste of freedom. Cool and sweet like rainwater. Like the kiss of a good woman. I wanted to drink my fill of it—but first, I must make peace with Old Cap, convince the old man to help me.

Truth be told, he wouldn't take much convincing. A long time ago, Old Cap had saved my life. Despite our rocky history, I knew in my heart my friend would gladly save me again. Once I had my letter, I could make my way north and over the border to freedom.

I rattled the knob, then bashed on the door.

"Beaumont!"

After a stretch, a woman answered. She was middle-aged, sporting a mop cap and grime under her fingernails. She frowned up at me, tugging a moth-eaten shawl around her shoulders.

"You know what time it is?" She grimaced, shaking her head. "A sparrow's fart, that's what. By crikey, you'd better have a good reason for hammering down my door this early, lad."

It was past eight, the rest of the world already up and about their business, the sun bright in the sky, but there was no point vexing her further. Time was ticking. The sooner I got my papers, the quicker I'd be on my way.

"I'm here to see James Beaumont."

For a moment, she looked blank. Then her mouth dropped open. She glanced past me along the laneway, then narrowed her eyes.

"Been a while since I heard that name."

"Tell him it's an old friend."

She scoffed. "I won't be tellin' him nothing, pet. Old Jim Beaumont's been dead ten years."

I gripped the door frame. "Dead?"

"Hanged. Strung up for horse thievery, so he was. And a good thing too. He fooled the whole town into thinkin' he was respectable. A fine saddler and a man of good character. Next thing we know, they're callin' him Captain Twilight, with a price on his head." She narrowed her eyes. "Who might you be, askin' after the old mate? Friend of his, ye say?"

I backed away. "Never mind."

As I retreated down the lane, I heard the woman's voice calling, a new urgency in her tone. A man's voice answered, gruff and enquiring.

I ducked into a grassy lane and strode downhill towards the river. The banks were muddy, the narrow trail dotted with mossy boulders. My feet skated under me as I picked up pace, cursing under my breath.

Dead. Dead. Old Cap was dead.

As it sank in, a hollow ache opened up inside me, turning darker. Darker. It began to swallow me, and I steadied myself against the sensation of falling. Dropping abruptly into a black chasm, the breath knocked out of me, my inside twisting in grief.

The world was a poorer place now.

A desolate place. Old Cap had saved me countless times, not only my body but my soul. In the time since I'd known him, I never made a decision without first asking: What would Old Cap do? I'd always strived to live in a way that would make my old friend proud, a tough ask for a bushranger and horse thief. In the chaos of my life, in the darkness, Cap had been my guiding light. My truest friend, my protector. Now he was gone, there'd be no more saving. No false papers. No chance at freedom. And no way to wipe out a lifetime of regrets.

No way to make peace between us.

I huffed out a ragged breath. Shadowlark stood tethered to a gum tree further along the embankment. When I whistled, she tossed her head and greeted me with a whinny. I unlashed the reins and leapt into the saddle, and the big mare took off at a trot towards the road.

I would swing for what I'd done. The botched escape from Cockatoo Island. My crimes before. I didn't fear death. Lord knew I deserved to swing. But inside my heart burned a spark that wanted desperately to live. To turn it all around. Old Cap's wife had often talked of redemption—as much for Cap's ears as mine—but back then, redemption was just a word for weaker souls to fall back on. Out of reach for the likes of me. I hadn't finished punishing the world for what happened to my pa.

The way I felt back then, I'd never be finished.

From the time I was eleven, I'd been punishing the world with everything I had, and it had punished me right back.

Not just punished, but crushed. Broken. I was ready for change. For something better. A different life. Maybe even the redemption Lottie Beaumont had talked about all those years ago.

Maybe it was in reach, after all. Maybe it was waiting for me up in Queensland, and all I had to do to attain it, to start my life over, was to cross the border and grab it with both hands.

8

SOLAINE

"Have you heard the news, Solaine?" Mrs Simmons, the haberdasher, stopped cutting silk from the bolt and leaned on the counter. She cast a quick look at Charlotte, who was choosing a hair ribbon from the display, and then raised her brows expectantly at me.

I straightened my hat, repinning the crown. "What news?"

She set down her scissors with glee. "A convict escaped from Cockatoo Island. Killed a guard and swam across the harbour. Some think the sharks got him. Others say he fled into bushland. That was well over a month ago, and he's still at large."

I averted my gaze to Charlotte, then pretended to rummage in the chatelaine bag at my waist. Taking out a hanky, I dabbed at my neck.

"Elliotville's a long way from Cockatoo Island."

Mrs Simmons adjusted her spectacles. "Trappers found a

fresh camp out at the old prospector's site. That's only a few miles from here."

"Uncle says the new mine attracts all manner of drifters."

"Drifters might leave behind empty mutton tins." Mrs Simmons glanced at Charlotte and lowered her voice. "But few discard their sawed *manacles*."

I doubted this was true. The manacles would have been sawn and abandoned long before Elliotville. But even so, I shifted closer to Charlotte. She was humming to herself, intent on the ribbons. The flush had returned to her cheeks, her earlier encounter with the runaway horses—and her dishevelled rescuer—hopefully forgotten.

I smoothed her dark head protectively.

"Seems everyone's coming here for the new gold mine, Mrs Simmons. It's worse than a locust plague. But what business would a convict man have here?"

Mrs Simmons shrugged. "Passing through on his way to Queensland, most likely. Once over the border, he'll disappear into the tropical wilds. Others have done it. It's a lawless place up there, mind."

"With luck, his wicked bones are bleaching on the harbour floor."

"My husband says he'll come into town for supplies. And men like that –" She captured a fistful of silk, then quickly smoothed it back on the counter. "*Desperate* men will do anything to get what they want."

My shoulders tightened. I could still see his face. Rugged and unshaven, a notch of white scar near the lip. The bruised brow, his eyes like wild rivers, or the ocean …

I eased out a breath. "I don't like his chances. If Uncle Niall catches him, he'll be marched to the gallows quick smart." I gestured at the roll of crumpled fabric. "Three yards if you please, Mrs Simmons. We've a luncheon at noon."

Black scissors whispered through the thin yellow silk like a blade through butter, slicing a length from the roll. Mrs Simmons prattled on with her gossip. *Mark me, Solaine. With that wretch on the loose, we're not safe in our beds. Just think, an outlaw from Cockatoo Island in our quiet little town, who'd have thought?*

Charlotte chose a pale gold ribbon, which Mrs Simmons wrapped up with the fabric. She stopped chattering long enough to write our order into her book, but as I turned to go, she called out to me.

"Be careful, Solaine. This man will be desperate. Dangerous. Go straight home, now. Stay on the main road and don't dally on the way."

I tipped up my chin. "Thank you, Mrs Simmons. I'll be sure to take care."

Out in the fresh air, I breathed a sigh. People like Dorothy Simmons thrived on excitement and scandal. The merest possibility of anything new in our dreary little backwoods sent ripples through the bush telegraph. Ripples that could be every bit as harmful—if not more so—than a desperately hungry and frightened man running for his life.

"Anyway," I murmured to no one. "If they catch the wretch, he'll certainly hang."

How ragged my voice sounded. How raw. I hadn't meant to speak aloud. Heat flushed my face, my damp fingers leaving smudges on the paper parcel.

Calm yourself, Solaine. No one's been hanged in Elliotville for over a decade. Not since ... well, anyway, if this man is caught, they'll transport him to Goulburn and do the hanging down there. You won't have to look. Or smell the wet rope. You won't have to hear the cheering crowd, see his poor body swing …

Charlotte tugged my hand, frowning up at me. "Mama?"

I unclenched my jaw and dashed my fingers under my eyes. Gave her the parcel to carry. "Look there, my love. Is that Deacon waiting for us on the curb?"

"Deacon!" She danced along the street and thrust her parcel at the slender man waiting with our carriage. "Mama says we're going on a surprise."

9

SOLAINE

We picnicked on a blanket in the shade of a sprawling gum tree, the grassy slope stretching down to a babbling creek.

The wild meadow, my father had called it, because of all the wildflowers that ran riot here. Yellow buttons, golden hibbertia, white and pink paper daisies and purple rock orchids, their honey-sweet breath attracting butterflies that whirled like scraps of bright silk.

Deacon spread a blanket over a patch of bare ground and then retreated to water the horses. I unpacked the basket of food the tearooms had prepared especially. Lemon cordial, sandwiches, and an iced cake with Charlotte's name written in tiny marzipan flowers.

She clapped her hands when she saw it, but then pressed them over her mouth. Her eyes were suddenly huge, and then they filled with tears.

"Oh, darling!" I reached for her small hand. "What is it?"

She threw herself against me and buried her face. Her little shoulders shook, and I took hold of them gently.

"Charlotte, whatever's the matter?"

She drew back and peered up at me. She was smiling, but tears clung to her lashes. "I'm too happy, Mama."

"*Too* happy? Most people are never happy enough."

She shook her head. "Uncle Niall says it's unbeeming for a little girl to …" She shrugged her narrow shoulders and bit her lips. "Be too happy."

I frowned. "Uncle says being happy is unbecoming?"

Charlotte dashed her fingers under her eyes and wouldn't look at me. I poured her some lemonade and plated some sandwiches, and she munched away contentedly. Soon she was chattering about the morning, pointing out the butterflies. Then declared she was taking some sandwiches and cake to Deacon and the horses.

I stayed in the shade. The branches creaked overhead. A bee buzzed around my own untouched sandwiches, and I waved it away half-heartedly. *Unbecoming for a girl to be happy? But Uncle, children are supposed to be happy! Heaven knows they grow up all too soon and then they're bound to be miserable.*

The bee alighted on a lettuce leaf, but this time I didn't shoo it away. Was I miserable? Charlotte was my joy, my light—but outside the world of the nursery, beyond the little bubble I had created around her, was I happy? Or was I as guilty as Uncle Niall for teaching my little girl that happiness had limitations?

I shut my eyes, listening for my heartbeat.

There was just the sigh of wind in the branches overhead.

A quiet chomping as the horses grazed. And Charlotte's voice piping like birdsong as she chattered to our coachman. *The horses nearly squashed me, Deacon. You should have seen them, big dusty things with hard feet that would have stamped me to bits. But then a man flew in and saved me, he said five's my lucky number* — Her laugh twittered and soared for a moment, then cut off abruptly.

I looked over.

There were the little hands again, clamped over her mouth. The wide eyes, as though she'd done something wrong. Deacon bent at the waist and tugged the tail of her plait. He said something, and it got her tittering again.

Such a joyful little girl.

Such a pretty laugh.

Uncle Niall, I could wring your neck for teaching her to be ashamed of it.

I waved her over. "Charlotte."

She came running, her dark hair frayed around her head, her cheeks flushed from the heat. The bright yellow flowers on her blue dress glowed in the sunlight, a pretty meadow in miniature.

"Mama?"

"It's time for your surprise."

She blinked rapidly, her eyes going wide.

I drew her close and settled her near me. "I must warn you, though, Charlotte. It's going to delight you beyond words. So if you want to jump for joy or laugh or giggle with glee, please do so. Today's your birthday. Everyone simply *must* be happy on their birthday. It's ..." I waved my hands about. "It's the *rule*. Do you understand?"

Her little fingers clasped together in her lap. Big brown eyes watched me, so trusting. She nodded.

I drew out a tiny parcel tied with a silver ribbon and placed it in her hands. She untied it carefully to reveal a velvet box. She looked up at me.

I nodded. "Go on, love. Open it."

Inside the box, strung on a silk cord, lay a silver charm in the shape of a piglet. Charlotte cradled it in her palm, head bent over it, transfixed. The silversmith I'd sent my sketches to weeks ago had exceeded my hopes. The miniature silver piglet with a bow around its neck was perfect.

Charlotte studied the piglet, touching its snout and ears, its curly tail, and the tiny bow. Her eyes gleamed.

"It's Miss Abigail."

I cupped her cheek and kissed the top of her head. "You were so sad when she went to heaven. Now she can be with you every day. Here, let me help you put it on."

She turned obediently while I pushed her plaits aside and fastened the cord around her neck. "There, let me see. Oh, it's every bit as lovely as I'd hoped."

Charlotte flung her arms around my neck. "Thank you, Mama."

I held her tightly, blinking up at the sky. She'd been heartbroken when Uncle Niall ordered the piglet slaughtered for Christmas lunch. Her sweet eyes round in shock, her rosebud lips trembling. *No Uncle, please. Not Miss Abigail. Take one of the other piglets and spare her. She's my best friend! Please …* And then the tears. I had gone to Uncle, begging him to spare Charlotte's pig. Couldn't we keep it as a pet and have turkey instead? Of course, he hadn't swayed. Not even for his heartbroken little great-niece.

And that was the problem, wasn't it? The thorn between us, the unspoken bane of my uncle's existence. While he had never queried taking me under his wing after Papa died, my child was another matter.

The shame of it, Solaine. The appalling shame. That you'd tarnish the Granger name with the child of a good-for-nothing wastrel. A talentless painter, of all things! And after all that scandal with your father…

"Tell me a story, Mama."

I settled back, finding my smile again. "But it's not bedtime."

"Let's pretend."

A laugh erupted out of me. "What would you hear?"

"The conbict."

Of course. The wretched convict.

No longer a dark, hairy, ogre-ish blur in my mind. But still every bit the villain.

I sighed. Billy would always be the hero of our stories, no matter how many times I told them. Especially now, surrounded by wildflowers and dancing butterflies, in the pretty meadow I'd once escaped to with him the night we conceived our daughter.

I sipped my lemonade and settled back against the tree, already conjuring the memory of my handsome young painting tutor. To imagine, if only for a while, how different our lives might have been had fate not stepped in and torn us apart.

Still smiling, I shut my eyes.

"There was once a clever princess who lived in the woods—"

"Marigold!"

"Who loved riding her horse to this very meadow …"

As the story unravelled, a face appeared in my mind. Not the pale, bespectacled face of the man I'd once loved.

This new face was unshaven and rugged. With eyes as blue and cold as an ocean storm, and wings inked into his muscular forearm. And a notch of scar on the corner of his wide, unsmiling mouth.

10

HENRY

I RODE north out of town, glad to put Elliotville behind me. Two miles. Three. Bushland on either side, the road a ribbon of yellowish dust, the sun blazing high in the sky like a hot penny.

Shadowlark whinnied sharply, tossing her head.

I eased her to a stop. Ahead on the road, a large black-snake meandered across the dirt, its sleek body catching the sunlight as it disappeared into the scrub on the other side.

Soon the sun would blaze over the horizon and set the air alight. Summer up here on the tablelands could be blistering, but I liked it better than winter. When you lived off the back of a horse, heat was a far friendlier companion than bone-biting winds and icy rain.

At the crossroad, I turned west onto the old drovers road and slowed my pace. The Queensland border was maybe a ten-day ride north on the main roads. More, along the back-roads I'd be travelling.

The detour I was taking now would likely set me back another full day. Worth it, though. To make it to the border alive, I'd have to stay the hell away from people. And arm myself in case they refused to stay away from me. I'd never buy a firearm without drawing attention to myself. But if luck held, there might be one ripe for the picking.

Sweat trickled down the side of my face, and I thumbed back my hat, scratching my whiskery jaw. Without my false papers, I wouldn't get far. There was no one else I trusted enough to ask. There'd be a decent bounty on my head, too. I was probably outlawed. Which meant thanks to the Felons Apprehension Act passed in April last year, I could be shot on sight without warning. Any man or woman could take a potshot, fill me full of holes, no questions asked. And collect a tidy reward for their trouble.

Shadowlark whickered, tossing her head. Her ribs still showed, but the gleam was back in her eyes, the gloss returning to her coat. I had planned to fatten her up a bit more and sell her on, make a few quid.

But she'd gotten under my skin.

"Shadowlark," I said, smiling. "I'd no sooner part with you now than turn myself in."

Saying her name made me feel closer to Old Cap. Even now, on this dusty road, his voice filled my mind.

Henry, my boy, let me tell you a story. Old Cap loved his stories. *There once was a beautiful lady who liked to ride alone out along the old station road. One day, I planned to waylay her, but ended up fleeced myself. She stole my heart right out of my chest, all the while laughing, her pretty eyes twinkling like a sky full of diamonds.*

I smiled. A sky full of diamonds. Who spoke like that?

Old Cap was a gentleman to the core, though God help anyone who found themselves on a lonely road at the business end of Old Cap's rifle. A teller of stories was Jim Beaumont. A poet. A magician. A kindly gent in a dusty top hat and waistcoat. But lurking behind that friendly smile was a wily old fox who'd been outwitting traps since year dot.

The chasm opened in my chest, dragging me into its darkness. *Gone. Dead. Strung up for thieving—*

"Whoa, girl."

I twitched the reins, and Shadowlark slowed.

Up ahead, a swirl of dust lifted over the road. And sure enough, when I tipped my head to listen, there was the faint thump of horses. I steered onto the verge, then down the incline into the trees. When I was well hidden from the road, I dismounted, smoothing the horse's sleek neck with my hand to quiet her.

Four riders trotted along the road in the direction of town.

Traps, I thought at first. Hot on my trail. I pressed back further into the shadows, stroking the mare's velvety nose to calm her. Watching the men approach.

A strange bunch.

Not trappers. I eased out a breath.

But not ordinary folk, either. These men were bushrangers. None I knew, though. Two youths, one a mere kid with wispy bumfluff on his cheeks, and an older grey-bearded man nursing a rifle. The two younger men wore the highwayman's uniform —waistcoat and moleskin trousers, battered cabbage-tree hats. The older man had knotted a flamboyant green sash around his waist and tucked an eagle's tail feather into his hatband.

A fourth man rode up from the other direction and joined them.

He was another breed entirely.

Narrow-shouldered and lanky as a beanpole, hair laced back under a wide-brimmed Panama hat. Gentry, by the looks. A toff with money. He sat rigid in the saddle, a stranglehold on the reins, the heels of his shiny Wellington boots tucked hard into the stirrups. He took out a bulging leather pouch and tossed it over.

The older man caught it, weighing it in his palm.

One of the youths drew his handgun and aimed the muzzle at the sky. "Hoo-ha! A hundred quid each, we're bloody rich!'

The thin man glared over from under his hat brim. "Put it away, you brainless clown! No shooting, you hear? It's a clean job. No one hurt, or the three of you hang."

The older man regarded the toff a moment, then said something to the youth. Like a scolded dog, the boy stowed his gun and hung his head, his mouth working as he silently fumed.

The toff's horse started tossing its sleek head, its hooves stamping up dust. He jerked on the reins.

"Once the job's done, make yourselves scarce. Get out of Elliotville and lie low for a while."

The man pocketed the money bag. "What about the baggage?"

The toff took off his hat and dragged a forearm across his sweaty face, the breeze catching a strand of damp, coppery hair.

"Take her to your ma's place on Gloster Road," he said

impatiently, jamming the hat back on. "I've already paid her and given instructions for what's next."

Without saying more, he rode away at a gallop.

The others continued along the old drovers road.

I waited long after the sound of their voices faded. Finally, I returned to the road and looked both ways. The dust had settled, but the man's words lingered.

What about the baggage?

I shut my eyes. If I'd learned one thing from Cockatoo Island, it was this. Not all criminals wore chains or had blood on their hands. Not all were dragged down by a system that locked a man up for stealing bread to feed his family. Some criminals sat up high and dry, out of the mire. Untouchable. Some, like the pasty-faced toff, were above the law. They *were* the law.

I spat on the ground.

Then there were men like me. Guilty as charged, a bushranger. A horse thief, a liar and cheat. Yeah, I was all that. But I was also a survivor. I'd learned that the night my father died. You stay above ground, no matter the cost. Whatever you have to do, you do it just to keep breathing.

LEAVING THE ROAD, I headed into the bush.

The meadow was west of town, and if I followed the arc of the sun, I'd arrive there mid-afternoon.

The meadow.

Old Cap had taken me there years ago, when my father's

death still rubbed raw. It was Old Cap who'd pointed out the big old gum tree. Melliodora, he'd called it. Yellow ironbark. *You see that burned section in the trunk left by a lightning strike, lad? Look closer, that's right. It makes the perfect hidey hole for stashing things you don't want anyone else to find.*

I grimaced at the sudden ache in my chest.

"Bloody old fool. Why'd you have to go and get yourself hanged?"

I could still see the pride in Old Cap's face as he slapped the smooth bark with his hand, grinning fit to bust. Years later, I had returned to the tree and stowed a precious bundle deep in that same hidey hole—just before I was captured.

I followed a wallaby trail past granite boulders, then veered further into the trees. Uphill for a way, then along an overgrown track and down into a gully. The shade grew thick and cool, the sound of creek water bubbling nearby. As I breathed it all in, the knots in my neck and shoulders began to loosen.

"What do you think, Shadowlark? Smells like freedom, eh?"

The black mare twitched her ears.

I laughed.

It was freedom, all right. The smell of green, the bubbling creek. The flecks of warm sunlight on my bare arms, my face. And my beautiful sleek mare whickering contentedly, tossing her head as if she felt it too. For the first time since Cockatoo Island, hope flamed in me. Yeah, I was gutted over losing my friend. A true friend. Family, even. But Old Cap was part of me, always would be. The best part. The part I'd carry with me over the border into my new life.

I clicked my tongue, urging Shadowlark across the

shallow creek bed. Soon we were climbing a narrow trail flanked by bottlebrush and the grey-gold trunks of yellow box. I was moments from the meadow. My pulse kicked up. Downhill a way, and then through an alleyway of tall-trunked ribbon gums, their bark hanging off in long strips like flayed skin.

I broke from the shadows.

At first, the meadow looked the same. Butterflies dancing woozily in the warm air, drunk on wildflower nectar. The old eucalypt casting shade over grassy wildflower patches.

Then I frowned.

Were those wheel tracks in the dirt? I dismounted and let Shadowlark loose to graze. Under the tree, I knelt and ran my fingers over the compacted sward. Someone had been here. Recently. Maybe they'd only just left.

My pulse began to hammer. Going around the back of the tree, I knelt beside a blackened cavity in the trunk. Green-gold splotches of lichen had grown over the deadwood, and grass sprouted from the base. I reached into the hole and groped around.

When my fingers brushed a solid bundle, I let out a breath.

Still here.

I dragged it out. My old deerskin coat had mostly rotted away, but it had done its job of protecting the treasures wrapped inside it. A gold sovereign wrapped in burlap. And a neat little 1849 Colt revolver.

"As faithful a friend any man could want."

The wooden grip slid easily into my palm. I curled my finger against the trigger and lined my sights at the sky. It needed cleaning, oiling. But once upon a time, it had fired like a dream and would again.

Not that I planned on shooting anyone. That was a last resort only. I'd been down that road, and it wasn't one I wanted to travel again. Blood on your hands got you locked up. Or strung up. Neither of those was an option for me. If I ever again had the misfortune of getting caught, I'd take a bullet—heck, a belly full if I had to—rather than let the traps catch me alive.

I got to my feet, sliding the Colt into my waistband. As I strode down the slope towards my horse, a sliver of gold caught my eye on the grass near my boot.

A hair ribbon.

Same colour as the one I'd collected off the street this morning. It was scored in my mind, passing it to the girl's mother, the brush of the woman's fingers shooting sparks down my spine.

"Were you here?" I whispered. "In my meadow?"

I followed the cart wheel tracks a little way. They led towards the old drovers road, which wound through the hills and over a bridge back in the direction of town. The folks who'd been here were long gone. No point going after them on account of a ribbon. I had a border to cross, a new life to get on with.

A chubby heart-shaped face filled my mind.

The little girl with the wide moonstone eyes. And the woman who'd unlaced me with her haughty stare. The woman who'd seen me. Seen beneath my tough old hide to … what exactly, I dreaded to think. But whatever she'd seen, she hadn't flinched away.

"Get a grip, Hawke. She's so far out of your league it's laughable."

Besides, the ribbon could have come off anything.

A lady's bonnet. A whore's garter. Anything.

I wound it around my finger and slid it into my pocket. Then I stalked down the slope and whistled to Shadowlark, swinging up into the saddle and clicking my tongue. Soon we were back among the trees, deep in the dappled shade. Riding north now towards the border. Towards freedom.

11

SOLAINE

THE CARRIAGE JOLTED along the road towards home, Charlotte dozing against me.

One hand was curled in mine, like a baby bird in the nest. The other hand rested on the tiny silver piglet around her neck. Her rosy lips were caught in a not-quite smile, her eyelashes fluttering on her cheeks.

On her lap sat the haberdasher's parcel. She'd worked her finger through the wrapping, tearing a hole to admire the buttery silk that would, with Daisy's expert seamstress skills, become her new dress.

I stroked her dark hair, still warm from the sun.

She'd remember today always. Not the runaway horses that had almost trampled her. Not the stranger with the fierce blue eyes and scarred hands. Those would fade. Instead, she'd remember our glorious picnic. The cake and cordial, the butterflies and Deacon's gentle teasing. The sunlight and blossom-scented air. The bluebells we'd collected for her flower press, along with the big scratchy blackberry stems for me to draw. Most of all, she'd remember the little silver piglet, and our story under the gumtree.

If only we didn't have to go back.

Uncle Niall would be furious that I'd disobeyed him and not returned straight home. He'd rant until his face turned crimson. *When will you learn to heed me, Solaine? To rein in your impulsive streak and do as you're told?*

"Never," I whispered, smiling out the window at the sun skimming the hills. "I'll be too busy doing as I please. Collecting my inheritance. Buying my own farm. Living on my own terms instead of following your stifling rules."

The carriage shuddered and slowed.

"Miss Solaine." Deacon's voice cracked with urgency. "Under the seat, there's a revolver. Grab it and pass it up."

My body went rigid, heart slamming against my ribs. "Revolver?"

"Under the seat. Quickly now."

I leaned to the window and moved aside the drape. We were at Wattle Tree Bridge, water rushing below.

"Deacon?" I kept my voice low. "What's happening?"

Easing Charlotte onto the cushions, I cracked open the door and peered out. Three men on horseback approached— a heavyset older man flanked by two younger men. Features hidden behind kerchiefs, weapons trained on Deacon.

"Bail up!" the burly man called. "Hands in the air, and quick about it."

"We've no cash or valuables on board." Deacon's voice quivered. "Let us pass."

"Bail up, I say!"

I pulled back inside, heart hammering. Groping under the

seat, I found a heavy burlap-wrapped object and dragged it out. Deacon's revolver, recently oiled and fully loaded. I placed it in my lap, dragging my shawl across it.

The burly man appeared at my window. The kerchief over his bushy beard made his face look misshapen. Lank grey hair hung to his collar, small eyes glinting from under his battered hat brim. A feather swayed jauntily from the hatband, and he wore an emerald-green sash for a belt.

"Well, well." His eyes crinkled. "What've we got here, then? A hen and her chick."

I tore off my necklace and thrust it at him. "It's all I've got."

He leered at my throat. "What, no purse? Returning from town, coin all spent?"

I untied my chatelaine and tossed it over. "That's everything. Now let us pass."

His leer travelled slowly over me, then fell on Charlotte. She still slept, tucked under my arm, her head heavy against me.

"Miss Solaine?" Deacon banged on the carriage roof. "Are you all right in there?"

A thump. Then the crash of something heavy against the carriage wall.

"Deacon!"

The burly man drew back and gestured to one of his companions. Another man appeared, a youth with shifty eyes. He climbed into the carriage, his lanky frame dwarfing the cramped space, the stench of tobacco clinging to him. He reached for me—fingers yellowed at the tips, bristling with black hair—and clamped his hand around my throat.

"Nice and quiet, now. There's a good lass."

I moved my shawl aside. Gripping the gun with both hands, I jammed the muzzle into his belly.

"My father taught me to shoot," I said with more steel than I felt. "I'm a decent shot. Kindly leave my carriage, or I'll be cleaning your guts from my boots."

The youth drew back, eyes wide, rolling a startled look towards the burly man.

"Lower your gun, missus." The leader's voice hardened. "No one needs to get hurt."

"I have a child." My hands shook violently, finger quivering on the trigger as I fought to steady my voice. "Let us pass, and you'll hear no more from us."

His eyes flicked to Charlotte. Then he gestured to someone outside.

A latch clicked.

The door on the other side wrenched open. Sunlight flooded behind the broad figure of a third man, dark hair curling over his collar, his hat pulled low and his masked face in shadow. Movement flashed in my peripheral vision, and I flinched out of the way. Too late. Something hard cracked against my skull. I buckled forward clutching my head, the revolver clattering to the floor.

Hot sticky blood streamed into my eyes, and the carriage blurred. I blinked, grasping for my daughter as the shadowy man gathered her into his arms. I clawed for her, screaming her name as someone seized my wrists.

Charlotte's eyes flew open, pupils wide with shock, face crumpling. "Mama?"

I wrenched free and lunged for her, catching her in my arms, trying to tear her from the man's grasp. Almost had her—then an elbow rammed into my head. Stars burst behind my eyes. The man wrenched my child from my arms and dragged her from the carriage.

"Charlotte—!"

The grey-haired man loomed over me, the stench of his sweat gagging me. As he retrieved the gun from the floor, I slashed at his cheek, nails drawing blood and dragging away the kerchief covering his round, sweaty face. I snatched at his shirt front, driving my knee up into his groin and shrieking in his ear. He bellowed, swinging the weapon, bringing it down hard against my temple.

My body crumpled, bones turning liquid.

The carriage dimmed as a black wave washed over me, plunging me down into a dark, bottomless void.

12

SOLAINE

"MISS SOLAINE?"

The dim interior of the carriage flickered as a shape moved across the window. Scraps of sunlight speared through the drapes, hurting my eyes.

"My dear?"

A wet cloth pressed against my face. I shoved it away, but it returned, cold water drawing me up from oblivion. I didn't want to surface. I only wanted my child safe in my arms. My baby. How could I bear to open my eyes and find her gone?

"You've taken a blow to the head, Solaine. Can you hear me?"

Deacon crouched beside me, his hanky crimson with blood. His hand trembled. I lay across the seat, my hand searching for Charlotte. Finding emptiness, I bolted upright.

"Where is she?"

"Those men ... oh my dear, they've taken her."

The gash on his forehead trickled blood, a bruise already blooming under his eye.

"We must go after her, Deacon." A wave of giddiness rolled me over. "Now, before they get too far."

Deacon gripped my shoulder to steady me. "We'll go home first. You need a doctor."

I shoved his hands away. "I need my daughter!"

"Mister Niall will find her, Solaine. Once we tell him what's happened, he'll send out a party. Troopers, the best trackers. They'll find her. Those men were thieves, not killers. My guess is they're planning to ransom her."

"Ransom?"

"Everyone knows of Mister Niall's wealth. They're desperate men in need of coin. Your uncle will pay up, and then little Charlotte can come home."

"But she—" My throat clenched, thoughts tangling in a haze of panic. She would be so scared. Terrified. My poor little wisp in the custody of those evil men. My knees crumpled, but I forced my legs to hold. *His face. You saw his face, Solaine. He won't be happy. What if he takes it out on her?* I squeezed my eyes shut, a hot tear burning down my cheek. "Deacon, we have to find her."

Deacon patted my hand. "We will, Miss Solaine. I promise." He climbed heavily to his feet, gripping the doorway. "Rest, my dear. You'll be all right. Rest now."

He was wrong. I would never be all right.

Not until my girl was safe in my arms again.

I clambered groggily from the carriage and searched our surroundings. Dust lingered over the trees towards the west, drifting like dirty clouds. Below the bridge, the stream gurgled noisily, and faintly in the air I could still smell the sweaty reek of rum and tobacco and unwashed male skin.

Deacon called down from the driver's bench. "Miss Solaine?"

A shiver swept over me as I studied the dust clouds. "I'll find you, little wisp. I promise." I climbed up beside Deacon, warm sticky blood trickling down the side of my face like the tears I refused to cry.

"All right, miss?"

I nodded, settling beside him on the hard seat, a thought pecking the back of my mind like a hungry bird. I'd seen one man's face. I could identify him. Another had been barely more than a boy, with straggly fair hair and nervous eyes.

The third, the one who'd ripped Charlotte from my arms, was a shadowy blur.

Tall, broad-shouldered. Dark-haired.

His face deeply cast by the sunlight behind him, his eyes—

I frowned, trying to remember them. Failing.

My heart began to race. One by one, the day's events fell silently into place, forming a new picture. The runaway horses in Elliotville, the terror of seeing Charlotte tumble into their path. The stranger who had swept her to safety like an avenging angel. A tall, dark-haired stranger with manacle scars on his wrist and a prison tattoo.

The haberdasher's words I'd dismissed before now rang in my head. *Most likely on his way to Queensland. Once over the border, he'll disappear.*

"Deacon." I grabbed the coachman's arm, digging my fingers into his wiry flesh. "Make haste, I need to speak to my uncle. I know the man who took her."

THE SITTING ROOM WAS AIRLESS, the windows shut tight. The walls seemed close, too close, as Uncle Niall studied the likeness I had sketched hastily from memory. He took forever before his gaze finally lifted to regard me with thoughtful eyes.

"You saw this man in Elliotville today?"

"Yes, Uncle."

"Why didn't you go straight to the police?"

My mouth dropped open. I shut it and swallowed, then tried again.

"He saved her, Uncle Niall. He saved Charlotte. Some runaway horses almost crushed her, but he pulled her out of the way. She might have died if not for him—"

"But you saw his manacle scars?"

I lowered my lashes. "Yes."

"And the rough state of his clothes?"

I nodded, my stare unblinking as I viewed myself through my uncle's eyes. A trembling woman hugging herself, hair askew, pacing back and forth as if deranged. Blood leaking down her face, dripping off her chin onto his expensive Persian rug.

"And you chose not to report him?"

My lips parted, but the words would not come, so I nodded again. I had recognised an escaped convict, a dangerous outlaw wanted by the police. But rather than reporting him or rushing immediately home to tell Uncle

Niall, I'd taken Charlotte miles out of town to the meadow and spent a lazy afternoon by the creek. I'd only wanted her to enjoy her birthday, but now, because of my recklessness, she was gone. *Plans have a way of turning sour, Solaine. You of all people should know that.*

Uncle Niall poured himself a drink. "Describe him again."

The clock ticked. My heart wanted to gallop, the reins of self-control already slipping from my grasp. Sweat trickled down my sides.

"He was tall, Uncle Niall. Even taller than you. Black hair in need of a trim. He wore a waistcoat, I recall. A kerchief tied round his neck. And there was …" I frowned.

There was something familiar about him, coming back to me now like a shiver from a dream. The way he tilted back his hat, so jaunty. That scar over his lip, the white notch. I had seen it before, yet the face it marked was unknown to me.

My uncle frowned at the drawing clutched in his long fingers.

"Are you sure this is the man you saw?"

I nodded. "I'm sure."

He swallowed the brandy and replaced the glass on the sideboard with a click, giving my drawing an ominous shake.

"My dear, this man is Henry Hawke. He escaped from Cockatoo Island almost two months ago, killing a guard before swimming across shark-infested waters to freedom. Evading search parties across the state. He's ruthless and dangerous, Solaine. God help anyone who crosses his path."

I clasped my hands to stop them trembling. "Why would he take Charlotte?"

He waved his hand at me. "A well-dressed woman of

means. Clearly with money to splash around. He might have planned it with the other men, taken the girl, intending to ransom her."

"So they might send a note?"

Uncle Niall gripped the doorframe, his face stony. "Not all kidnappings go to plan, Solaine. You coddled the girl. Made her wilful and headstrong. Do you really think she'll survive long in the company of bushrangers?"

"Uncle, they'd never hurt her." I clamped my fingers to my throat. "Would they?"

His eyes gleamed darkly. "What else can you tell me about this man? Did he mention his whereabouts or intentions?"

I shook my head, casting back. It was all a blur now, the horses and dust. All except the man's eyes, the ocean blue depths that had swallowed me whole. Then I remembered Mrs Simmons. "The haberdasher said he might be heading north."

Uncle Niall frowned. "North?"

I nodded. "Towards Queensland. She said others have done it. Desperate men. Taking the backroads. Crossing over the state border to escape the reach of the law."

A narrow look came into my uncle's eyes. "Others, perhaps. But not this one. I'll send my best troopers immediately and notify the station up at Wallangarra. We'll catch this Henry Hawke, I promise you, my dear. He'll hang for what he's done to Charlotte."

13

HENRY

THE HORSE'S rolling gait lulled me in the heat, her flanks gleaming, and the landscape we rode through crackling in the hot sun. Lifting my hat, I elbowed the sweat from my face. The sun was high, the air ablaze. Even the tall eucalypts that flanked the road seemed to be holding their leaves very still, as if to conserve moisture and energy.

I'd been riding since dawn. It was now midday. White froth stained Shadowlark's muzzle, and she was favouring her right foreleg.

I looked back.

In the distance, almost too faint to see, a cloud of dust hovered over the road. I'd noticed it earlier. Probably a farmer droving his herd towards the sale yards in Glen Innes. Or another traveller like me, making slow progress along the dusty road towards the sweet promise of the north.

I steered off the road just in case, weaving into the trees.

On the rocky ground, the mare's limp was more

pronounced. When we reached a crop of boulders, I dismounted and uncorked my canteen. Filling the crown of my hat with water, I let Shadowlark drink and then poured what remained in the flask down my own parched throat, looking around.

I'd come this way as a kid.

Back when Pa and the other cedar getters came in search of red cedar. Those times were hazy in my mind, but one spot by the river was brightly alive. Cool blue glimpses through the trees, the icy splash of water on my sun-scorched limbs. The tang of fresh-cut cedar. Like the meadow, it was a sacred place. Where my good memories lived, tucked safely out of reach, untarnished by the bad.

I looked back at the road.

No sign of the dust cloud. I was alone out here. Exactly how I liked it.

Taking a curved hoof pick from my pocket, I leaned against Shadowlark's shoulder and patted her foreleg until she raised it. Gently holding the hoof, I scraped away the road dust and debris that clung to the shoe. Then I located a tiny stone wedged in the groove near her sensitive heel. I rubbed it out with my thumb and flicked it on the ground.

"There you go, girl. Good as new."

Staying close to her, I did her other hooves and then scratched her ears. Back in the saddle, I headed further into the trees and along a shallow gully until I saw the water.

On the bank, I dismounted again and let the horse graze in the shade. I placed the Colt on a rock and stripped off my clothes. In the cold water, my scars changed from faded pink to bluish white against the weathered tan of my skin. I dived under, scrubbing the dust and sweat from my hair, my eyes, my beard. Would be good to have a shave, a decent feed, but time was fleeting. These back roads were already holding me up, dragging out a journey that was already taking too long—

Shadowlark whickered.

Shrill in the quiet.

Then a metallic click. I jerked around. Three traps stood on the bank. One held Shadowlark's reins as she skittered and rolled back her eyes. Another was going through my saddlebags. The third—a burly dark-haired fellow with pock-marked cheeks and a sour smile—stood at the water's edge, the business end of his rifle pointed straight at my head.

14

SOLAINE

After church on Sunday, at my uncle's bidding, Deacon drove the carriage along Hill Street to the edge of town.

Elliotville's police residence was a humble structure—built of local granite, small and unimposing—but it wasn't the residence that made my breath catch.

Next to it, on a vacant paddock, sat a wide timber platform built from Cypress pine, though Uncle assured me the hanging beam was hardwood. Rough steps led up from the ground on one side, while in the centre of the gallows platform gaped a wide rectangular hole.

"The drop," Uncle Niall said, as though reading my thoughts. "Built so the fall is sharp, the break clean and quick. A small mercy, God knows the mongrel doesn't deserve it."

I swallowed the knot in my throat. "When?"

"We're awaiting the authorisation papers from Goulburn." He brushed his lapel, biting back a grimace. "No point taking him down there ourselves and risking another escape. A couple of days at the latest."

"Can I see him, Uncle Niall?"

He winced, surprised. "Why would you want to?"

"That yellow ribbon they found in his pocket, it was Charlotte's, I'm sure of it. He must know where she is."

"No, Solaine. He's already been questioned for many hours, to no avail."

"But, Uncle—"

"No." He frowned, tipping back his hat with a sigh. "Try to be patient. The police know what they're doing. You must have faith in them. We may hear news this very day."

"You keep saying that. And she's still missing."

He patted my hand. "I know it's been hard for you, my dear. I only thank God you're here, where I can help you. It galls me to think of you alone on some farm, having to cope with all this by yourself."

I plucked at the bandage squeezing my brow. "I'm grateful for all you've done, Uncle. But how can I bear another day not knowing if she's even alive?"

"You will bear it, Solaine." He glanced past me to the gallows, his eyes hard. "You must brace yourself to bear the worst."

I raised my eyes, my uncle's thin face blurring before me. A solitary tear slipped over my lashes and streaked hotly down my cheek. I hated him for saying so. Damn him, it was a cruel blow in the midst of my grief.

Yet wasn't he right?

After three horrible days, there was still no trace of my daughter. No ransom request, no sightings, not even a whisper that anyone knew a thing. But wasn't bracing myself the same as admitting defeat?

Uncle seemed to perk up. "Let me buy you a new horse, my dear. A lively distraction. The saleyard auctions are on Wednesday, what do you say?"

My lips parted to argue, but Uncle Niall reached up with his cane and rapped sharply on the carriage roof. "Move along, Deacon. We've seen enough."

As the carriage lumbered around, spraying gravel and dust from its wheels, I twisted in my seat to peer through the drape.

From here, the small dark building at the rear of the police residence was only just visible. I couldn't see the bricked window. But I could picture it. With *him* inside the cramped cell. His lean frame huddled in the gloom, his black hair tangled over his face. His heart beating in time to the clock that was ticking away his wicked, worthless life.

"Rot in hell, Henry Hawke." My breath burned hot on my lips. "For taking my child. For causing me all this grief. I pray your soul writhes in horrible misery for the rest of eternity."

THE WIND SURGED up on Wednesday as I stood on the back verandah staring across the garden. It stung my cheeks and tore my hair from its pins, whipping dark tentacles across my face. The tail of my bandage fluttered against my cheek, and I unwound it and tossed it into the garden, the wind catching it like a long white flag, whipping it away.

"Do your worst," I whispered to the wind. "Blow us all into the hereafter, for all I care."

Almost a week had passed since Charlotte was taken, but still no ransom note had appeared. My hopes withered more with each passing day. I'd barely eaten or slept, so when Daisy reminded me that Uncle Niall was taking me to the livestock sales today, my mood only plunged further.

We travelled in silence, my uncle's face grim as he stared through the carriage window.

He thought a new horse would distract me. But our stables were full of horses. What was one more? In a few days, when the authorisation arrived from Goulburn, Henry Hawke would swing. Whatever he knew of Charlotte would follow him into the grave. Uncle Niall would be congratulated for stopping another bushranger, and for everyone else, life would go on.

Everyone but me.

I slipped my hand through my hair, feeling for the scarred knot on the side of my head, left there by the bushranger's pistol. Uncle Niall and his network of police troopers might be satisfied to let Charlotte's trail grow cold, but I would never give up on her.

Never.

"I'll find you, my angel."

Uncle Niall looked over. "What was that, Solaine?"

I pretended not to hear, turning my face to the window, my gaze flitting over the wide dusty roads flanked by shops and houses, and little wooden market stalls that came and went with the weather.

I needed to return to the meadow, to the bridge where she was taken. It was a long shot, but I didn't care.

A long shot was better than nothing.

When Deacon pulled the carriage up at the saleyard gates, Uncle Niall climbed down, extending his hand to me.

Ignoring it, I managed the steps myself. "Thank you, Uncle. I'm quite capable."

Once inside the busy yards, he linked his arm through mine, steering me through the throngs of farmers and cattlemen to the showing pens. Only stopping when we reached a large fenced arena.

A beautiful chestnut mare stood patiently with her handler. When he clicked his tongue, she followed, her sleek coat turning copper in the sunlight that streamed inside. As prospective buyers shouted their bids, she did not flinch. Her large eyelashes fluttered gracefully. When the handler dug his fingers between her lips, she bared even white teeth.

"She's perfect," Uncle Niall breathed. "Worth the fortune her owner is asking."

I went closer. "She's a beauty, all right—"

A ruckus cut me off. Over by the corals, two men were trying to restrain a glossy black devil with wild eyes and a mane that whipped and snapped as she bucked against the tethers. My heart skipped. My palms went damp. Without a word to my uncle, I unlinked my arm from his and hurried over. As I approached, the horse let out a whinny so shrill the hairs stood up on my arms.

I nodded greetings to the handler. "What price for her?"

He ran his gaze over me. "Fifty quid, miss."

"I can see her ribs. I'll give you thirty-five."

He nodded, casting a nervous glance back at the horse. "She's a wild'un, miss. Needs a firm hand."

"Does she have a name?"

"That'd be Shadowlark, miss."

My blood quickened, and I took a step back, frowning at the man. "Who named her that?"

"The man who owned her before."

"Who was he?"

"A bad'un, miss."

"Why did he sell her?"

He cleared his throat. "You might say he's not long for this world, missus."

I was already reaching into my chatelaine. "I'll take her."

Uncle Niall jostled up beside me. He was pale, glancing over his shoulder before gripping my arm with firm fingers.

"Solaine, what are you doing?"

The handler scribbled a ticket, pointing me towards the collection yard. I turned to my uncle, brandishing the ticket triumphantly.

"I've found my horse, Uncle Niall. Gorgeous, isn't she?"

"But I've already paid for the chestnut mare." He huffed a sigh, hooking his hand into my arm, trying to tug me away. "Come, my dear. Once you ride her, you'll see she's the one you want."

"No, she's not." Ignoring his clutchy fingers, I went over to the black mare, approaching near her shoulder. She shied from me until I slowly lifted my hand palm-down. She extended her neck and sniffed, finally letting me stroke her velvety nose.

My heart softened.

What a beauty. Large, gleaming dark eyes and a proud neck. Faint scarring on her rump and flanks, ribs jutting through her skin, but her spirit sang to me. She'd been broken once, like I was now, and something told me we needed each other.

I ran my fingers gently up her face.

"Someone mistreated you, didn't they? Well, never again. I'll take good care of you, Shadowlark." Her name sent a shiver over my skin, a cascade of memories and hurt that I quickly shoved down. "You'll be safe with me, I promise."

15

SOLAINE

SHADOWLARK WAS SUREFOOTED, even on the bumpy trail that skirted the small township. She stayed nimble and light, her head high, her muzzle twitching in the fresh air.

We left Elliotville and rode west towards the wild meadow. The day had turned glorious, the wind settling, the sun burning brightly overhead. A faint haze hung in the air, pulling brilliance and colour from the most mundane of things, making everything glow. Pale tree trunks became luminous, and leaves caught shards of sunlight. As if under a fairytale spell.

I leaned forward, smoothing my hand along the horse's neck, tangling my fingers in her mane. She was warm from the sun, smelling of straw and fresh green grass and oiled leather.

"Shadowlark."

Shivers rippled through me. My mama had once owned a black mare with the same name. *Swift as a lark, dark as a shadow*, she'd say. *My beautiful Shadowlark.* It seemed impossible. Or perhaps a good omen.

Papa teased that Mama had loved that horse better than she loved him. Oh Jim, she'd coo, her face softening as she wove her fingers through his beard. You say the most ridiculous things. And then she'd smile, and my father's brim and bluster would melt clean away.

When Mama lay on her deathbed, her bandaged head seeping and foul-smelling, her last words were about that horse. *Don't let them hurt her, Solaine. Promise me, won't you? Take good care of my Shadow, and one day you'll be big enough to ride her and love her as I have …*

Mother had fallen while riding and bashed her head on a rock, and never quite recovered. She became forgetful. Irritable. Portions of her life were lost to her, whole memories gone. People and places swept under the fog, buried deep in those parts of her mind where she could no longer go.

That last day, she had found a moment's lucidity. Drawing me close, she whispered in my ear. *Don't let them hurt her, Solaine.*

I was ten. My mother was the queen of fairyland in my eyes. My father, the king. They were deeply in love, despite their age gap. He was older by twenty years, yet she adored him and he worshipped her. Both of them utterly absorbed by their closeness, by the world of romance and belonging they inhabited together.

There were times when they seemed oblivious to the rest of humanity, even to me. I never minded. How could I? Even as a child, I saw how rare and precious their love was.

The only thing they ever argued about was my mother's

black mare. *She's too wild, Lottie. Unpredictable. Every time you ride her, I die a little inside.*

That last day, I held her hand and reassured her. "I'll care for Shadow, Mama. No harm will come to her, I promise."

When she sank back into the pillow, her smile trembling in thanks, I bent and kissed her. Glad that I'd lied. Glad that, at least for now, I'd protected her from the truth. Maybe next time we spoke, I'd have the courage to tell her.

But there was no next time.

She grew more wasted, her body all bones as she retreated deeper into her mind. Perhaps in those final days, she was with her beloved Shadow. Riding like the wind through her dreams, free and unfettered. *Take good care of my Shadowlark, Solaine.*

My last words to her were a lie.

The very day of Mama's accident, my father had taken his shotgun and gone after the half-wild mare. Poor Shadow had broken her leg in the fall and would never run again. More than that, though, I think he couldn't bear to see the horse suffer my mother's absence as he would soon suffer it.

"Shadow, shadow," I murmured, dashing the wetness from under my eyes. "Swift as a bird, fleet as the dark. My very own Shadowlark."

The mare flicked her head, her mane whipping her face as one large eye rolled back to regard me. I leaned forward in the saddle, stroking my gloved fingers along her neck, scratching her mane.

"I can't wait for Charlotte to meet you." My heart gave a pang, darkness uncoiling in my belly. But I refused to let the fear take hold. "She'll be home soon, and the three of us will go riding together."

We rode onto Wattle Tree Bridge, pausing halfway so I could stare down at the creek rushing below us. I searched the banks and the sludgy water, but all I could see was my daughter's startled face as the man ripped her from me. All I could hear was her cry. *Mama!*

My brave little wisp, where was she right now? Still calling for me, wondering why I'd abandoned her?

The rocky banks blurred, but I gritted my teeth against the tears. Bending low over the mare, I urged her into a gallop.

Soon we reached the meadow with its butterflies and trickling creek, so beautiful, but suddenly so nightmarish to me. I slid from the saddle and walked unsteadily to the big tree, where—four days ago—our picnic rug had flattened the grass.

I stared around.

What are you looking for, Solaine? A footprint, a broken stem? Look over there, what's that white tatter on the ground? Another of Charlotte's hair ribbons, a handkerchief?

I ran over, heart thudding.

It was only a butterfly. Or what remained of it. Ants crawled over its wriggling body, its delicate wings in tatters.

Wiping my eyes in the crook of my elbow, I stomped the poor thing out of its misery. Crushed it under my heel until no shred of it remained. Then I ran about, searching the ground, absently plucking at the grass seeds that clung to my sleeves.

"Charlotte!"

Shadowlark whickered, as though to warn me. *You're doing what you said you wouldn't do, Solaine. Giving in to the fear. Letting it crack you in half.*

My ears rang, eyes streaming from the bright sunlight. My hat had fallen in the grass, but I left it there, climbing into the saddle, mopping my face on my sleeve. Another wave of panic gripped me, but I breathed until my vision cleared.

I rode the mare hard along the old drovers road, galloping up over the hill and down around the rim of the valley. Slowing again to stare across the landscape.

Boulders pushed from the thin grey soil, and narrow stock trails meandered through the trees. A dry wind dragged leaves through the dust, lifting them in swirls, tugging my hair as though trying to carry me off, too.

"Take me home," I murmured, leaning forward to smooth my palm down Shadowlark's sleek neck. "My baby's not here."

Shadowlark took off at a trot, her lean strength rippling under me, her pelt gleaming like tar in the sunlight. I nudged her with my heels, and she broke into a gallop, her long legs pounding the craggy trail.

As her muscular body moved under me, a feeling of raw power radiated from her, somehow seeping through me. It spoke to me in my mother's voice. *Failing is not the problem, Solaine. You will fail, and then you'll fail again—but that is how you learn. The real danger is in giving up.*

"Then I won't give up."

The wind picked up suddenly, as if electrified by my words, snatching my hair from its fastenings as one mile and then another sped under us. Soon, the oppressive helplessness I'd felt since losing Charlotte lifted.

The fog of my grief burned away. In its place, a hope so luminous I half-convinced myself that Charlotte would be waiting for me at home, her eyes bright as she threw her little arms around my neck.

And me squeezing her tightly, vowing never to let her go again.

CHARLOTTE WAS NOT WAITING for me at home. Instead, Daisy met me at the door and ushered me through to the parlour, where Uncle Niall greeted me, his face ashen.

"Solaine." He linked his thin hand under my arm and led me to a chair, tried to ease me into it. "Please, sit down."

I pulled out of his clutches. "Why, what's happened?"

He gripped my arm again. "My dear, the police found something. It's not good news, I'm afraid."

His pale face swam in front of my eyes, my heart impaling on my ribs. I brushed off his hands, stalking out of reach to the other side of the room, turning on him with shaky legs.

"Charlotte?"

He nodded, trailing after me, taking a scrap of fabric from his pocket. It was pale blue linen printed with tiny yellow flowers, the torn edge stained with reddish-brown splatters.

"It's hers," he said quietly. "Isn't it?"

My legs buckled. I wanted to deny it, but all I could see was Charlotte in the meadow on her birthday, her cheeks flushed as she ran towards me, her pretty dress glowing like the meadow in miniature.

"Where did they find it?"

"Near Wattle Tree Bridge. Caught in some briars by the water."

I tore the remnant from my uncle's hand and lurched across the room to the chair he'd offered earlier. I sank into it, the heaviness settling in my stomach, buckling me over.

Words of denial flooded my mind, a torrent of *no, no, of course it can't be hers*, but my throat was closed. My jaw clamped shut. My heart clenched so hard I couldn't breathe, let alone speak. *Charlotte loved flowers … she'd chosen the fabric herself, and would have worn it every day if I'd let her …*

Niall placed a glass in my fingers, the brandy swirling, its smell sharp as acid. I dashed it onto the floor, staring at the shattered mess as if from another life.

Another world.

"It doesn't mean anything," I whispered, crushing the blood-stained remnant in my fist. "She might have tried to run away from them. Tripped and hurt herself." I looked at my uncle, then sprang up, glass crunching under my shoes. "You must keep looking, Uncle Niall. Question Hawke again, force him to tell you what he did with her."

Uncle Niall shook his head. "The brute refuses to say a word. The more we ask, the more he mocks us with his silence."

"But can't you—"

"No, Solaine. My men have scoured the state already. This —" He gestured at the fabric in my hand. "This is the only bit of evidence they've found, and it's damning. I'm sorry, but your daughter's trail ends here."

He crunched over the broken glass to the drinks cabinet and poured himself a brandy, gulping the golden liquid before turning his dull grey eyes to me.

"It's time to unburden yourself of any foolish false hopes you still carry, Solaine. Your child is gone. And the sooner you face up to it, the more quickly you'll be able to recover enough to move on."

The bottom of my world dropped out from under me. The room began to revolve, and stars exploded in bright streaks behind my eyes. My vision tunnelled until it was just Niall's hard face before me, his words tolling like a death bell in my ears.

"Foolish false hopes?" I swallowed, gripping the blood-stained linen like a lifeline. "But, Uncle ... There must be something more we can do?"

"There is, my dear." Niall topped his glass again and drained it, grimacing. "Tomorrow at dawn, Hawke will hang. And you and I will be there at the gallows to witness his last gasping, dying breath."

My uncle's words rang hollowly in my head as I hurried across the dark yard towards the stables, the full moon's sour face peering down in disapproval. *Tomorrow at dawn, Henry Hawke will hang.*

"Yes, Uncle ... and he'll take to the grave any last hope I have of finding Charlotte alive." I slipped my hand in my pocket, rumpling the scrap of blood-stained linen between my fingers. "But I'm not giving up on her, no matter what you or anyone else says."

I approached the stables, shadows nipping at my heels,

the bright moonlight painting everything silver. Behind me, the house was dark and silent, everyone retired for the night.

"Deacon?" I called softly into the dark. "Are you about?"

I'd already checked his cottage. It was not like him to vanish so soon after dinner. Normally, he lingered by the kitchen door to carry out the scraps or share a glass of beer with Daisy. He wasn't in the garden, nor down in the paddocks. Unlikely he'd be in the stables at this hour, but faint lantern light glowed under the door. I shoved through and peered across the gloom.

A thin figure was bent over a broom, collecting slivers of hay. Slow sweeps, as though his heart wasn't in the task.

"Deacon."

He startled and turned around, mopping his face with his sleeve. His eyes gleamed, his lids puffy and swollen.

"Ah, Miss Solaine. Forgive me, I ahhh ..." He cleared his throat. "Miss Charlotte was so happy about learning to ride. Figured I'd tidy the place up for when she gets back."

"You heard they found a piece torn off her dress?"

He nodded. "I'm sorry, my dear."

I slumped. "It's my fault, Deacon. If only I hadn't taken her to the meadow that day. Uncle Niall warned me—"

"Hush, girl." He set aside the broom, fishing out a handkerchief and blowing his nose. "You wanted her to have a happy birthday, is all. No crime in that."

"I'm not myself. I hardly recognise the person I see in the mirror. What's happening to me?"

Deacon patted my shoulder. 'It's grief, miss. Your poor heart's broken."

"How do I fix it?"

"I wish I knew."

"I hate feeling helpless. Uncle Niall says the police are still searching. He says I need to trust that they know what they're doing. But after finding that torn piece of her dress, it feels like everyone's given up."

"But not you, miss."

I shook my head. "Deacon, I want to see Hawke. He's my last link to knowing what really happened to her. I need to talk to him, plead with him as a mother."

Deacon's face hardened, and he straightened his narrow shoulders.

"I'll come with you, of course."

"No." I glanced back at the doorway, to where the house sat like the shadow of a sleeping beast. "It's best if I'm alone. Hawke will be easier to persuade if he sees it's just me."

"Then let me ride with you."

"Thank you, but I need to do this alone. If you're there, I might lose my nerve."

I half expected a lecture about the dangers of a woman riding out unprotected, slipping into the jailhouse to face a dangerous criminal without backup.

But Deacon only smiled.

"You're stronger than your uncle lets you believe, Solaine. You are your father's daughter—and that's not the curse Niall says it is. It's your greatest strength."

A chill skated over me, and I rubbed my arms. He was wrong about me being like my father. I'd gone to great pains to be everything Papa wasn't—stable and respectable, doing my best to follow Uncle's rules. But right now, I was desperate enough to hope that maybe a few small drops of Papa's reckless blood flowed in my veins.

"So you'll help me?"

Deacon's smile widened. "My word, I will."

He rattled out the keys to the shed where the carriage was kept, and I followed him through into the cavernous darkness, waiting while he lit the lamp. The smell of kerosene sharpened the dry air, its glow flickering over the gleaming carriage.

Deacon climbed up into it, returning with a small revolver. It was newer than the one the bushrangers had stolen. The one I'd failed to defend Charlotte with. Since that day, I'd rehearsed holding the handgrip and cocking the hammer over and over in my mind, confident I wouldn't hesitate a second time.

Deacon placed it in my hands.

"Remember how to fire it?"

"You and Papa were exacting teachers."

"Just don't get too close to the man, Miss Solaine. He's dangerous. And far more cunning than you'll be expecting."

"Hmm," I murmured absently.

I opened the cylinder, counted six bullets, and then clicked it back in place, smoothing my fingers over the cool, burnished metal. So heavy. So deadly. And now that it was in my hands, so powerful a persuasion for getting what I needed most of all.

16

SOLAINE

In the stables, Deacon helped me saddle up the black mare. Shadowlark snorted quietly as I swung into the saddle and patted her glossy neck.

"Be careful," Deacon said, peering up at me in the lantern light, his eyes worried. "Don't turn your back on Hawke for an instant."

I nodded, then guided the horse along the drive, her hooves crunching softly on the gravel until we reached the road.

When the house lights faded behind us, I urged her into a gallop. The cold night air stung my bitten lips, my palms damp around the reins as we raced towards Elliotville. Towards Hawke. Towards the answers I prayed he would provide.

The streets lay in darkness, the walkways and shopfronts empty.

Shadowlark trod quietly, as though sensing my need to

stay unnoticed. We kept to the dark places, making our way behind the main road and then east along Hill Street.

Outside the police station, I dismounted and tossed the reins over a fence post. Moonlight rippled over the iron roofing, picking out the sharp angles of the gallows in the paddock. The station house was dark, the tiny lockup behind it swamped in the blackest shadows.

As I approached, a bright pinhead of light flared in the window, like a match being lit. The faint scent of tobacco warmed the air.

I paused a moment, my breath held.

The night guard was awake. Even if I spoke in a whisper to Hawke, we might be heard. I would have to keep our exchange quick, our voices low. If we were caught, what then?

I drew the gun from my waistband, holding it steady by my side. I would have my answers, whatever it took. Whatever the consequences.

Rounding the house, I crept towards the lockup yard and its two cells. At the first cell, I pressed my face to the bars and peered into the inky blackness.

"Hawke?"

The shadows inside the cell moved, fluid as spilled ink. I hastily stepped back as a man raised himself from the floor and, in a single stride, was at the bars.

"Who's there?"

His voice was ragged, though probably not from sleep. On a man's last night on earth, I couldn't imagine he'd care much for dreams.

"My name's Miss Granger."

"You're breaking me out?"

"I ... ah ..." Stealing a glance over my shoulder, I wet my lips. I'd memorised my questions, but in the excitement, they were suddenly stuck. "We met a week ago," I whispered urgently. "You saved my daughter from a runaway cart."

"You've come to thank me, then."

A flare of anger, my fingers tightening on the gun. "You'll get no thanks from me, sir. I want information."

A huff of annoyance as he pulled back from the bars.

"Can't help."

"Wait! My child was taken by bushrangers the day we met. They bailed us up on Wattle Tree Bridge. I know you were one of them. If you help me get her back, I'll have your sentence remitted."

Silence.

My palm grew damp around the gun grip. I risked a step closer. "Mr Hawke? My daughter's only five years old. Please, I need to know if she's still alive ... and where she is."

A heartbeat thundered past. Two.

His face appeared in the gloom, up close to the bars. Unshaven, his eyes blackly hollowed, the stern line of his lips pressed hard. A fearsome face, with a frown that smashed my hopes.

"I never took your child," he whispered. "Why would I pull her from danger, only to steal her from you?"

"To ransom her, of course. But if you help me, I'll give you money. All the money you need."

"It won't help me in the grave."

"Please."

"Why are you here yourself, a fine lady in the middle of the night. Where's Mr Granger?"

"My uncle's at home asleep."

"I mean your husband."

I inhaled the night air, suppressing a shiver. "Dead."

Hawke growled softly. "I left town soon after our paths crossed, Miss Granger. I never saw the girl again, I swear."

"You're lying." I raised the revolver and trained it on his face, pleased when his eyes widened at the sight of the weapon. "They found her hair ribbon in your pocket. You attacked our carriage with the other men. I saw you. It was you who ripped her from my arms."

A dark brow shot up. "You saw me?"

"The sun was in my eyes, I admit. But how else would you have her ribbon?"

"Maybe I found it in a lonely meadow." His eyes cut to the weapon. "That thing loaded?"

"It is indeed, Mr Hawke. And I know how to use it."

He sighed, slumping forward and spreading his arms wide, gripping the bars so his broad chest was in full view.

"Go ahead. I'd rather be shot by a wild-eyed beauty than choke to death from a poorly tied gallows rope." He eyed me in the darkness, the glint of a wolfish smile. "You'd be doing me a mercy."

Heat stung the back of my eyes. He was taunting me. I'd risked everything by coming here, and it was all for naught.

"You'll get no mercy from me," I hissed. "Tomorrow you swing! And I'll be at the front of the crowd doing a jig."

He started laughing, a booming echo that rattled the bars. "Your jig will cheer me immensely, miss. I look forward to it. A fine send-off to the afterlife."

"You fiend—!"

Footfall sounded behind me, the flare of lanternlight. A man's curse, and the click of a weapon being cocked. I whirled around, my revolver clenched tight, its sights now levelled on the night guard who stood at the edge of the lockup yard. In his ghostly underthings, with the barrel of a rifle pointed straight at us.

He motioned the rifle at me. "Drop your weapon, miss."

I did not want to drop it. I still needed answers before Hawke swung tomorrow, taking my last chance of finding Charlotte with him.

I took a step back.

A hand slid around my waist, light as a lover's caress. It gently eased me towards the bars. As I realised what was happening, I stiffened, but the brute held me firm. His other hand took the gun from my fingers and tucked the muzzle under my chin.

"Careful now, son," Hawke said calmly to the guard. "I'd hate to see the lady harmed. Lay the rifle on the ground and step back."

The guard hesitated.

Next to my ear, a click.

The guard heard it too. He swung out his arms and slowly lowered the rifle, his youthful face ruddy in the fluttering light.

"You won't get far," he warned.

Hawke's breath rasped hot on the side of my face. "The keys," he said softly. "Slide them over to the lady."

The guard did as he said.

Fingers dug into my waist. "Pick them up. Open the door."

I slid to a crouch, my thoughts tumbling. I could spring up and run, be around the corner in a flash. Shriek for help, and pray that Deacon's gun misfired when Hawke pulled the trigger …

I picked up the keys.

They jangled as I slid them shakily into the lock. It took three tries, but then the door lurched inwards. Henry Hawke stepped out.

He pulled me beside him, turning the gun on the young guard.

"One move," he rasped at me, "and the trap gets it between the eyes. Understand?"

I nodded.

He gestured at the guard. "Get in the cell."

The man hesitated. Letting a prisoner escape was bad enough, but one as dangerous as Henry Hawke could ruin a career. His eyes flicked to the rifle on the ground.

Hawke lunged at him, fast as a striking snake, walloping the revolver across his temple. The guard grunted and dropped to the cobbles, his face slack.

Hawke sent a warning look my way, the gun steady in his hand. He grabbed the front of the guard's shirt and hauled him easily into the cell. Then he kicked shut the barred door and took his eyes off me to lock it.

I turned and ran.

Ducking around the residence, I raced along the path and into the front yard. My hair torn free and whipping my face, my skirts hoisted over my knees as I ran towards my horse. If I could make it into the saddle, we'd be gone in a flash.

"Shadowlark!"

She whinnied at the sound of my voice and stamped her hooves. With a toss of her head, she freed her reins from the post I'd tossed them over and trotted towards me, her tail swishing and her nose held proud.

I lunged for the reins, but she danced straight past me.

Right up to Hawke, who stood in the moonlight behind me, dark and shadowy as a demon. Except for his smile. It rivalled the moon in its brightness. He gathered the reins and then did the most unimaginable thing.

Laughing, he scratched my horse's ears and kissed her velvety nose. And Shadowlark—my beautiful, loyal black Shadowlark—whickered and chirped and whisked her tail as if the murderous brute was her long lost love.

17

SOLAINE

NIGHT TURNED TO DAWN. The sun came up, and still we rode. All the while, Hawke's gaze was fixed on the horizon, as though he could already see freedom shimmering ahead of him.

He had buckled his belt around my wrists, forcing me to lean against his back and grip the saddle with my thighs to stay upright.

Inside my riding boots, my toes cramped from digging into the saddle straps. Dust billowed around us, gritty between my teeth and gumming my eyes.

Even the horse seemed to be suffering, her coat glossy with sweat, froth flecking her muzzle.

I thumped Hawke's back with my bound hands.

"You're pushing her too hard."

"She can handle it."

The muscles in my neck tightened. She was his, he'd told me as we rode through the night. Before he was arrested and

104

dragged to the lockup, Shadowlark belonged to him. Hawke had stolen her from a man who had abused her into the ground. *Was he the one who named her?* I wanted to know. *I named her,* he replied gruffly. *Now stop asking questions.*

He claimed the shine on Shadowlark's coat and the healthy gleam in her eyes were all thanks to him. She adored him. Anyone could see it in the way she gentled at the sound of his voice, whickering softly when he stroked her muzzle or patted her neck.

Her adoration was a thorn in my pride.

I thumped him again. "She needs to rest, you brute. Carrying two riders is wearing her down."

"She'll cope."

"She's exhausted!"

"We'll rest when those gallows are far enough behind me."

"They'll never be far enough behind. My uncle won't stop till you're caught."

"He won't catch me, Miss Granger."

I scoffed. "You sound very sure."

"You're my guarantee against arrest."

"How do you figure that?"

"With you at my side, the traps won't fire. And if they won't fire, they can't catch me. You're my insurance policy."

My jaw dropped, my brows pinching into a line. "And you, sir, are a monster."

His laugh rumbled, briefly eclipsing the quiet thunder of Shadowlark's hooves. I thumped his back again, but that only made him laugh harder. Then the rough terrain forced me to lean against him once more, swallowing tears.

He was right. They would not shoot.

Uncle Niall, for all his faults, would never let them.

At least not while Hawke had me.

Uncle Niall was a hard man. But beneath his stony facade was a soul whose passions ran deep.

Once, years ago—in the early days when my love for Billy was kindling—I was rummaging in Uncle Niall's office for some paper on which to pen a poem. And I came upon a sheaf of letters that my uncle had written to his sister—my mother.

They were dated in the year before my birth, the very year Mama had eloped with my father, turning her back on her wealthy family and breaking her brother's heart.

Dearest Lottie, my uncle had written, *your flight from our family has bedevilled me. I can't sleep or eat or drink. What can that man give you that you cannot find here at home? Love, you say? Did we not have love enough, you and me? Our moments in the garden or by the lake, our laughter trailing us like birdsong, your fingers caught in mine?*

I shouldered the dampness off my face.

Uncle Niall had stifled her. My father told me that later, after Mama died. Her family cut her off when she married him. They put her considerable inheritance in trust for any children she might have—which turned out to be only me— and refused to speak to her ever after.

It broke Mama's heart, but not her resolve. She would never go back to the Granger fold, my father said. Never. *Your mother was a wild bird, Solaine. Born in captivity and trapped all her life in a gilded cage, her beautiful wings clipped. Until I came along and set her free …*

In my uncle's eyes, I resembled her—my dark hair, my lean build, my lanky tallness—but sadly for Niall, I was also like her in nature. A wild bird. And now he would think that I'd flown his golden coop, too.

And I would not return.

Not until I found my daughter.

That night, we camped at the bottom of a deep gully. Hawke had ransacked the guard house last night, retrieving the saddlebags he claimed were his, adding supplies and ammunition, an old leather hat for me, and a knife that he strapped to his ankle.

I spent the entire night propped against the gully wall. Wrestling against the belt binding my wrists, as I glared at Hawke's dozing form. In the morning, he filled a green beer bottle with water from the stream, and at dawn we started out again, Hawke urging Shadowlark onto yet another back-road trail.

Further from Charlotte.

"Where is she?" I cried, ploughing my elbow into his spine. "What did you do with her? At least have the decency to tell me."

This had been my constant refrain for days, and his reply was always the same.

"I'm telling you, Miss Granger. I never took your girl."

I shouldered away more tears, driving my elbow into his back for the hundredth time, taking scant pleasure from his pained grunt.

"You had her hair ribbon."

He twisted in the saddle to look at me, the horse slowing under us. "Your daughter reminded me of someone," he said, almost under his breath, his eyes full of shadows. "A little one I knew as a boy. Her pa saved my life. Her mama was kind to me, took me into her home, and treated me like a son. Miss Granger, do you really think I'd corrupt their memory by hurting a little child who reminded me of theirs?"

More lies, no doubt. Whether to ease my nagging or his own conscience, I did not know or care. Just that his mere proximity was turning my stomach.

"I don't know," I snarled. "Would you?"

He clicked his tongue, and the horse walked on. "I'd rather carve out my heart and feed it to the crows."

"Now there's a happy thought."

He stared ahead, his face grim, ignoring me.

I clenched my jaw, looking down at my bound hands. He was a criminal. A liar. Wanted by the law. But his eyes just now … the shadows I'd seen in them, the raw pain.

Was he telling the truth?

I forced myself to remember Charlotte's birthday picnic in the meadow. It was a blur. The carriage ride, my daughter's sleeping weight against my side. The men muscling their way inside the carriage, tearing my baby from my panicked clutches.

A sob broke out of me.

Think, Solaine. Remember. Was Henry Hawke among them, or not? An older man, bearded and solidly built, had approached our carriage first. His clothes were too snug, the hair that hung past his collar lank and grey. The other men were younger. Big, robust fellows who might have been brothers. One clearly a teen, the other with the sun against his back, his face in shadow, his brown hair curling to his collar—

"Oh," I murmured.

Hawke's hair was longer, darker. Straight and glossy, fraying about his head like a thick black mane he'd only barely managed to constrain with a length of cord. Not a single curl, and well past his collar.

I slumped, my bluster deflating.

"Why is your hair so long?" I accused. "I thought they sheared it all off in prison?"

"Only the lucky ones."

I waited, but he said nothing more, not that it mattered. Lifting my shoulder, I rubbed dust from my eye as the truth finally dawned.

In my grief, I had needed someone to blame. Latching onto Hawke, convincing myself—and then Uncle Niall—that he'd taken Charlotte, had given me purpose. Hope. But I was wrong. Hawke hadn't been on the bridge that day. He hadn't stolen Charlotte. Rather, he'd saved her from being trampled by the horse's deadly hooves that same morning and returned her safely to me. And I'd repaid him with a close encounter with the gallows.

Buckling forward, I crumpled against his sweat-soaked back.

"Hawke."

"What?"

"I believe you. About Charlotte."

A soft huff.

I shouldered the dampness off my face. "I was confused. Panicked. Angry. If only I'd listened to Uncle Niall and gone straight home that day. I might be in the parlour right now, sipping sherry and quietly reading, Charlotte sleeping peacefully upstairs. I might have avoided this whole sorry mess."

Hawke twisted his neck and looked back at me, his blue eye glittering darkly.

"I'm glad you didn't avoid it, Miss Granger." Twin spots

of colour rode high on his cheekbones, and for the first time since our paths crossed, his mouth relaxed, not quite a smile but less of a grimace. "If you hadn't come to question me the other night, you'd be safe at home with your uncle in Elliotville. And I'd be six feet under the cold earth getting feasted on by worms."

"Where are we, anyway?" I shoved a strand of hair from my eyes, glaring at my captor. "Surely far enough from Elliotville that you can let me go?"

"Not yet."

"When?"

"Once I'm safely over the border."

We had spent the night beside a patch of granite, boulders eclipsing the small patch of sky barely visible through the treetops. No fire, and no decent food this morning, just a small hunk of leftover rabbit. At least he'd had the decency to untie me while I ate.

Hawke climbed to his feet and pulled me up after him, then unwound his leather belt.

"Put out your hands."

I inched back. "I refuse to be tied another day. Look at the welts on my arms."

"Stop struggling so much, and the leather won't bite."

"Then let me go!"

He patted the gun tucked into his belt. "Don't make me threaten you, miss. Put out your hands."

"I'm quite sure that *was* a threat."

A growl. "Put them out."

I thrust my fists at him. "Then buckle it nice and tight, Mr Hawke. Because if I get free, I'll throttle you with my bare hands."

"That a threat, Miss Granger?"

"No," I murmured, looking up at him as the leather bit into my wrists. "It's a promise."

The corner of his lips twitched up, but his eyes were hard as steel. He buckled the belt, tugging it to make sure it would hold against my efforts to get free.

"It's pinching already," I grumbled as he led me to his horse. "And the buckle's digging into my thumb."

He squinted at the horizon. "You'll survive."

"Unless I slide off and get trampled."

He mounted the horse and then hauled me up after him, swinging me around so I sat pressed close behind him.

"Hook your fingers into my waistband, if you like."

I twisted sideways, jabbing the bony point of my elbow into his ribs.

"I'd rather die than touch you."

He grinned over his shoulder, blue eyes peering back at me. Then with a click of his tongue, he urged the horse out of the shade and up along the ridge. After a while, he leaned forward and spoke to her, and suddenly we were cantering up the incline, and then a little while later skating down the rubbly slope on the other side.

"Hang on tight," he said. When we reached flat ground at the base of the hill, he kicked the horse into a gallop. "The ride's about to get rough. Be a shame for you to tumble off and snap your pretty neck."

My teeth clacked together, and my backside began a downward slide to the edge of the saddle. I had no choice but to renew my grip on him. No mean feat with my hands tied before me. But if I gripped the saddle with my thighs and pressed myself hard into his back, my fingers locked into his waistband, I could keep my balance.

Just.

"I hate you," I murmured as the horse's motion thrust my face against the sweaty dampness of his shirt. "Lord knows, I hate you so much I could scream."

His laugh cut through the warm air, his body shaking so hard with mirth that I feared I might take a bone-breaking tumble after all. If I did, I'd be sure to drag the hateful wretch of a man down with me.

18

SOLAINE

HALF ASLEEP IN THE SADDLE, with the full force of the afternoon sun on my face, I began to drift.

I was walking on a midnight path, dark flowers blooming where I trod. Up ahead, a little girl called out and started running towards me. *Charlotte, is it really you?*

Her little legs were sure and fast as she ran along the path laughing, her dark eyes alight. *Mama, where did you go? I missed you!*

Oh, my heart. I opened my arms, craving the solid warmth of her strong little wriggling body, the mulberry scent of her skin, the violets in her hair. But as she reached me, she blurred and began to dissolve, a charcoal sketch in the rain. Terrified of losing her again, I lunged forward those last few steps and snatched her up, held her tight, so terribly tight in my arms, hot tears scalding my neck, hers or mine I could not tell, only how right it felt to hold her once more.

For the instant it lasted, my fractured heart was healed—but then, then …

A rough hand gripped me.

"Miss Granger?"

I jerked back to attention, lopsided in the saddle, my foot swinging free. Hawke's hand gripped my sleeve, holding me upright. Another moment and I'd have slithered onto the ground.

"Did you fall asleep?"

I shook free and scowled at him.

"No, I fainted from your stench. When did you last bathe?"

He considered this, then frowned over his shoulder at me. His eyes were red-rimmed, dark in the shade of his hat brim. His whiskers thickening into a beard, his hair full of dust.

"I stink?"

"Believe me, sir. Stink is too mild a word."

My eyes still stung from the sleepless night. From holding in tears it seemed pointless to shed. Being mean to Hawke felt good. A relief, almost. It kept me from thinking about other things. Charlotte's face as the shadowed man ripped her from me, her eyes wide with shock. And just now, my dream. Clasping her so tightly, she dissolved in my arms.

"You know, Mr Hawke, I've come to hate you for making me endure that stink. Of course, I also hate that you've kidnapped me against my will, and that your self-serving mission is bound to fail. And you *will* fail, have I mentioned that?"

"Many times."

I opened my mouth, then closed it. The wind had left my sails as quickly as it filled them. I slumped against him. He wasn't the only one who needed a bath. My own clothes were filthy with dust, my hair lank. Welts all over my skin from scratching. Nerves, most likely. Or an infestation of something horrid.

I thumped his back for no reason. He barely seemed to notice. Even Shadowlark was fed up, her tread heavy. From time to time, she snorted dust from her nostrils and tossed her head from side to side as if to say, *This infernal journey, this dusty road! When will it all end?*

Lord, she was right. The dust.

I wrangled my handkerchief from my skirt pocket and awkwardly blew my nose, then spent forever trying to tuck it back in. It almost fluttered away, but I managed to pinch it into a ball and jab it far enough down into my pocket to stay there.

I nudged Hawke's spine with my elbow.

"How long to the border now?"

He stared across the horizon. The bush was bright with birdsong and glittering ribbons of light. In another lifetime, I'd have itched for my sketchpad and paints, to stop and poke among the wildflowers, admire the wild beauty.

Now I just itched.

Hawke pointed. "That's northwest to the border. A week away, maybe ten days. Or more."

I squinted, my heart dropping. "Why so long?"

He leaned forward to pat the mare's neck. "Shadowlark's still skinny as a broom handle, and carrying the weight of two riders. She needs to rest. Depending on the terrain, I'll only push her to travel ten or fifteen miles a day. Any daylight hours leftover, we can walk."

"A week." My shoulders drooped. I blinked at him, praying I'd misheard. "Seems like forever."

"Providing the good weather holds." He tipped the brim of his hat lower over his eyes and glared out from under it at the dusty track. "If it rains, we'll hole up somewhere. I won't risk her falling."

I peered up at the sky. A solitary cloud drifted overhead in an expanse of heartbreaking blue. Fluffy and white, but over the distant hills, more were gathering.

"Mr Hawke? Take me back to Elliotville. Please."

"I can't."

"My uncle will pay you handsomely."

"He'll slip a noose round my neck."

"He's a powerful man. He can arrange a pardon, I'm sure he would—"

"I don't trust him, miss."

"Then leave me at Glen Innes. I can get the coach, and you're surely on the home stretch now."

"We're bypassing Glen Innes. The traps there will be on high alert. Can't risk it, Miss Granger."

My throat was raw from dust and weariness, from holding back tears. My head was light, my stomach knotted from hunger. Around and around it went, the worry. The dread. A whirlpool sucking me under.

"Charlotte's been gone ten days. With every passing moment, every breath I take, she gets further and further away from me. How am I supposed to bear it?"

"Ten days?" Hawke twisted back to look at me. His eyes were narrowed against the glare, unreadable—but I knew what he was thinking. The same thing everyone else thought.

What five-year-old could survive for ten days in this rugged land? In the company of armed ruffians?

My shoulders sagged. "She's out there, I know she is. Alive. Frightened. Such a timid thing, she startles at shadows. But she's smart—as smart as any five-year-old could be. I only wish ..." My voice trembled and a tear escaped, tracking down my dusty cheek. I used my shoulder to wipe it away, but another trickled down in its place and came to rest on my upper lip. This time, I left it, too weary and heartsore to bother.

Hawke's hand loomed. He smudged the dampness with his thumb, then pulled away. With a click of his tongue, he urged Shadowlark back into a canter.

I swallowed the dry knot in my throat.

Had I imagined *that*?

A flush blazed across my skin where he'd touched it. My cheeks and neck began to burn. No man since Billy had touched me that way. Gently, almost tenderly. Not knowing what else to do with it, I shoved it to the back of my mind.

I had bigger worries to occupy me.

Somewhere, out there in the wide world, a little girl was crying for her mama. Despite what Uncle Niall said, and despite the evidence of the blood-stained linen fragment they had found under the bridge, my heart *knew* she was alive. The torn piece in my pocket did not tell the full story.

Charlotte was out there, I sensed it with all my being. And whatever it took, whatever I had to do, I was going to find her. Find her and take her safely home.

19

SOLAINE

The afternoon was fading.

My thighs trembled and burned from gripping the saddle. The leather belt had cut a bloody welt around my wrists. My mouth was dry and my backside numb, my skirts heavy with dust. My stomach, past rumbling, was now a tight hollow that ached.

Still we rode.

I clung to Hawke, resting my forehead against his muscular back as I watched the landscape roll past. Sparse farmland receded behind us as we entered rocky terrain and rode deeper into bushland.

Hawke ignored my curses, my screams. My pleading. *Take me back, I beg you. My child is out there alone and probably hungry. Scared. Every mile we cover is another mile between her and me …*

Once in sheer frustration, I tried to fling myself off the saddle, but he merely reached around and righted me, the horse barely breaking her stride.

I fell silent. If he refused to help me, then I'd have to help myself. In a few hours, night would blanket the world. Better to risk escaping now than wait till after dark when he would have the advantage.

I thumped his back. "I need to go behind a tree."

"You went an hour ago."

"More like three! The sun was high when we last stopped, and now it's sinking over the hills."

"You'll have to hold." He pointed at the horizon to a rocky hillside shadowed by pine trees. "We need to make that ridge by nightfall. It's barely an hour away."

"I feel an accident coming on."

With a frustrated growl, he pulled the horse to a halt and slithered off. Reaching up, he grappled me down and loosened the belt from my wrists.

"Make it quick."

I shook the feeling back into my hands. "Aren't you afraid I'll run off?"

He looked around at the stony granite landscape. Shrugged. "Be my guest. There's nothing out here for miles —aside from dingoes and snakes. You wouldn't get far."

I glanced nervously at the shadowy trees on the far edge of the open expanse, a shudder rippling through me.

"Dingoes? I've heard horrible stories … about how they stalk in packs. Thank goodness you're armed."

Hawke shaded his eyes from the sun, staring thoughtfully towards the trees. "You know, Miss Granger," he drawled, "if it came to that, I'd be sorely tempted to let them have you."

"Indeed?"

He nodded. "In the few short days of our acquaintance, you've proved worse punishment than solitary confinement and the cat-o'-nine-tails combined." He jerked his chin at some scrubby bushes. "Now, hurry up."

Gripping my hips, I looked around. The bare sloping plain was dotted with granite lumps, the air sweet with the scent of cassinia flowers, but the surrounding bushland seemed an unreasonable distance. The scant bushes he'd indicated provided no cover at all.

I upturned my palms. "You expect me to go out here in the open?"

He pointed to a large rock. "Your throne awaits, highness."

Fuming, I hobbled over behind it.

Above me, a rocky slope met the forest edge. As the sun dipped behind the ridge, deep shadows crawled through the trees. Shadows that looked dense enough for me to hide in.

For a pack of wild dogs to hide in, too.

"Better them than him," I murmured, ignoring the damp sheen of fear that washed over me.

I picked my way across the rocky ground towards the trees, glancing back through the curtain of my tangled hair. Hawke had filled his hat with water from our bottle and was holding it for Shadowlark to drink.

I took another step.

Another glance back.

Then I ran.

The incline was steeper than it looked, and halfway up I stumbled. The ground hit me hard, my hands and knees taking the brunt of the fall. My palms stung and my torn wrists jarred from the impact, but I sprang up and ran on.

I never heard him behind me.

When he caught me around the middle, I shrieked and

swung my elbow backwards into his face, connecting with a cheekbone. He bellowed out, but his grip stayed strong. Wrenching back my arm, he kicked my feet from under me.

As I fell, I clawed at him, fisting his shirt front. We both went down, Hawke grunting as he hit the stones. I landed hard on my back beside him, the breath exploding from my lungs. I tried to fill them again, but the air would not return. Every inhale was barely more than a strangled wheeze.

Hawke leapt to his feet, hauling me up beside him. "Damn fool woman! You trying to kill us both?"

Unable to reply, I slumped over, gasping. My eyes streamed as I gulped at the air, inhaling noisy hacks, certain I'd never breathe again.

A large hand settled on the back of my neck.

The fingers warm and rough, his touch—as it had been the night at the jailhouse, slipping through the bars to catch my waist—gentle, almost familiar. I wanted to knock the hand away, but it felt heavy and soothing. My throat unclenched, and air began to trickle back in.

The hand dropped away.

"Did you really think you'd outrun me?"

I glared at him through streaming eyes, rubbing his touch off the back of my neck. "Was worth a try."

He nodded, seemingly pleased.

Pleased he'd caught me? Or pleased that I had the gall to run?

He led me back to Shadowlark, hauling me up behind him into the saddle. This time, he didn't bother restraining my hands. The belt went back into his trouser loops, and he clicked his tongue at the horse. I held onto the back of his hide jacket, a butterfly clinging to a leaf, my thighs doing their best to grip the saddle.

When I nearly toppled, he dragged my hands around his waist, making me hold on to him.

I sank closer in the saddle, hating his warmth and the feel of him so near. His hard body was unfamiliar, the ripple of his muscular stomach under my palms filling me with horror and panic. My uncle's words boomed in my head. *Men like Hawke destroy families … they corrupt good men and lead them to the gallows.*

I tried not to inhale the scent of fire smoke and saddle oil lifting from his clothes, tried not to let it affect me. But the combination pulled up a memory of my father from long ago—

I'd gone to him with skinned knees after taking a fall by the stream and losing the bucket of frogs I'd been catching. He smiled, his cheeks rosy and his eyes bright as he dabbed my scrape with his hanky. "Don't cry, little sparrow. You'll catch other frogs." He tipped my chin with gentle fingers and then dug in his waistcoat. "Let's see what we've got in here. Oh, look, a sixpence." He slipped it into my palm, closed my fingers around it. "Our little secret, eh?"

I shut my eyes, swallowing the ache in my throat, the stab in my heart as I tucked the memory back out of sight. Clinging only to the warm glow it left behind.

My body soon relaxed. My poor chafed thighs unclenched, and with my hands unbound, the knots in my shoulders unravelled. Breathing more deeply, I settled into Shadowlark's plodding rhythm, already planning my next escape.

20

SOLAINE

THE PINE TREES on either side of the trail seemed dark and foreboding, the sun sinking fast, the rocky slope streaked with shadow. As we climbed, a crude hut came into view. Its roof was a mess of weathered bark shingles, its walls rough-hewn logs.

I sat up in the saddle. "Who lives here?"

Hawke shrugged. "No one."

"Why," I asked darkly. "What did you do to them?"

He glanced back at me. "It's an old cedar getters' hut. They came through here decades ago. Built these huts to get them through a tough winter or wet-weather autumn, if the need arose. Folks still come and go. You fill the lantern if you can. Leave behind supplies you can spare. Keep the hospitality alive."

"You've been here before, then?"

He reached forward, smoothing his scarred fingers deliberately along Shadowlark's neck.

"I stayed here with my father once or twice. When I was a boy."

We dismounted and he unsaddled Shadowlark, letting her roam in search of fodder while he lugged the saddle and the guard's rifle into the hut.

I trailed after him, my legs jelly, my stomach growling. I could barely hobble, let alone even think about trying to flee again. Hawke made no move to restrain me, though he kept close watch.

The hut was spare inside. A large tin trunk served as a table and a pair of wooden boxes as chairs. A small kerosene lamp hung from the rafters. In the far corner, someone had fashioned a crude cot from four stumps and a frame, with lengths of branchwood for slats. All it lacked was a mattress, blankets and a pillow.

Hawke found a box of matches on a ledge and lit the lantern. A cosy glow filled the hut, softening its rawness.

I dragged my hair into a bun and tied it off my face, straightening my shoulders.

"I'm hungry."

Hawke unlatched the table trunk and pulled out a moth-eaten blanket, tossed it onto the bed. Then he fished in the trunk again and drew out a can of mutton, one of beef, and another of green apple slices. And thankfully, a small hooked can opener and a handmade fork, its tines buckled but sharp.

He closed the trunk and arranged the cans on its lid.

"No point making a fire. This time of year, smoke can travel miles. How does cold mutton straight from the tin sound?"

"Revolting, but I'm too famished to care."

He gestured for me to sit, and then opened the cans of

meat one by one. The gamey smell of mutton filled the hut. It was not the fare I was used to at home—roast duck most nights because my uncle favoured it, and huge platters of baked potatoes with carrots and ham. But sitting at the makeshift table, scooping chunks of gooey mutton into my mouth, felt like a feast.

When the can was empty, Hawke passed the beef. I took it and got halfway through before looking over, my eyes narrowing.

"Saving yourself for the apples, are you?"

He leaned back, appraising me with an almost-smile. Hands on the back of his head, stretching, his muscular shoulders rippling.

"They're all yours, Miss Granger. I'm not partial to apples."

"You're not eating?"

"Just enjoying the sight of a woman's healthy appetite."

I set down the fork.

The only fork.

Heat flushed my cheeks. On the table, one can empty and the second begun. I hadn't even stopped to think. Hawke must be hungrier than me. Days in the jail cell, and heaven knew how many more lean weeks while on the run.

"When was your last meal?"

He shrugged. "They fed me in lockup."

"Let me guess, tinned mutton?"

He almost cracked a smile. "Nothing that fancy."

I polished the fork on the hem of my underskirt and slid it across to him, then pushed over the beef.

"It's not so bad," I said, getting up. "A little soggy. But I'm sure it'll do the trick."

"What about the apples?"

"You have them. I'm full."

I went over to the bed and sat carefully. The slats creaked but held my weight. It would have to do. My arms were bug-bitten and itchy. My muscles ached. Mattress or not, tonight I would sleep like the dead. I sat on the edge of the cot and began unpinning my hair.

Hawke cleaned up the table and went outside, returning a while later with an armload of cassinia branches. He cross-hatched the branches over the bed slats and then tucked the blanket on top of them. Then he took off his hide jacket and rolled it into a pillow.

"It's not what you're used to, of course. But it's up off the ground and under cover. At least you won't have snakes crawling in with you tonight. Or scorpions."

"You certainly know how to make a girl feel secure."

"All part of the service, miss."

He regarded me for a moment, as if with more to say. His gaze dipped to my mouth, and his fingers came up briefly and rested on his chest. An oddly vulnerable gesture.

I went very still.

The precarious nature of my situation became abruptly and shockingly real. Until now, I had assumed this man beneath me, a common criminal to be despised and even pitied. Of course, I feared what he might do to me. He was a convicted killer after all … but not what *else* might be done.

A solitary bed.

A hut in the middle of godforsaken nowhere.

And that look in his eyes, the way he looked at me with a hunger that no amount of apples or beef would sate. His hands restless. Tugging his collar, dragging through his hair.

I sat rigidly, knowing what came next. My pulse sped up as I stared around for a weapon. The guard's rifle was propped near the entryway. Nearby, the saddlebags that now held Deacon's revolver. On the lid of the trunk sat the clean fork with its sharp tines, and the jagged can opener. Weapons galore, but none within reach.

"Miss Granger …"

I swallowed. "Something on your mind, Mr Hawke?"

He nodded. "If it wasn't for you, I'd be lying in my grave tonight."

I hugged myself, saying nothing. Waiting.

"I know all this—" He gestured around at the hut. "Well, it's an inconvenience for you."

I blinked. "You drag me off at gunpoint and hold me hostage as an insurance policy, and think it's *inconvenient*?"

My shrillness made him flinch. He collected his hat from the table and jammed it on his head. From the saddlebag, he took Deacon's gun and tucked it in his waistband, then collected the rifle by the door. In the entryway, he turned back.

"You're fretting for your little girl. I'm sorry for that. Once we're near the border, I'll get you on the soonest coach back to Elliotville. Until then, I'll keep you safe, Miss Granger." His gaze became pointed. "You needn't fear me. No harm will come to you in my care, I promise."

He ducked through the entryway, settling on the ground with his back against the hut wall, just outside. Leaving me alone and feeling strangely chastened.

I'll keep you safe, Miss Granger.

Odd words from the lips of a convicted killer. A

dangerous man with blood on his hands and a price on his head.

They did not reassure me.

I went silently to the table. Removed the little iron fork and stowed it in my skirt pocket, then crept back to the cot. Wildflower stalks whispered and crackled as I lay back on them.

No harm will come to you in my care.

Dragging the moth-eaten blanket over me, I settled my head on Hawke's coat, inhaling his horsey, woodsmoke scent.

My gaze drifted around the hut. Making out dim shapes. The table and box chairs, the saddle and now empty saddle-bags. And the rectangle of moonlight in the doorway where Henry Hawke's slumbering body had begun to quietly snore.

THE NIGHT WORE ON, and sleep eluded me. At my uncle's house in Elliotville, nighttime had been a quiet affair—just the soft ticking of the downstairs clock and an occasional whinny from the stables.

But way out here in the rugged wilds, it seemed the bush came to life. Possum shrieks and insect chatter, creaking boughs. And the constant swish of night air ruffling through an endless sea of eucalypt trees and wild whispery grasses.

I glared up at the roof.

Gaps of sky poked through the rough shingles, and even the stars seemed noisy, prickling and crackling like minus-cule flames.

The hut trembled lightly as Hawke shifted his weight, murmuring to himself. I punched my lumpy makeshift pillow into submission, picturing his smug face growing bloody under my fist.

"If only."

His voice rasped, sandpaper in the darkness. Something unintelligible. He tried again.

"All right in there, Miss Granger?"

I ignored him and flopped back onto the rolled jacket. The rough hide rasped my cheek, the buttons jabbing like stones. I could have wept for one of my hand-loomed silk pillowcases I'd taken for granted at home.

I closed my eyes and breathed slowly until the tension in my muscles began to unwind. Various scents wafted from the jacket. Bootblack. Fire smoke. The faintest tang of male perspiration, but not just any male.

Henry ...

My eyes snapped open, my heart stalling. Had I spoken aloud? Cold dread flushed through me, and I held my breath. Was that a chuckle from outside? Or maybe just the dry branches of my makeshift bed creaking and crackling under me.

I inhaled slowly, savouring the peppery tang of eucalyptus and cassinia flowers. Breathing it in, taking comfort from it, I settled back, my thoughts whirling through the events of the last few days.

Not my failed inquisition at the jailhouse—I'd already mulled over that until it gave me a headache. But rather the days on the road. The dust and flies. The thirst and hunger. The fear that constantly scraped my ribs like the talons of a great dark, horrifying bird.

The brute who'd taken me hostage,
But also, the open spaces.

The scent of wildflowers every morning at sunrise, the prickle of stars watching over us at night. And the call of something ancient inside me, a whisper that I hadn't heard since childhood. *Freedom*, it sang. *No one to hold you back, no one to judge.* And it was getting louder every day.

I rolled onto my back, inhaling the sweet scent of crushed wildflowers lifting from the cot, staring up at the weathered bark shingles.

Once I found Charlotte, did I really want to return to Uncle Niall's house? To his strict rules, his frowning disapproval? My inheritance was still almost a year away, but could I wait that long?

"Just find Charlotte first," I whispered. "This ordeal is playing havoc with your mind. Once she's safe again, all this will fade away."

But would it, though?

And did I even truly want it to?

I stared up at a glimmer of sky through the shingles, a solitary star peeping through.

Imagine living life on your own terms, the way Hawke does. Free to make your own rules, not caring a fig about anyone.

"Ridiculous." And utterly impossible for a woman.

Uncle Niall was right about one thing. Money spoke with a language of its own. A universal language. That everyone, from the night soil collector all the way up to people of power like my uncle, understood. So why couldn't women learn to speak it, too? Once I had my inheritance, less than a year away, I'd be free to do as I pleased.

Then why go back to Uncle Niall? When you find Charlotte, why not just keep going, see what lies ahead?

A full-bellied moon drifted into view through the door-frame. The landscape beyond the hut glowed gold and silver, the moon a shining sovereign, an omen. Touching all below it with a magical golden blush.

I shivered.

The night seemed fully awake. Insects chirped and wild things rustled in the bushes beyond. Branches creaked, and the wind whispered, speaking to a part of my soul that I'd taken great pains to keep buried.

Until now.

Don't go back, Solaine. Take a chance and run, make a new life. Not the life that's been chosen for you … but the life you choose.

21

HENRY

My dream felt a little like dying as it dragged me under, swallowing me down into the black mud of memory like a great whale drinking in a minnow.

I tried to push back to the surface, where it was safe, but suddenly there were stars overhead and the river rushing by me. And the night air reeking of blood and desperation—

I was crawling.

Always crawling.

On my belly in the mud, along the river's dark bank. My hands sloshing in the grit, my skinned knees finding every sharp rock and pebble in my path.

Wake up. You're a long way from Pelican Creek—miles and years and a lifetime between now and … then. You're not that boy anymore, Henry—you're a man, and anyway they're all dead. All of them, dead and gone. Wake up …

I kept crawling.

The further away I got from the blood and stink of death,

the better. Navigating by moonlight, my fingers digging into the sticky mud, I forced myself on. Run. Get up and run. But my legs shook so violently they wouldn't have held me, and anyway, where would I run to? There was just the shelter of the ragged trees and shadows along the river's edge that hid me from the men.

The men in masks.

A twig cracked behind me.

I jerked around. *They've found me. They're going to chop me the way they chopped Pa.* But behind was just the swaying grass and the looming river gums, their thick trunks glowing white under the low-hanging moon.

A trickle of something sticky ran down my cheek. Not tears. Never tears, I'd been taught that from a babe. I raised my hand and wiped the horrible stuff away. It smelled of metal and salt, of fear. I shut my eyes, but the vision assailed me anyway. My father on his knees in front of the masked men, his face pinched so tight that it didn't look like Pa at all, the features blanched bone-white, the lips drawn in a grimace. A skull.

Don't think of it, don't.

But then a flash of what came next—steel whispering in the night air, the cries of the four men, the cedar getters, my father among them, and as each man fell, a pattering on the soft earth that sounded like rain.

I stopped crawling.

Not rain. Rain fell on the earth and nourished it. This was hot and reeked of iron. Blood. My father's blood. The blood of the others who'd come to help my father.

Two weeks' work, my father had declared back then. And a mighty swag of coin for our trouble. So the other getters had travelled to this remote spot to haul the giant cedar logs out of the forest and down the slippery banks to the river. I was there to help. To fetch and carry. To look out for snakes and gather leaves and bark dross into piles for burning.

Where my father went, I went too. Working alongside him, eager to learn. To please. The other men ruffled my hair and teased me, but they treated me like a man, though I was only eleven. Young Henry, they called me, because my father was Henry too, but woe betide anyone who called Henry Hawke the elder old. The men liked my father and respected him. They called him boss and joked with him, but they'd been loyal. Even at the end. Even as they all lay dying …

Keep going. If you stop, they'll find you.

I pulled my fist from the mud and drove it in front of me, dragging my trembling body. Ten yards ahead, a fallen trunk lay half in the water. I would rest when I got there. I needed to rest. Get myself up out of the mud and decide what to do next. I couldn't think straight. If I lay down now, on the boggy river's edge, I'd die. The mud was sucking the life out of me. My only injuries were the skinned knees and elbows, the wallop I'd taken to the face as I'd fled the cedar getters' camp. *But I'm dying. I can feel the life bleeding out of me into the mud. Just like Pa …*

"Well, now."

I jerked backwards at the voice.

The shadow of a man stood over me, a giant eclipsing the moon. A big, ragged man cradling a rifle. Hunkering down, he thumbed back his hat, his eyes catching the starlight.

"Is that blood you're covered in, lad?"

I scrambled back, my heart pounding. A branch whipped my face, jabbing into my lip, hot blood filling my mouth. Big rough fingers gripped my scruff and hauled me up. *Pa, I'm sorry! The men with the masks, God help me!*

I bucked wildly, limbs flailing as the man dragged me along the river's edge towards the log. Then up a slope onto drier ground. I went limp. This was it. I'd be chopped like Pa, my body left to rot in the summer sun. When the riverboat arrived at the camp later that morning to collect the logs, they'd find my pa and the others. Find their bodies. But they'd never find me. My bones would bleach and fall apart, and then one day the river would swell up and wash them away, and they'd be gone.

A horse snorted nearby.

My captor dropped me on the ground and hunkered next to me again. Brought his whiskery face up close until his eyes were large as moons. "You're a sorry wee mess, that you are. You'd better come along with me."

SOLAINE

"Mr Hawke?"

I bent closer. The fork in my hand, just in case. He didn't stir. Arms crossed over his chest, fists clenched tight, he hunched protectively into himself against whatever dream or nightmare was making him mutter and murmur so desperately.

Should I shake him, wake him up?

The image of a sleeping bear came to mind. A bear who might not take well to being prodded awake in the darkness of night. Maybe I should simply return to my cot, stuff strips of handkerchief in my ears? I had thought my exhaustion would drag me into oblivion, but instead it had wired me up, and now this racket of Hawke's was making sleep even more impossible.

Hawke stirred. A small huff escaped his lips. Black shadows hollowed his cheeks, and a week's worth of whiskers darkened his jaw, making him seem somehow demonic and really quite like a sleeping bear.

So much for keeping guard, if that had been his plan.

I crouched beside him, reaching over to shake him anyway, prepared to jump out of harm's way if he sprang up swinging. But again I hesitated.

The moon's silver light was playing tricks. Beneath his whiskery ruggedness lay a powerful beauty. The strong jawline and tender mouth, the half-moon shadows of his lashes. If only I clutched a pencil instead of a fork. If only I had my sketchbook and paints, and a whole sunny afternoon to study that intriguing face …

He grunted softly, his eyes opening.

His large fingers swooped around my wrist, dragging me down on top of him.

"What the heck?"

His voice was hoarse from sleep, his words slurred. Yet his grip was vicelike. The fork landed on the ground with a soft thud. He retrieved it with the hand that wasn't gripping me, and stared at it for the longest time, as though he'd never seen one before. His face was close, his breath warm on my lips.

"What are you up to?"

I tried to scramble away. "Let go, you're hurting me."

He loosened his clasp but kept me trapped. On his lap like a naughty child, I struggled. My cheeks burned, and the breath I had been holding now panted out of me.

"You were dreaming."

"Ah …"

"Your cries kept me awake."

"And so you thought to silence me with this?" Pocketing

the utensil, he captured my free wrist and held that too. "Really, a fork?"

"It was for my own protection."

He hung his head a moment, as though to gather his wits. Or maybe in shame. When he finally looked back at me, his face was gaunt. He seemed on the brink of saying more, perhaps an explanation for his night terrors, or an apology for his gruff accusations.

But then his features sharpened. He looked out into the blackness. Somewhere nearby, Shadowlark softly snorted.

Hawke sprang to his feet, dragging me with him. He spun me so my back was pressed hard against his front. His hand slid over my mouth.

My body went rigid. This was it. I had approached a sleeping bear, and now my moments were numbered. I was going to die. Hawke reached into his pocket and took out the fork.

"Take it." He pressed it into my hand. "You might need it. Don't make a sound, promise?"

Gripping the fork, I nodded. He released me, and I whirled on him, bracing for a struggle. But he was gazing past me into the night.

"We've got company."

The heat in my body turned cold. I twisted around, following his gaze down the moonlit slope. Tree shadows, pale trunks, lumps of rock. Somewhere a boobook hooted, its ghostly call sending shivers up my arms. Then, into the silence, drifted other sounds. The faint clop of hooves. Voices, gruff and drawling. And there, halfway up the hill, the blazing glow of torchlight.

"Mounted troopers." I whirled on Hawke in triumph. "Uncle Niall sent them to find me. I'm saved!"

Hawke made a scoffing sound and shook his head. He was focused on something in his hands. Deacon's revolver. Snapping open the chamber, he ran his fingers over the cartridges. "A full load," he confirmed, then looked back down the hillside. "The slope's too steep for traps. They wouldn't risk their horses this far from town, nor in the dark. Besides—" His eyes flashed in the gloom. "It's near midnight. Most traps I know would be tucked up in their swags by now, dreaming their law-abiding dreams."

He pushed the chamber shut and grabbed my arm.

I shook free. "Who is it, then? Friends of yours, I suppose."

"I don't have any friends. Not anymore." He tucked the gun into his belt and then pressed a finger to his lips. "Go back inside the hut, gather what you can. We need to make ourselves scarce."

"Why?"

He glanced down the hillside, his face grim in the half-light. "If you don't know for sure someone's your friend, Miss Granger, you'd best assume they're your enemy."

He picked up the rifle and headed down the slope a little way to where he'd tethered Shadowlark.

I trailed after him. How easy just to flee. To run a little way into the dark and call for help. I was barefoot and wouldn't get far. But the approaching riders would hear me and come swiftly to my rescue.

Wouldn't they?

Voices drifted from the dark, men's voices. Thick with

drink and overly loud, probably thinking themselves alone in this remote spot.

A bottle smashed. Someone cursed.

Hawke's concern infected me. Silently, I ducked into the hut. Slipping on my boots, I laced them and then gathered the rest of our things—Hawke's rolled coat and the unopened tin of apples, the water flask. Stowing them in the saddlebags, I hauled them to the doorway. Hawke met me in the darkness outside and we hurried down to the horse. He buckled the bags onto the saddle and stowed the rifle in the holster.

I took the reins and we moved noiselessly down the slope into a thicket of trees. Treading carefully until the shadows swallowed us. Hawke murmured in the horse's ear and stroked her quivering nose.

"Quiet as a dove, my beautiful. Not a sound." He spoke softly, but his voice had an edge of command I'd never heard before. He took my arm and drew me near to him. "Don't do anything foolish, Miss Granger. We might both pay with our lives."

I pulled away. "Why are you so worried? Who are they?"

"With luck, we won't find out."

"They're on the run from the law? Like you."

"Or on the chase."

Suddenly, I understood his fear. He had a price on his head. Was outlawed. Anyone could shoot him stone-cold dead and claim that reward. *The traps won't fire at me while I've got you, Miss Granger. And if they won't fire, they can't catch me.* But the men approaching the hut from the other side of the hill were not troopers. They were, perhaps, desperate convict bolters like Hawke.

Or worse.

A shudder gripped me and I gasped quietly, inhaling the dark. Men like the ones who took Charlotte. Men with guns and knives and no conscience. Bounty hunters. Bushrangers. They could shoot Hawke and claim the reward, but what would a band of men like that do to me?

I slid my hand into my pocket, my fingers pricking against the sharp tines of the fork I had stowed there. It wasn't much of a weapon, but I'd use it if I had to.

Behind us, the voices got louder.

You, boy! Get that torch over here, there's tracks. Fresh ones by the look. Take a gander, lad. Yeah Pa, them's tracks all right. You think it's him? Pray it is, my boy. He's worth a cool two thousand quid now. We'll be rich. Gawn, now. Arm yourselves and take a look around.

I glanced back. There was only one flaming torch, but its light was intense, eclipsing the moonlight and burning my eyes. The shadow of the man who held it loomed large and threatening.

Hawke bumped against me, steering me deeper into the trees. A twig snapped underfoot, the sound like an explosion in my ears, even louder than my pounding heartbeat.

We stopped walking.

Hawke slipped the reins from my hands and patted Shadowlark's rump. As if understanding his unspoken command, she trod quietly through the trees and down the hillside. Hawke took my arm and we ducked behind a boulder, pressed close to the ground in the shadows.

I lay there shivering, the fork clutched in my fist. If only I'd had the presence of mind to grab the rifle, or even begged Hawke for the knife strapped to his shin. If they killed him, I'd have no chance on my own.

Footfall came along the way towards us. The man stopped ten feet from us, swinging the light. Torchlight blazed up tree trunks and into the canopy, the flame crackling and tainting the night air with the smell of tar. Beside me, Hawke eased the revolver from his belt and silently cocked the hammer.

He rolled back, aiming at the shadowy man, the length of his body pressing warm and heavy beside me. I held my breath and shut my eyes, my fingers damp around the fork handle.

Behind my lids came a procession of images—that day on Wattle Tree Bridge, the barking commands of the men who had waylaid us. The stink of horses and sweat and fear, and the shattering moment my little girl was torn from my arms.

By a man just like the one lying next to me.

I shivered. Insane, sheltering here on the ground, the body of a rough-mannered convict pressed alongside me. I was afraid. But not of him. Not anymore. Henry Hawke wanted freedom, and he was using me to get it. But these men ... what did they want? What were they willing to do to get it?

Hawke nudged me.

I opened my eyes. The torchlight had gone, and the surrounding bush returned to shadows. The men had regrouped inside the hut, clattering and banging, probably looking for food. A fire had begun to crackle outside, and a rank smell clung to the air, like putrid meat. Something sharper, too. Liquor. And the waft of tobacco smoke.

Hawke climbed silently to his feet and pulled me up after him. My trembling fingers went slack around the fork handle, and it thudded softly to the ground. Without a word, we made our way downhill into the dark.

23

SOLAINE

WE WALKED FOREVER, our footsteps hushed in the moonlit wilderness.

Hawke led the way, picking a path between boulders and through tussocky grass. I followed, my muscles burning, my throat parched. The weight of our escape from the cabin and those men pressed down on me, making each step heavier than the last.

Would they follow our trail? Creep up silently while we slept, cut our throats? Or would they cut us down in broad daylight in a blaze of gunfire?

My shirt grew damp, my tread unsteady. By the time we were approaching the bottom of the hill, the sound of hollering and rough talk had faded behind us. The first blush of dawn glowed on the horizon, trees and boulders emerging from the darkness.

My exhausted legs trembled so violently that I stumbled on the rough ground.

Hawke reached back to steady me. "All right, Miss Granger?"

I nodded, and we walked on, him ahead of me, his shoulders silhouetted against the pre-dawn sky, his stride confident despite the gloom. My tightly strung nerves began to relax, but a dull forboding still clung to me.

At the foot of the hill, Hawke stopped suddenly, head tilted. Giving a low whistle, he scanned the shadows.

"Why bother?" I rubbed my gritty eyes. "We've lost her. Lost everything in the saddlebags, too. Poor thing, she must have startled and taken off into the bush." My throat tightened. "I hope those men don't find her. Do you think she'll be all right?"

"Listen."

The soft pad of hooves approached. Then, out of the darkness, the black mare emerged, true to her name—light-footed as a lark and black as midnight shadows. Hawke reached her first, gathering the reins in one hand. He pressed his face against her muzzle, his shoulders relaxing as he breathed her in.

Something shifted inside me as I watched them.

The outlaw who'd dragged me away against my will, showing such tenderness to an animal. It didn't fit the monster I'd constructed in my mind. Back at the cabin, he'd positioned himself between me and danger, protecting his insurance policy, I thought. But he gave me the only food, as humble as it was, while he must have been starving. Then collected flower stalks to soften my bed.

Steadying me just now, when I stumbled.

The mare nuzzled Hawke's neck, and he murmured something I couldn't catch.

The backs of my eyes prickled.

Shadowlark. I'd been a fool to fall so hard and fast for a creature who was never truly mine to begin with. She belonged to him first. He'd named her, bonded with her before I even knew she existed.

I rubbed my hands together, glancing back up the hill, trying to ignore the hollow feeling in my chest. That was love for you. Fragile as summer mist. Giving you false hope, raising your spirits. Making you think you had a chance to be happy—only for fate to blow through like a storm and whisk it all away.

"Why'd you call her that, anyway?" I asked, drifting closer, hugging my ribs. "Shadowlark. Unusual name for a horse."

Hawke's hands stilled on the mare's neck. In the growing light, I could see the tension return to his shoulders.

"It suited her."

"Shadow, maybe. But Shadow*lark*?"

He ran his hand along the mare's sleek neck, his face half-hidden in the gloom. "Must've heard it somewhere." He paused, nodding me over. "Come closer, Miss Granger. She wants you near."

"How can you tell?"

"Her ears," he said, his voice so quiet it might have been the breezy scrape of leaves. "The way they quiver towards your voice."

I moved forward, suddenly conscious of Hawke's gaze on me. Conscious of my dishevelment. My tangled hair, my skirts torn and muddied. Ridiculous, to care what I looked like now, after everything. In the dark pre-dawn, with so many other concerns weighing on me. Worrying for Charlotte, and my need to escape so I could find her. The bounty hunters behind us in the dark, who did not care about Hawke's insurance and would fire on us both to claim the reward—

A soft nose nudged my hand. Shadowlark whickered softly, nibbling her hairy lips over my fingers. I scratched her cheek absently, keeping my distance. Keeping the protective shell around my heart. She leaned closer, nosing my hand, blowing warm snorts over my palm, working her way up to my face.

Her liquid ink eyes gleamed in the moonlight. *You can trust me*, those eyes seemed to say. *Wild things like us only have each other. If we can't be true to ourselves out here in the night, then where can we be?*

I sank forward, pressing my face against her forehead, breathing in the warm musky scent of her coat. A moment ago she was lost to me, but suddenly she was mine again—at least for now. Hope flushed through me. If Shadowlark found us in the dark, when it seemed impossible we'd ever see her again, then maybe there was still a chance to find my daughter—

The tears came without warning.

A torrent I'd bottled up these past few weeks since Charlotte was taken. All the fears I'd held at bay. All the heartbreak. Out it rushed, a river breaking through my carefully built dam.

Shadowlark nudged and whinnied, stamping her hooves, as if letting me know I was safe here. Safe to unravel. Safe to mourn what I'd lost and still hope for its return.

Hawke moved behind me, his hand settling lightly on my shoulder.

"Miss Granger?" he whispered. "You'll see her again. I know it in my bones."

I turned to face him, tears still streaming.

"How can you know it?"

In the growing light, shadows and sharp angles carved his features, but his eyes—eyes that had seemed so cold and dangerous before—held something else now. Understanding. Maybe even a reflection of my own pain.

"The ones we love sometimes find their way back to us, Miss Granger."

"Is that what happened to you?"

His hand dropped from my shoulder. For a moment, I thought he wouldn't answer.

"No," he said finally. "Nothing ever came back to me. Until now."

His gaze held mine for too many heartbeats, then flicked to Shadowlark.

"We should move on," he said, stepping back, the moment breaking. "Those men'll be on our trail by sunrise."

I nodded, wiping my face with my sleeve.

Hawke checked the saddlebags and then helped me onto the mare's back, his hands lingering at my waist to steady me. As he pulled himself up behind me, his chest warm against my back, my breath caught. *What, no hauling me up like a wench behind you? No binding my hands?* The barbed words died on my tongue as Hawke's arms circled me to hold the reins, his breath steady against my hair.

I was simply too exhausted to argue.

So I sank back against him, taking what comfort I could from his warmth. From the gentle sway of the horse, and the waking chatter of magpies in the trees around us.

We rode north as the sun broke over the horizon, bathing our quiet world in amber light.

I didn't know where we were heading or how long it would take us to get there. I only knew that the shell I'd grown around my heart since Billy's death had begun to crack—and through those cracks, something dangerous and bright was seeping in.

24

SOLAINE

"Knot it like this," Hawke said, his fingers working the string with practised ease. "Not too tight, or the noose won't slide properly when the rabbit pulls."

It was late afternoon. We'd ridden all day, finally stopping in a small clearing where the ground sloped down to a river and the grass grew thick and lush.

While I bathed at the water's edge, washing my petticoat and using it to scrub the dust from my body, luxuriating in the shady coolness, Hawke stalked further along the bank, examining the ground.

When I joined him after my wash, his hair was damp and he smelled faintly of soap. He had sharpened a pair of sticks with his knife and beckoned me to follow him.

Now we stood by a narrow hole in the ground—a rabbit burrow, he claimed.

"Why do we need a snare?" I peered into the hole, wondering if anyone was home. "Can't you just shoot it?"

"Waste of cartridges." He unravelled the knot, passing the string to me. "Your turn."

I thrust it back at him. "Can't you do it?"

"Learning to snare your own food might come in handy one day."

I botched the first few tries, but Hawke showed me until the string finally curled around itself and the little noose appeared. I beamed, holding it aloft. "I did it!"

Hawke nodded his approval. "Now bang those sticks into the ground on either side of the burrow, hang your noose from it, and then secure the other end of the string to that sapling over there."

An hour later, Hawke was stoking the embers under our catch. As I bit into the crispy flesh, he wandered down to the river's edge to collect water in his billycan to brew some tea.

I sat back against a boulder, ferns tickling my arms as I licked grease off my fingers. I could have devoured a whole rabbit by myself, even a second one, but at least our meagre feast had stopped my belly rumbling. Made me drowsy, too. I shut my eyes—

"Miss Granger, stay very still."

I blinked. Hawke stood several paces away, frowning at the nearby ground. Slowly, he set the billycan down by the fire.

My stare slid sideways. My heart stopped beating.

"Oh," I breathed.

A large blacksnake was slithering through the grass towards me, approaching too quickly for me to fly safely out of its path.

"Easy," Hawke murmured, stepping closer with agonising slowness. "Stay exactly where you are, Miss Granger."

He leapt gracefully at the snake and, in a fluid motion, collected it by the slender tail. It dangled there at arm's length, its head swaying over the ground. It tried to swivel back at Hawke, its tongue flicking, its long body writhing. But as it moved one way, Hawke rotated his wrist and the snake swivelled back the other way, unable to curl back enough to strike.

I sat frozen. "Why isn't it biting you?"

Hawke cut a glance at me, then stared back at the snake. "His body weight holds him down. See, I'm using it to control him. His spine won't bend back on itself, so if he twists one way, I just rotate him back the other." He looked over again. "He's good eating, you know."

I recoiled, clutching my throat. Then I licked my lips.

"Are they tasty?"

"Very."

"So you've eaten one?"

The snake swung suddenly, but Hawke calmly pivoted his wrist, forcing it back down. "A few. Only, the last one I had must have bitten itself before I killed it, injecting itself with venom. They do that, you know."

I eyed the creature. "Lord."

"I spent the night curled in a ball, sweating through the worst pain of my life. Which," he added, casting a frown at the swaying creature. "Is saying something."

"Can you let it go? Safely, I mean?"

He threw a wink in my direction, then sauntered down the slope towards the river. A splash echoed through the quiet, then footfall returned through the bush. Hawke appeared again.

I drew my feet up under me. "You threw him in the water? Won't he drown?"

Hawke shook his head, stumbling a little as he came up to the fire. "They're good little swimmers. And the current swept him off before he could whip around and—" He rubbed his wrist, inspecting his forearm, his face slackening. "Damn."

I straightened, my eyes wide. Pulse picking up.

Hawke staggered sideways, swaying on his feet. His eyes found mine in the firelight, hard and unreadable as steel.

"Miss Granger—"

"What is it?" I scrambled to my feet, my heart lurching.

"Damn thing must have bit me as I let him go." He sounded husky, uncertain. "I can feel the venom already ..."

I rushed to him as his knees buckled. "Sit over here, quickly. Let me see."

He sank heavily against my tree where I'd been a moment before, his breath becoming laboured.

"It's burning through me, miss. Like liquid fire."

I knelt beside him, reaching for his wrist with trembling fingers. "Give me your knife, Hawke. I'll slash the bite and suck out the venom."

He eased out a shudder. "You'd do that for me, Miss Granger? After how poorly I've treated you?"

"It's the decent thing to do. Now, where's your knife?"

Panicked, I began to fumble at his belt before remembering the guard's blade he'd strapped to his ankle. I turned from him to reach for it, but his hand shot out and caught mine, pulling me up against his chest.

Strong arms wrapped around me, and unwittingly I sank into them.

Suddenly, his face was close, burnished by firelight, his breath puffing warm against my lips.

Such an intriguing face. The bony angles framed by wild black hair that refused to be tamed. The strong jawline and tender mouth, the notch of scar above his lip that only increased his beauty.

A shame he was going to die. Despite my offer, I knew nothing about sucking out venom. Tremors were already racing through him. He didn't have long. He was going to die painfully, horribly. It could take all night. If only I didn't feel so ill-equipped to help him in his hour of need …

My fingers twitched, my tongue darting to the corner of my mouth as I considered his lips. Ten years in prison, he must have been wretchedly lonely. Craving a woman's touch, longing for a moment's tenderness. Perhaps there *was* a way I could ease his passing?

I leaned closer, hesitating. Then closer still, until we were almost touching—

He smiled.

A lazy, sizzling thing that crawled into my chest cavity and wrapped itself python-like around my heart, rendering it unable to beat. His eyes were liquid onyx in the firelight, his skin flushed—not with venom, but with something far less wholesome.

My lips parted in shock.

He dropped his gaze to my mouth, the tip of his thumb grazing my jaw.

"You'd really do that for me?"

"You absolute scoundrel!" I yelped, pushing against his chest, scrambling away. "You weren't bitten at all!"

He smiled, wider than I'd ever seen him, and then his

laugh crashed out, rumbling around the clearing, scattering the shadows.

"Guilty as charged, miss. Worth it, though. To see that look on your face."

"What look?" I demanded, heat flooding my cheeks.

"The one that said you might like to kiss me."

I jumped to my feet, planting my hands on my hips. "It said nothing of the sort!"

"Not even a little?"

"I'd sooner kiss a toad."

That set off another chuckle. "Glad we've cleared that up, then."

I stalked past him and collected my shawl from where it lay on the ground, shaking it out and wrapping it tightly around me like a shield. "And for the record, Mr Hawke. That was a terrible thing to do. Frightening me like that."

"I'll remember for next time."

"Next time?" I lifted my head to look at him, my brow raised.

"It's dangerous country, Miss Granger." His eyes sharpened on me, bright with mischief. "Can't promise there won't be more snakes between here and the border. We should be prepared for anything."

25

HENRY

THUNDER ROLLED ACROSS THE VALLEY, black clouds drawing closer with each rumble.

I guided Shadowlark up the rocky hillside, her hooves pounding the thin soil. Lightning split the sky, casting the rugged terrain in harsh white light before plunging it back into shadow.

Miss Granger flinched behind me, her hands tightening at my waist.

I pointed towards a cluster of boulders higher up the slope. "There's a cave up there."

"A *cave*?" She frowned up at the hillside. "Oh, lovely. Does it have a bath?"

"No, but the sky's about to drop a deluge on us. I'll get a fire going and heat some rainwater for you."

"Ah," she murmured, her breath warm on my neck. "Some luxury at last."

Two days had passed since the snake incident, and in that time, we'd barely said a dozen words to each other.

I seemed more aware of her now—acutely, uncomfortably aware. The memory of her in my arms, her dark gaze trailing my face, her breath puffing hot on my lips. The way she'd leaned in, melting against me.

Lord help me. I'd thought of little else since.

I reined Shadowlark to a halt at the cave's narrow opening. Lightning threaded between banks of dark cloud, briefly illuminating the valley below. Rain hadn't started yet, but I could smell it—the rich, earthy promise of a downpour.

I dismounted and tethered Shadowlark to a sapling beneath an overhang of granite, helping Miss Granger down from the saddle. "We'll stay till the storm passes."

She nodded, her face a blur in the fading light. "What about Shadowlark?"

I smoothed my hand over the horse's sleek neck, feeling the strong pulse beneath my palm. "You'll be all right, girl. Won't you? Seen more than a few storms in your time, I'll bet." I removed the saddle and saddlebags, ducking as I carried them through the cave's entrance.

Miss Granger followed, her skirts brushing against the stone wall. "How did you know this place was here?"

"Used it before." I laid the saddle and bags on the ground, then moved deeper into the cave, crouching to gather dry twigs and branches banked against the walls. "Back when I was—"

"A bushranger?" There was no judgment in her voice, just curiosity.

"Among other things." I arranged the kindling in a small pile. The cave wasn't large, but it was dry, and the overhang at the entrance would keep the rain from blowing in. "It's not exactly Elliot House, but it'll do for the night."

A smile ghosted across her lips. "I've slept in worse places."

I struck a match, carefully shielding the flame as it touched the dry kindling. "Somehow I doubt that, Miss Granger."

The kindling caught, flames licking upward, casting warm light across the stone walls. I added larger sticks, building the fire slowly. When I glanced up, she was watching me, her dark eyes reflecting the firelight.

"You'd be surprised," she said softly. "My father used to take us mushroom picking in the forest. Mama craved them grilled over the fire, and we always ended up staying overnight. Huh," she added, biting her lips and glancing into the shadows. "I'd forgotten until now."

Outside, the first heavy drops of rain began to pockmark the dirt, striking the ground like tiny, insistent fists. Within moments, the patter increased to a steady drumming, a wall of water cascading past the cave entrance and streaming down the stony hillside.

Miss Granger took a handful of oats to Shadowlark, speaking to the horse in a singsong voice. The same voice she'd used with her daughter, the day I'd first seen them on the street.

A pang twisted my gut.

The daughter who'd been ripped from her arms.

The daughter she might have found by now if it hadn't been for me.

I gritted my teeth. "You bloody fool, Hawke. You'll be at

the border in under a week. She'll be on a coach back to Elliotville before you know it."

"Whispering to yourself again, Mr Hawke?"

I glanced up as she ducked through the entryway, damp tendrils clinging to her face where the rain had caught her. She brushed them back, settling by the fire opposite me.

I pulled our tin plates from the saddlebag, along with the remains of yesterday's rabbit and the leftover damper. Not much of a meal, but it would do. Tomorrow I'd have to hunt again. Rabbits were plentiful further south, but their numbers grew scarcer up this way. Luckily, the northern rivers teemed with fish, and I was skilled with a spear.

We ate in silence, the fire crackling between us, the storm raging outside. I found myself watching her more than I should, noting the graceful way she moved, how the firelight caught in her hair, turning the dark strands to burnished copper in places.

My lips twitched, thinking of my snakebite prank. *I'd rather kiss a toad*, she'd declared afterwards. But I wasn't fooled. I'd seen her eyes soften when I pulled her against me. Seen the way she'd leaned in close, her lips parting—

"You yelled in your sleep again last night, Mr Hawke."

I stiffened, my mood plummeting.

Her eyes met mine across the fire. "You were thrashing, calling out. Like you did back at the cabin."

I shrugged, looking away. "War leaves its mark."

"What war?"

"My own." I prodded the fire with a stick, sending sparks spiralling upward. "It doesn't matter."

"It matters to you." She shifted closer, the rustle of her skirts loud in the small space. "Did your time at Cockatoo

Island cause your nightmares? I've heard it's a terrible place."

I considered deflecting again, but something in her face—an openness, a genuine interest—made me pause. It had been a long time since anyone had looked at me that way, as though what I had to say might actually matter.

"The island was no picnic, miss."

"Did you really kill that guard?"

I glared down at my hands. "No, Miss Granger. The feller I escaped with had his shiv ready before we jumped."

She blinked across at me. "They blamed you, though."

I nodded, not liking where this was going. Talking about the island opened a pit in my heart, reminded me of the worthless mess I'd made of my life. Especially sitting across from someone I'd much rather be impressing.

Miss Granger pulled a smouldering stick from the edge of the fire and tossed it back on the flames.

"Why did they send you there?"

"Horse theft." I leaned back against the cave wall, resigned to her questions. She didn't seem condemning, though … just curious. "The judge was more concerned with who I was than what I'd done."

"Who were you?"

"A ghost. A rumour." I shrugged. "The son of a cedar cutter who didn't know when to keep his mouth shut."

"About what?"

"About things that happened years before. Corruption. Murder. Covered up by them in power."

Miss Granger leaned closer, eyes wide. "That you witnessed?"

Lightning flashed, briefly illuminating the cave entrance. Thunder followed, rumbling through the stone around us.

"My pa was a cedar cutter," I continued, surprising myself as the words flowed. "He and four other men travelled up the coast to Pelican Creek, where boats delivered provisions to a storehouse and picked up loads of red cedar. There was a dispute over territory between local squatters and the cedar cutters."

I fell silent, the memories washing over me. Not memories of that night, I'd bolted those down deep in the dark. But safer memories—my father's laugh around the campfire, the smell of fresh-cut cedar. The way the stars glittered like possum eyes, watching from the dark.

Miss Granger shifted, her skirts rustling. "What happened? Did they resolve the dispute?"

I inhaled through my teeth. Years ago, I'd patched together the events of that night for Old Cap, buckling under the weight of my horror and grief. I thought I'd hardened since then, but inside, I was still that hurting kid. Still just as scared to unbolt my recollections. And worse, share them.

I glanced up at Miss Granger.

Found her gaze in the ember light. Her beautiful eyes, her angel's face. The strong set of her shoulders, her unflinching regard.

"They came at dawn," I said hoarsely, barely above a whisper. "White men on horseback, their faces covered. Slaughtered the cedar cutters while they were stumbling from their bedrolls." The words felt like stones in my mouth, my throat clicking as I swallowed. "I was eleven. Fetching water from the river when I heard the shouts. I dropped my buckets and raced back to the camp, but I was too ... they had already ..." I hung my head, the past rushing back, bowing me under its weight. One horseman saw me standing there and gave chase, his machete swinging. The blade whistled behind me like demon-song, the blood in my veins freezing to solid ice as I stumbled away—

I looked up.

Miss Granger had gone very still, her eyes awash in the gloom. "What did you do?"

"I hid in the bushes along the river. Watched them loot our camp, take our horses." I swallowed hard, fisting my hands to stop the tremors. "After they left, I went to fetch help, but somewhere along the riverbank I lost my nerve. Possibly my mind, too. I thought the men in masks had returned for me. So I ran like the devil and never looked back."

"Were the men apprehended?"

I shook my head. "Authorities blamed a local Aboriginal tribe for the massacre. Landowners put a party together and slaughtered them, wiped out the entire tribal group, no questions asked. Bloody toffs," I added softly. "I've spent my life trying to take back what they stole from me. From my pa and the others. The Aboriginal clan they wiped out. But nothing I did ever seemed enough."

She watched me steadily. "And that's why you went to prison? For taking back what was stolen from you?"

"No. That came later. I was young, angry. I fell in with some men known for stealing horses, bailing up the merchant coaches and rich travellers. I tried to go straight. Got a job working in an old man's stables for a few months." I tried to smile, but it felt forced. "Then at sixteen, I took another man's horse after a bad debt. He had connections. I didn't."

The rain pounded harder outside the cave, the downpour deafening.

"Ten years," she murmured. "That seems ... excessive."

"It was a twelve-year sentence, miss. The judge had a particular dislike for bushrangers. Made an example of me." I shrugged. "Might have been worse. Could have hanged."

Silence settled, broken only by the crackling fire and the steady drumming rain outside. I prodded the embers, feeling oddly light. I'd only ever spoken about my father to Old Cap, and then in reluctant bursts. Confiding in Miss Granger hadn't been easy, but it seemed to ease a weight I'd grown so accustomed to carrying that I'd forgotten it was there.

"You lost your pa," Miss Granger said in a whisper, sorrow glittering in her eyes. "I lost mine. And Charlotte lost hers. Why is fate so cruel to us, Mr Hawke?"

I considered the grief that had torn through me since learning about Old Cap. After that night on the riverbank as a boy, the air reeking of cedar and blood, I'd avoided letting anyone close, wanting to avoid the sting of loss that always followed. But Cap and his family had gotten under my skin. I'd loved the three of them more than life itself. Loved them so damn much that in the end, I'd run from them.

I raised my gaze to the woman opposite, the soft orange glow of embers lighting her beautiful face. The dark wilderness of her hair, still damp from the rain, falling freely over her shoulders.

Something inside me cracked open.

A delicious heat flooded my veins. Hope, maybe. Or just a momentary ceasing of the pain.

"Maybe it's not cruel, Miss Granger. Just preparing us."

She frowned. "For what?"

I shrugged, smiling as a flash came to me. Her in my arms after the snake bite, the soft look in her eyes as she leaned in …

"To be ready for things we've secretly prayed for but never dreamed possible."

She watched me for a long time, her dark gaze steady. Then she rolled her shawl into a pillow and lay beside the fire.

"Goodnight, Henry Hawke."

"Night, Miss Granger."

The rain fell harder, drumming the earth outside their shelter. Wind gusted occasionally, sending sprays of water into the cave entrance. The fire began to die down, the embers glowing orange in the darkness.

Sleep came in fits and starts, as it always did. Alert for sounds beyond the cave, for danger. The fire dwindled to embers, the cave growing colder as the night deepened. I pulled my coat tighter around myself, listening to the storm outside and the soft breathing of the woman across from me.

Sometime in the darkest part of the night, I felt movement beside me. The soft rustle of fabric, then warmth against my back. Miss Granger snuggled in behind me, her body curving against mine.

For warmth, I told myself. Nothing more.

But when her cold fingers burrowed under the edge of my shirt, seeking my body heat, I turned slightly, taking her slender hand in mine and tucking it against my chest. Her fingers were like ice, but my heat quickly warmed them.

"Better?" I murmured.

She made a small sound, her breath tickling my neck.

I smiled in the darkness, listening to the rain and the soft sound of her breathing as it evened out into sleep. Her hand remained inside my shirt, palm flat against my heart.

For the first time in longer than I could remember, I drifted off without fearing what dreams might come. Whatever ghosts haunted me, at least for tonight, they seemed very far away.

26

SOLAINE

BIRDSONG WOKE ME, and I sat up, alone in the cave. The rain had stopped, bright morning light streaming through the entrance. Last night's fire was now a pile of ash, the saddle and saddlebags gone.

I stood, brushing dust from my skirt. Where was Hawke? Dragging my shawl about me, I hurried outside, stopping in my tracks when I saw him buckling the bags onto Shadowlark's broad back.

He glanced over, a faint smile touching his lips, his eyes wary. "Sleep well?"

A deep flush burned up my throat, flooding my face. I curled my fingers—the ones I'd slipped into his shirt last night, too bitten by the cold to care—into my pocket, as if that might somehow save me from the shame of a night spent curled next to my captor.

No matter our talk last night.

No matter that my heart had turned to mush as he untangled his past for me. A past that he kept well-guarded. The young boy on the riverbank. The nightmares that still haunted him. The yearning in his eyes as he talked about hope. *Things we secretly prayed for but never dreamed possible.*

As if he'd reached inside my soul and trawled through everything I kept hidden there.

"Well enough, thank you," I managed, my voice stiff.

"We'll get an early start," he said, passing me the green beer bottle we'd been using for water. I took a sip, savouring the faint malty taste that always lingered, and passed it back.

"Nature calls," I said crisply, stalking away down the hill. I needed a moment alone to clear my head.

Last night we crossed a line.

My enemy had revealed a different face. A gentle face that glowed softly in the firelight, and eyes that were one moment fierce, vulnerable as a child the next. A beautiful face that, in other circumstances, I might have liked.

Very much. Maybe too much.

But in the bright light of morning, the reality of my situation slammed back around me. I needed to be in Elliotville. Searching for Charlotte, or at least waiting in case her kidnappers brought her home.

Not here.

Miles from anywhere. Travelling north when I should be heading south. Going silly over a man with a target on his back. An infuriating man with the soul of a poet.

Things we secretly prayed for.

"Lord." I shut my eyes, resting back against a tree trunk. "Why does he have to be so sweet at times? Then a moment later, I'd gladly wring his blasted neck?"

"All right down there, Miss Granger?" His voice carried from above.

It had to end. Today. Before I got pulled under his charming spell.

A magpie warbled shrilly overhead, its call cutting through my thoughts, as if saying *Remember how it was with Billy, you fell so willingly under his spell.*

I looked up at the bird. "Billy was different. Decent and genuine. Hawke spent a decade rotting on an island with hundreds of other desperate men. Heaven knows the unsavoury tricks he picked up. Or the lies he learned to tell."

I shuddered, remembering the heat he radiated last night. Heat that had drawn me like a cold, shivering moth to a deadly flame. My frozen fingers burrowing into it, the glorious relief as his body heat thawed me. And him quivering at my touch, drawing my hand over his heart with such tenderness.

He was lonely. Underneath his tough facade, he ached for gentleness. For love.

I smiled, smoothing my skirts as I made my way back up the hill. Henry Hawke might be dangerous in more ways than one, but I'd seen his weakness now. The loneliness in his eyes, the way he'd drawn my hand to his heart.

He thought I wanted him.

Maybe part of me did.

But Charlotte needed me more. And if playing with Hawke's newfound affinity was my ticket back to Elliotville, then that's exactly what I'd do.

BRIGHT SUNLIGHT WARMED my face as we crested the ridge. Two days of playing the sweet, compliant captive had Hawke practically eating from my palm. The way his eyes followed me when he thought I wasn't looking—hungry, hopeful. Almost possessive.

The sun skimmed the distant horizon as we descended into a leafy glade ringed with brambles and spindly saplings, golden light spearing around us. A dry creek bed cut along one edge, stones bleached in the unrelenting sun. Shadowlark slowed, her sides glossy with sweat.

Hawke dismounted first, reaching up to help me down. His hands lingered at my waist, and I leaned into his touch, just slightly, feeling the tension ripple through him. Feeling his gaze roam over me as I arched backwards, stretching my spine.

When he started removing his belt to bind my wrists, I sagged, blinking up into his eyes.

"Please don't bind me, Henry." My voice was almost a whisper. "My legs are like jelly, I'm not going anywhere. I just want to rest."

He hesitated, searching my face, his pupils blooming as he took in the weary shadows I could feel hollowing my cheeks, the raw pleading in my eyes.

He nodded, then took the rifle from the saddle holster and wandered into the bush, his boots crackling through the leaves. I slumped against Shadowlark, resting my head on her flank, closing my eyes.

My bones ached. My stomach was growling. A bath would be heaven. A hot meal, followed by one of Daisy's rhubarb tarts. Most of all, holding my little girl in my arms again, her smile bright as a penny, her skin pink from the sun. Squeezing her so tightly that no one would ever take her from me again.

"I'm not giving up on you, Charlotte."

Even if everyone else had.

I straightened, working the kinks from my shoulders. My legs really were quivering, my entire body creaking and sore after more than a week in the saddle. Of rough living. Of heartbreaking worry and fear for my child.

I rubbed the chafe marks on my wrists, studying the trees. Holding still, listening. Birds twittered in the distance. The wind rustled through the leaves. No sounds of a man returning.

Hawke was taking his time in the scrub. Perhaps another snake had found him, truly bitten him this time?

A girl could hope.

I moved quickly, gathering Shadowlark's reins and reaching up to grip the pommel. Hooking my foot into the stirrup, I prepared to swing myself up—

"Going somewhere?"

I froze. In the twittering afternoon, the faint metallic click of a rifle hammer being cocked was barely audible. But inside my head, it was explosive. Slowly, I let my boot slide from the stirrup. Taking a breath, I turned.

Hawke stood at the edge of the glade, the rifle slung loose in his arms, Deacon's gun tucked into the front of his belt.

He strode over to the horse and took the reins off me, threw them over a tree limb. Then he thumbed up the brim of his hat and frowned.

"Thought you'd charm me into letting down my guard, did you?"

I blinked widely. "What on earth are you gabbing about?"

He shifted closer. "Batting your lashes. Pressing up real close in the saddle. You think I don't know what you've been up to?"

"Up to, Mr Hawke?"

He leaned closer, his cheeks flushed, his eyes glassy bright.

"Clever woman like you. Thought I'd be putty in your hands after that night in the cave. Softening me up with your questions. Getting me to spill my secrets so you could pick through them, find my weakness. Outsmart me. I'm right, aren't I?"

He sounded bitter. Almost like a lover betrayed, the way his eyes were grazing my lips, a ragged edge to his words. He took a step nearer, his big scarred hand inching towards the weapon tucked into his belt.

Heat pulsed in my cheeks. I lowered my eyes, breaking contact, letting my stare drift to his throat, skimming the broad, muscular chest, dropping down to the big scarred hand and the gun it hovered near ...

My gaze drifted lower.

Once, almost six years ago, I had lain with a man in a glade not so different to this one. It was night, and we kept most of our clothes on, less out of modesty, and more for fear of Uncle Niall—or one of his spies—catching us, not that it mattered. A few months later, we were married, free to do as we pleased, despite my uncle's shadow always seeming to loom.

Yet it was that night in the glade that always came back to me. I hadn't seen much of Billy's body then, but I had an artist's memory. The pale glimpse of a muscled shoulder, the flash of a moon-pale thigh. I chewed my bottom lip, remembering the silky press of him, hard against my softness, the way his hands had explored and teased, and then gripped me tightly as his breath rasped in my ear. Every moment of our first union was scored into my mind, as if somehow I'd known even then that our time together was fleeting—

The spell of memory broke. I looked up.

Hawke had gone very still.

His lips were parted, his breath deep and slow. His stare locked with mine. As though my memories of Billy were written all over my face for him to clearly see.

I wet my lips, tried to look away.

Failed.

Hawke took a half-step nearer.

My limbs were suddenly hot, as though fever gripped me. The flush began in my throat and flooded upwards until it was burning the roots of my hair. Blazing across my scalp, then scorching down over me and settling low in my belly.

Was that written on my face, too?

Hawke took another half-step. We were almost touching.

I swayed on my feet, my breath suddenly hoarse. And then I did the only thing a woman of my station in life could do under such circumstances.

I fainted.

SOLAINE

HE DRAGGED me into the shade of a sapling and fanned my face with his hat. When that didn't rouse me, he retrieved the bottle from his saddlebags and trickled the last of our water between my lips.

I coughed weakly. "I ... I can't breathe."

He hesitated, then began unbuttoning my blouse, his big fingers struggling with the tiny embroidered buttons. When my shirt gaped, he picked up his hat and fanned me again.

"Better, Miss Granger?"

"My stays," I gasped softly. "Reach up under my blouse at the back and unlace them."

He hesitated. "It's been a while since I—"

"Hurry!"

He made as if to turn me around, but this drew a loud choking noise from my throat. I found his hand and moved it around my waist, bringing him closer, almost into an embrace. "Up under the blouse. Like this."

He pressed close, his breath hot on my ear. Hooking his fingers through the soft lacing, he fumbled to untie the intricate pattern of loops.

Meanwhile, my own fingers went to work, light as butterflies, swift as wasps. Locating the buttons on his waistcoat, fluttering lower, lower until they reached the waistband. I breathed a prayer as my touch found the hard object I sought. Deacon's revolver. I took hold of the grip and, in one fluid move, I jammed the muzzle against Hawke's belly.

"Not a move, Mr Hawke." My thumb clicked back the hammer. "I'd hate to accidentally blast a hole in you. Blood is such a nightmare to get out, and my blouse is from Paris."

"What the heck?"

"Back away now, sir."

He was on his knees before me, his face like thunder. Slowly, he got to his feet.

"You fainted … I thought—"

"A ruse to get you near. Now, please step back, and I'll be on my way."

He did as I said, grumbling under his breath.

I motioned with the gun. "Over there by that tree. Oh, and Mr Hawke?"

"What?"

I couldn't stop a little smile. "The year is 1866. Women's corsets lace at the back, of course, as they've always done. But these days we have front-buttoning as well, thanks to hooks and eyes."

"I'll remember that for next time."

"Oh, Mr Hawke. There won't be a next time. Now, over by the tree, if you will."

He did as I said. Keeping my sights trained on him, I

moved out of range. Six cartridges sat in the chamber. Hawke had counted them himself last night. If I missed the first time, even on the second, I had enough rounds to at least immobilise him.

Shadowlark snorted, pawing the ground.

Hawke's eyes softened. "Your aim's all over the place, Miss Granger. You'll blow your head off if you fire now. Here –" He raised his hands and shuffled nearer. "At least let me show you how it's done."

"Stay back!"

The gun shook in my hands.

I swallowed. I was doing the right thing. Of course I was. Rather than spending another week travelling in the wrong direction, trusting the word of a convicted killer who was probably planning to shoot me once we crossed the border, I could be riding back towards Elliotville to pick up my daughter's trail this very afternoon.

My grip on the revolver tightened.

Think of Charlotte. And think of poor doomed Billy, his sweet life cut short by someone exactly like Henry Hawke, a highwayman and bushranger, ruthless to the core. Think of the home we shared, the little cottage with its garden and duck pond, the wooden bed and feather mattress that Billy had made for us. Nights curled together in the warm darkness, far from the goings on of the rest of the world ...

Hawke smiled, patting his heart. "Go on, Miss Granger. Do what you must. I dare you."

I took aim.

Just as Papa had shown me all those years ago. Sliding my finger into the guard, settling my finger on the trigger, a butterfly's kiss. Holding my breath.

My vision of the sweet cottage vanished. The garden, too. And Billy curled around me, his fingers laced in mine. All gone. In their place, I thought of the crude cedar getters' hut with log walls and a tin trunk as a table. A bed of stalks and the spicy scent of wild cassinia flowers invading the night air.

And Henry Hawke, sitting watch at the door. Shadows caressing that face of his. The sculpted jaw and wide unsmiling mouth, the jagged cheekbones and storm-blue eyes that seemed to see beneath my skin.

"You're a criminal," I whispered.

An outlaw. A murderer. A dangerous man who, if I didn't stop him now, was going to cross the border and continue killing, everywhere he went, leaving behind a murderous trail of blood. He might not have taken my girl, but he was keeping me from finding out who did. Keeping me from finding her.

I fired twice.

The first shot tore bark off a sapling.

The second struck the ground near Hawke's feet, spraying up dirt and forcing him to stagger backwards. He raised his hands in surrender, swaying in the tree shadows as he eyed me narrowly.

"The heck, Miss Granger. What'd you do that for?"

"Because you're a monster and I need to make sure you don't follow after me."

Keeping the gun trained on him, I backed towards the horse. I collected the rifle from where it lay on the ground and jammed it into the saddle holster, then climbed into the saddle.

Hawke stepped forward. "For God's sake, Miss Granger. Don't ride off like this. It'll be dark soon. It's too dangerous."

"Once I find the road, I'll be fine."

"Elliotville's a good week away. How will you eat, find water?"

"I'll trap rabbits. Maybe catch a tasty snake to snack on."

He shuffled closer, shadows crawling over him. "Stay here, why don't you? We'll talk it out."

"I've nothing more to say to you, sir."

Nudging my heels into Shadowlark's flanks, I eased her around, my sights still trained on the man in the clearing. As I reached the trees, I loosened my stranglehold on the handgrip, moved the hammer into the safety notch and tucked the weapon into my waistband.

Spurring the horse again with my heels, I steered her southwards and soon we were galloping back along the narrow trail we had followed to get here, the wind of freedom finally lifting my sails.

28

SOLAINE

SHADOWLARK'S HOOVES drummed against the earth as I urged her faster, the narrow road unfurling before us like a dusty ribbon.

Each stride carried me closer to Charlotte—or so I prayed. More than two weeks had passed since she was taken, and Uncle Niall's grim warning echoed with each beat of the horse's gallop. *Do you really think she'll survive long in the company of bushrangers?*

"You're wrong, Uncle," I murmured, nudging my heels into the horse's flanks. "Sometimes, the ones we love find their way back." Hawke's words, but they had comforted me before, and now again they settled around me like a blanket of hope.

A blaze of light appeared up ahead. I tugged lightly on Shadowlark's reins, slowing her down. Sorry now that I'd stowed the gun in the saddlebags.

A figure darted onto the road, arm waving frantically. A

woman. She loped towards me, her voice cutting through the air as she shouted for me to stop, the lantern in her fist momentarily blinding me.

As she veered suddenly across my path, Shadowlark shied sideways, the reins yanking from my grasp. I tried to recover my balance, but my feet slipped from the stirrups. The ground rushed up to meet me.

I lay stunned for a moment, dust filling my lungs. Wincing, I climbed to my feet and brushed dirt from my skirt, then limped towards Shadowlark to collect the reins.

"Good evening, miss."

The woman approached cautiously. She was tall and bone-thin, her thick hair falling over her shoulders in twin braids. She wore a ragged skirt topped with a man's shirt and waistcoat, and she stepped closer, holding her lantern aloft. Her face was a map of grimy wrinkles, her bright gaze travelling over me.

She raised a gnarled hand, and I squared my shoulders. She was old, seemingly harmless. But the glint in her eyes made my hackles rise.

"I'm all right, thank you kindly," I said. "Had a bit of a tumble, that's all. I'll be on my way now."

"Not so fast," she said, placing the lantern on the ground and edging closer. One grimy hand disappeared into her waistcoat, and she withdrew a small curved knife that gleamed in the moonlight. "You'll be handing over your purse and valuables, miss. Then I'll be on my way."

Her words were sing-song, melodic, yet they scraped against my nerves like a dull blade. My jaw tightened as I flashed back to the day of Charlotte's kidnapping. No one— armed or not—would take anything from me again.

"I've no valuables on me."

The woman tensed, stepping closer, bringing with her the rankness of unwashed clothes and skin. I shrank against Shadowlark's warm flank as the woman cornered me.

"That's a fine mare you have there." Her gaze flicked over the horse, then back to me. "Once, I rode a horse like this, a black mountain brumby. Perhaps I will again. Give her to me, beauty. Hand over those tethers and you can go on your way."

Her filthy fingers reached for the reins. I pushed her away, but she lunged forward again. This time I shoved harder, my fingers catching in the neckline of her threadbare shirt. A button popped from her collar, and her shirt gaped open.

A thin leather cord hung around her neck. From it dangled a silver charm. A tiny sterling piglet with a silver bow.

My heart stopped. "Where did you get that charm?"

If she'd laughed or simply dismissed my question, I might have doubted myself. But when her wiry brows furrowed and a wary uncertainty came into her eyes, I knew. Without a grain of doubt, I just knew.

"It belongs to my daughter." The words flew out of me, harsh as the cry of a broken bird, my hopes soaring briefly before plunging into icy fear. "Where did you get it?"

The woman's face paled, her eyes narrowing to slits. Her grimy fingers went straight to the silver piglet, covering it protectively.

"You're talking rot, miss. I'll just relieve you of this fine mare now and be on my way."

I lunged forward, grabbing her collar, tearing it further.

My fingers fisted in the thin fabric as I clawed for the charm, trying to drag it from her neck.

"Did you see her? A little dark-haired girl, taken by bushrangers. This necklace was hers, so I know you've seen her. Lie to me and I swear you'll hang for it, that's a promise. Where is she?"

The woman shoved me backward with such force that I stumbled against Shadowlark and fell sideways onto my hands and knees. Trembling, I scrambled up and threw myself at her again. She knocked me down a second time, and when I hit the ground, she drove her boot into my chest.

Shadowlark grunted and swung her huge head at the woman in warning. The woman stumbled back.

I gulped air into my burning lungs. "Where's my child?"

The woman tugged her torn collar. "You'll tell no one you saw me, hear? If you do, I'll come for you in the night and cut your throat while you sleep."

I opened my mouth, but the words were jammed in my airless lungs. *I'm not afraid of you! And I don't fear death. Come after me all you like. You can't kill someone who's already dead.*

"Where is she?" I could barely whisper the words. "Please, is she ... alive?"

The woman stared at me for several heartbeats, her craggy face unreadable. "I lost a daughter, too," she said quietly. "Long time past, but it cuts now as fresh as it did then."

"So you understand—"

Her eyes gleamed darkly in the lantern light. "You should have held onto her more tightly, miss. Her loss is no one's fault but your own. Now hand me those reins and I'll let you live."

Gripping her knife, she came at me, but Shadowlark lunged forward and nipped her on the shoulder. The woman hollered in pain, then raised her blade and swiped it at the horse.

"No!"

I lunged at the woman's legs, but she leapt back, the deadly blade glinting in her outstretched fingers. With a swift motion, she flipped the knife, caught it by the blade and drew back her arm to throw it—

Shadowlark reared with a roaring squeal, her front hooves pawing the air. The woman froze, momentarily transfixed by the towering black mare. The horse lunged forward, knocking her to the ground, and the knife flew from her hand. She scrambled for it, then rolled sideways as the mare's hooves struck down, missing her by inches. The horse squealed again, and this time the woman heeded the warning.

Staggering to her feet, she zigzagged away along the track, blood streaming from the bite on her arm. A moment later, she veered into the trees and disappeared, curses trailing behind her.

29

SOLAINE

I SAGGED AGAINST SHADOWLARK, my fingers trembling as I curled them into fists.

I could still picture the piglet charm dangling from the woman's neck so clearly in my mind, and I clung to it like a lifeline.

Charlotte's alive.

And I was going to find her. Find my little wisp and take her home, never let her out of my sight again—

Shadowlark blew sharply, pricking her ears towards something behind us. I glanced back, half expecting to see Henry Hawke stalking me from the gloom.

But it wasn't him.

"Well, now." A stocky man strode towards me, his rifle aimed at my face. A tall, gangly boy appeared behind him, gripping a pistol. "Who've we got here?"

The boy retrieved the lantern from the road, which cast light on a third figure stepping out of the shadows.

"This her, Mum?"

"Yeah, that's the wench." The old woman's hard voice cut through the night as she stepped forward, her wrinkled face twisted in a grimace. She clutched her bleeding shoulder. "She tried to steal my charm … and her damn horse bit a chunk out of me!"

I glared at her. "That charm belongs to my daughter, who was kidnapped two weeks ago. And you know where she is."

The older man's eyes narrowed. "That true, Ma?"

"Course not," she spat. "Found it at that miners' camp. In the mud, so it was. Could have come from anywhere."

My heart leapt. "Miners' camp? Did you see a little girl there, with dark hair, about five years old? Wearing a light blue dress with yellow flowers?"

The woman and her sons exchanged glances.

"Listen," I said, desperation rising. "My uncle is Niall Granger. He's an important man in Elliotville. He has connections, resources. If you help me find my daughter, he'll reward you handsomely."

The older man lowered his rifle slightly. "Granger, you say? The commissioner?"

"Yes." Hope flickered. "Please, if you know anything—"

"Shut your mouth," the woman hissed. She turned to her sons. "We can't let her go now. She'll send the traps after us, sure as day follows night."

The younger son nodded. "She's seen our faces."

I stepped forward, holding up my palms to the woman to reassure her. "I won't say a word about you, I promise. Keep the charm, it's yours. Just tell me what you know about my daughter."

The woman studied me for a while, then her stare went

to the horse behind me. "Don't know anything about your girl. But I'll be having that pretty mare, only no funny business this time. Hand over the reins and back away."

When the younger man's weapon drifted towards the horse, I shifted slowly, passing the reins to the woman and soothing Shadowlark with my quiet words. She gave a loud snort, tossing her mane, but went quietly.

The older man tipped his head towards me. "We can't just leave her here, Ma. She'll send her bigwig uncle after us."

"Tie her up, Bram. We'll take her with us for now, figure out what to do later."

"No!" I scrambled backward, but there was nowhere to run. "My uncle will have every trooper in New South Wales looking for me!"

"All the more reason to keep you close," the woman said with a cold smile, her gnarled hand tightening on the reins. "You might be worth something to us, after all."

The younger son pulled a length of rope from his belt and advanced towards me, the older man grabbing my arm. I tried to elbow the boy in the chest, and when he pinned both my arms, I shrieked as loud as I could in his ear.

He staggered back, palm slapped to the side of his head, his eyes popping wide in shock. The older man gave me a shake so hard my teeth rattled, then bound my wrists himself.

My mind raced. From one captor to another—except this time, I had proof Charlotte was alive. The silver piglet around the woman's neck was a tiny glimmer of hope in my darkening world.

Mama's coming for you, my sweet. Just hold on a little longer.

30

HENRY

I STOOD IN THE GLADE, watching the space between the trees where Miss Granger had ridden away on my horse. A large dust cloud still lingered, taunting me.

Oh, Henry … My legs are like jelly.

I growled under my breath. Of all the stupid things I'd done in my life, this one was the stupidest. Falling for her tricks. Believing, even for an instant, that the closeness I'd felt in the cave was actually real.

"You bloody fool, Hawke. You're turning soft."

And now I had a long walk ahead of me to the border. Because I'd be damned if I was going after her. My horse, the supplies, the ammunition. Weapons. Water. Snaring twine. All of it, gone.

I stared at the sky, quietly fuming.

She was probably still twittering happily to herself about my gullible groping. *Reach around the back, Mr Hawke. That's right, lift my blouse and unlace my stays.* I'd gone willingly to the slaughter, a big dumb lamb falling under the spell of a wily little fox. That raspy choking sound she'd made had nearly derailed me. I'd fumbled her buttons in haste, my pulse darting all over the place, fearing the worst. As I'd gone in close and reached around her waist. Lord. The shock of warmth. Her strong body. The hot sunlight scent of her hair. The way her neck smelled faintly of soap.

I was the one being unlaced, not her.

And when I sensed the flutter of slender fingers at the front of my trousers, the earth had shifted under me. Everything stopped. My heart. My body. My mind. There was just the wild rush of hope and dread and fear and unimaginable longing …

It's been a while, Miss Granger.

"Oh, man."

I deserved to be shot at.

And yet. Who could blame me?

Ten years in Cockatoo Island, and in all that time, I'd never seen a woman, let alone held one in my arms. Of course, I'd dreamed about it enough times. The women in my dreams were always faceless creatures, an assemblage of the whores I'd known before. Busty girls with pretty faces and bad skin who ushered me into their rooms, riding me in a hurry and then ushered me out again, pocketing my banknotes as they peered over my shoulder at the next man waiting in the hall.

Miss Granger wasn't like that. She might be a proper pain in the neck, but she was still a lady. Educated and cultured. Spirited. Funny. Droll, even. I smiled. *The year is 1866, Mr Hawke. These days, we have front-buttoning corsets, thanks to hooks and eyes.*

"A lady," I reminded myself. A lady that the likes of me—an outlawed bushranger with a price on my head—had no right getting all hot and bothered over.

I crossed the clearing and picked up my hat. Dusted it off. Raked back my hair and jammed it on my head.

The sun was sinking. Shadows creeping through the trees. Night would fall quickly. Old Cap used to say that night was a big old raven swooping to earth and gathering all the sunlight in its wing feathers, hoarding it away till dawn. That was Old Cap for you. The way he saw things that no one else could see. Stories in the shadows. Poetry in a woman's face, a sky full of diamonds in her smile.

I was no poet, not like Old Cap. To me, night was night and stars were stars. Cold little pricks of light in an endless universe that cared nothing about the chaos going on down here on earth. I frowned up at them. There was nothing poetic about the black void of heaven. The coldness, the dark. No crow feathers and sure as heck no diamonds.

I hated the dark. The night.

Usually, once it fell, I'd be holed up somewhere with my eyes jammed shut and my mind fleeing back to what I thought of as my safe place.

The only place I'd ever known peace.

The hewn log cottage where Old Cap's wife had drawn a hot bath for me out in the yard, and then cleaned up my cuts and bruises with her small, steady hands. She cooked me up a feast, the best I'd ever tasted. Scones and gravy, fried pota-toes. Thick juicy slabs of bacon. I'd eaten ravenously until the fat ran down my chin. The woman, Lottie—who really did have diamonds in her smile—had beamed at me and passed over a clean cloth to mop myself with. Later, I'd basked outside in the sunlight, the little dark-haired girl sitting at my feet, peering up at me like a mesmerised doll. I didn't mind. Chatter drifted from the kitchen, gusts of laughter. Old Cap and his wife. I'd never seen two people love that way before. It was in everything they did, every movement, every glance. It warmed my heart ... yet hurt it too.

How long had I stayed? A year or more? It was so long ago now. Time and regret and heartbreak had carved a deep chasm between me and those happy times. Old Cap was gone. The woman with diamonds in her smile had died, and maybe the little girl, too. That was life for you. Everyone I loved ended up dead. And somehow I seemed to carry on, death snapping at my heels, but always managing to stay one step ahead of it.

I WALKED FOR AN HOUR, north towards the border. Then I slowed, slumping onto a hollow log. I was light-headed. Dry-mouthed. Weary. It was dark, cicadas raising the dead with their shrillness, gum leaves crackling in the night air.

I needed water. My teeth were full of grit and dust. I swallowed drily, hollowness gnawing in my gut.

My last real meal had been outside of Tamworth. Almost a week ago, an elderly woman on a homestead had let me chop firewood in exchange for a plate of food. Beef and potatoes, a hunk of bread. Gravy so thin and watery it might have been dishwater, but the flavour blew my mind. She'd given me a bundle of lucerne for Shadowlark, too, bless her.

I swallowed the unexpected lump in my throat.

Kindness was something I rarely encountered. When it came, it hurt something in me, like a stab to the chest. Usually, I avoided connecting with folks. Growing close to them. Needing them. I'd always been so much better off alone.

Miss Granger's face came back to me, the way it had been that night in the cave. Watching me spill my dark secrets, her eyes gleaming softly in the firelight, as though my confession had touched her deeply, and later, her cold fingers warming over my heart.

"All of it, bloody lies."

I'd been a fool to believe them. Believe that someone like her could see through my hard shell to what lay beneath. Being locked up for so long had made me soft. Gullible.

Wanting things a man like me had no right to long for.

I got to my feet and started walking again.

The night air was cool against my skin, carrying the scent of eucalyptus and dry grass. Above me, stars wheeled in their ancient patterns, cold and distant as everything else in my godforsaken life—

My nostrils flared as I caught a hint of fire smoke. I glanced back along the trail. Couldn't be Miss Granger, she'd be miles away by now. Probably just an old bushman, brewing himself a billy of tea—

A scream cut through the night.

A woman's scream.

Shrill and violent, bolting through my bloodstream.

I turned and started running, navigating through the trees

by moonlight as I raced towards the sound. A branch tore my face, a stump caught my foot, but on I ran, praying I'd find her in time.

"Hold on, Miss Granger," I whispered into the wind as I ran. "I'll find you."

Whether she wanted me to or not.

31

SOLAINE

THE ROPE BURNED my wrists as I twisted them, but the knots only seemed to tighten. The tree they'd tied me to bit into my spine, but I was glad of the pain because it kept me awake.

Across the clearing, the woman and her sons huddled around a campfire, passing a bottle between them, their faces lit by the dancing light. The woman sat closest to the flames, her hands extended to the heat despite the night's warmth. Her shoulder was wrapped in a filthy rag, dark with blood where Shadowlark had bitten her.

"We should just slit her throat and be done with it," she muttered, glaring in my direction. "She's seen our faces."

The older son poked the fire with a stick. "You heard her, Ma. Her uncle's the commissioner. We could ransom her."

"Ransom?" The woman spat into the fire. "Granger won't pay it. He'll bring the traps down on our heads, that's what."

I swallowed, tasting dust. She was right. Uncle Niall

wouldn't pay a ransom—he'd hunt them to the ends of the earth. And me along with them. I needed to know more about the miners' camp where the woman said she found Charlotte's charm. After weeks of thinking my daughter's trail was cold, this might be my last chance to find her.

"I'm thirsty," I called. "Can you bring me some water?"

The youngest son glanced over, but the older man kicked his boot, shaking his head.

"Please," I said. "Just a few sips."

The woman left the fire, limping towards me with a tin cup. Water sloshed over the rim as she approached.

"Here." She thrust it at my lips, slopping lukewarm liquid down my chin. "Drink."

I took a gulp, and then I turned my face away. "I want to know about the necklace. My daughter's charm. Where did you get it?"

Her mouth tightened to a thin line. "Told you. Found it."

"She was wearing it when she was taken." My voice cracked. "Please. She's only five years old. She's been gone two weeks, and I'm sick with worry. You said you had a daughter—?"

Something flickered in the woman's eyes. "Just drink the bloody water," she growled.

I lifted my chin. "Did you see her? At the miners' camp you mentioned?"

The cup trembled in the woman's hand. She glanced back at her sons, still arguing by the fire, then crouched down beside me.

"You're wasting your breath," she whispered harshly. "No use asking after the dead."

Ice spread through my chest. "She's not dead."

"I didn't say she was." The woman's face softened almost imperceptibly. "But that camp ... many were."

"What are you talking about?"

She hesitated, eyes darting to her sons again. "Just before we arrived, there was trouble at the camp."

"What kind of trouble?"

"The kind that ends with bodies in the ground. Lots of bodies." She swallowed hard, her throat working. "I had a daughter once. Long time ago now."

She was talking in circles, hoping to dodge my questions, or maybe she just wanted to chat. Either way, I needed her to open up.

"What happened to her?" I whispered.

"Fever took her. Wasted away in my arms." Her voice roughened. "Six years old, she was. Not much older than yours."

"I'm sorry."

She barked a bitter laugh. "Sorry don't bring them back, does it? Nothing does." Her gnarled fingers reached into her waistcoat pocket, drawing out a tarnished locket. "Keep a bit of her hair in here. All I got left."

I glanced at the men around the fire. They were passing the bottle, still discussing the ransom, the younger one slumped forward as though drunk. I strained against my ropes, leaning closer to the woman. "Tell me about the camp. Was my daughter there?"

The old woman sighed, her shoulders sagging. "We were passing through. Heard there might be easy pickings—these Chinese fellows had been doing well. Apparently found a big vein. Gold nuggets, not just specks from the creek." She looked away. "Wasn't our doing. When we got there, the place was ... blood everywhere. And bodies. Some still warm."

My stomach lurched. "And ... children?"

"Didn't stay long enough to notice. Took what we could and ran." She pulled something from her pocket—the silver piglet charm. "Found this trampled in the mud by the river. No child attached to it that I saw."

"Cut me loose," I pleaded. "Let me go to the camp so I can look for her. You can keep the horse, the little charm, everything. Just let me go."

The old woman studied me, a line carving between her wiry brows.

"Ma!" one of the men called. "What are you telling her?"

"Nothing," she snapped back. "Girl's thirsty, is all."

But her fingers were already working at the ropes around my wrists, hidden from her sons' view by her body.

"Cold Mountain Creek is northwest of here," she whispered. "Two days' hard ride. Follow the ridge until it breaks, then head for the tallest peak. The mining camp's in the valley below."

The ropes fell away. Blood rushed painfully back into my fingers, but I didn't move.

"Why are you helping me?" I whispered.

She pressed the silver piglet into my palm, closing my fingers around it. "Because I'd have crawled through hell itself to save my Jessie. A mother should get the chance to try."

"Thank you."

She stood abruptly. "Stay put till I'm back at the fire. Then slip away quiet-like." She nodded towards where the horses stood tethered. "Don't try for your mare. The boys will notice. Just go on foot, and don't look back."

I nodded, keeping my hands behind me as though still bound.

The woman returned to the fire, her sons too engrossed in their argument to notice anything amiss. I waited until their attention was fully diverted before sliding sideways into the shadows.

32

SOLAINE

THE NIGHT EMBRACED ME, dark and cool against my flushed skin. I moved silently through the underbrush, the silver charm clutched tight in my fist.

Charlotte must have been at the Chinese camp, but the woman's warning rang through my mind, settling like frost in my bones. *Blood everywhere. And bodies. Some still warm.*

I was nearly to the tree line when a hand clamped over my mouth. I thrashed wildly, kicking backward, connecting with something solid.

"Stop fighting, damn it," a familiar voice hissed in my ear. "It's me."

The hand released me, and I spun around, heart hammering. "Hawke?"

He stood before me, a dark silhouette against darker trees. "I heard you scream. Did they hurt you?"

"Only my pride, but that boy will think twice the next time he tries to pin a woman's arms." I nodded to the flickering campfire, the trio visible through the trees. "Once they realise I'm gone, they'll come after me. Anyway, why are you here?"

Hawke shifted closer, finger against his lips as he cut a glance behind him. "To steal back my horse. And take you with me."

Anger flared, sudden and hot. I took a step back. "I'm not your prisoner anymore, Hawke. I'm going to Cold Mountain Creek. There's a mining camp there where Charlotte might be."

"I heard." He glanced towards the firelight, the faint glow catching the hollow angles of his cheeks. "That woman is Mrs Landy, an ex-convict. Lives down near Elliotville. Knew her as a kid. She's a bad sort. A liar and a thief."

"I don't care what she is. I'm going to that Chinese camp."

His expression changed, softening in the moonlight as he looked at me. "That camp's not safe, Miss Granger. The attackers could return any time."

I lifted my palm, the silver charm glinting faintly in the gloom. "This was Charlotte's. It's proof she was at the camp. There might be other signs there. Signs that will lead me to her."

He blew out a breath, staring back at the firelight.

Voices rose around the campfire, a man's harsh laugh echoed into the trees as bottles clinked. Soon, they'd notice me gone and come after me. And this time, they wouldn't bother tying me up. I took a step into the darkness, but Hawke followed, catching my arm.

"Miss Granger, wait. I'm coming with you."

"What? No—"

He drew closer, tightening his grip. "Since you don't have a map, can you navigate by the stars? Do you know how to avoid the main roads? Or what you'll do if the attackers return to the miners' camp while you're there?"

Each question landed like a blow. I hated that he was right.

"I'll be fine." I searched his shadowy features, the urgent glint in his eyes. "We're close enough to the border for you to make it, Mr Hawke. Without me. I'll just slow you down."

"Is that what you think?" His voice was low, intense. "That I tracked you for miles, risked my neck sneaking up like this, just to reclaim my insurance policy?"

"Why else?"

He looked away, jaw tight. "That camp won't be easy. You heard Mrs Landy. Blood and bodies everywhere. No one should have to face that sort of devastation alone."

I searched his flinty face, flashing back to what he'd told me in the cave—how the masked men had come in the night and murdered his father, leaving slaughter and destruction in their wake.

"You faced it alone."

He went very still, his stare turning hard. "Like I said, Miss Granger. I'm coming with you."

A shiver rippled through me. The catch in his voice, the way his big shoulders hunched suddenly as if expecting a blow. Of all people, Henry Hawke knew the desolation I'd probably find there. The bodies and bloodshed. The horror. But if there was even a slim chance of picking up Charlotte's trail, I didn't care.

I bundled the tiny silver charm tightly in the scrap of

fabric torn from Charlotte's dress and shoved it deep into my skirt pocket. Then I looked at Hawke.

"Shadowlark," I said, nodding past the campfire. "She's tethered over there."

He nodded. "Then let's get her. We could use an extra mount, too."

"They'll hear."

"I'll cut loose the other horses, distract them. You get Shadowlark and be ready to ride."

We moved silently through the trees to where the horses stood tethered to some low branches, restless in the moonlight. Shadowlark lifted her head at our approach, ears twitching.

I peered back towards the camp. The woman, Mrs Landy, sat with her back to us, shoulders hunched, her sons dozing by the fire.

I untied Shadowlark's reins, silently climbing into the saddle while Hawke crept among the other horses. He untethered them, keeping the reins of one horse in his hand. He slapped the others on the rump, sending them scattering into the night, snorting and stamping the hard ground.

Shouts erupted from the camp.

As Hawke was mounting the horse, a gunshot split the night. Air rushed past my face, and something struck a tree trunk close by me, the bark exploding. I let out a stifled shriek, my heart lurching painfully, and Shadowlark reared up, whinnying. Hawke abandoned the other horse and leapt up behind me in the saddle, taking the reins.

"Time to go." His chest pressed warm against my back, arms encircling me as he urged Shadowlark into a gallop.

As we plunged into the dense scrub, branches whipping

my face, a second shot cracked through the night. I ducked low over the mare's neck, trembling hard, Hawke's body shielding me as the mare navigated the dense undergrowth.

Another shot, closer this time.

Hawke jerked against me with a strangled grunt, his breath hot and ragged against my ear. His arm around my waist tightened convulsively.

"Henry?"

"Keep going," he gasped, his voice tight. "Back onto the road."

We burst from the scrub onto the track, following until it widened onto the road.

Shadowlark's hooves thundered beneath us as she stretched into a full gallop, putting distance between us and the shouting behind. Hawke's weight was shifting, becoming unbalanced. Something warm and wet soaked through my blouse where his arm pressed against me. I reached down, my fingers coming away slick with blood.

"You're hit."

"I'm all right," he ground out, his voice thin and strained.

I fumbled for his hands. "Let me take the reins."

He resisted for a moment, then relented, his trembling fingers releasing their grip. I took control, guiding Shadowlark along the road towards the ridge the woman had mentioned, northwest to Cold Mountain Creek.

Hawke slumped against me, his forehead coming to rest between my shoulder blades. His breathing grew harsh, each exhale a warm ghost against my back. Tremors went through his big body, and I gripped his forearm, praying he'd stay in the saddle.

We'd have to stop. He could bleed to death. The bullet

might have already nicked an artery or done irreparable damage to his organs. Shattered bone.

"Why did you come after me?" My words were harsher than I meant, my throat tight with fear. "Back there, while I was tied up ... you could have just taken Shadowlark and ridden to freedom."

For a long moment, he didn't answer. I thought perhaps he hadn't heard me, or had lost consciousness. Then his voice came, barely audible over the drumbeat of Shadowlark's hooves.

"Couldn't let you go," he murmured. "Not alone. Not after everything."

"I don't understand."

His arm tightened around my waist, blood-slick but still strong. "You will."

My lips parted to ask what he meant, but part of me already sensed the answer. After our night in the cave, my flirtatious arrows had found their mark in his lonely heart, just as I'd hoped. I thought my betrayal in the leafy glade would have crushed his tender feelings, but I was wrong.

He'd come after me tonight, found me in the darkness. Helped me escape. Taken a bullet to shield me. And now he was bleeding to death, far from the Queensland border. Far from safety. If the gunshot wound didn't kill him, then the troopers or bounty hunters on our trail surely would.

I gripped his arm more tightly, pulling his weight closer against my back, his face snug on my shoulder blade, his blood slicking my side. Knowing, with an increasing sense of helplessness, that he was going to die.

"What have you done, Solaine?" My words caught in the

cool darkness, hot puffs against my cheeks. "How will I find her without him?"

The night stretched before us, the stars a glittering map I couldn't read. Mrs Landy's directions whispered in my mind. *Follow the ridge until it breaks, then head for the tallest peak.* Two days hard riding, she'd said. And now with Hawke wounded, how many more?

It seemed an eternity. Not knowing if my baby's delicate bones were bleaching in the sun, or if she was alive in cruel hands. Or if she lay somewhere injured, crying for a mother who never arrived.

I felt for the silver charm buried in my pocket, taking comfort from its hard shape. *Hold on, Charlotte. Wherever you are, Mama will find you.*

SOLAINE

WE RODE FOR HOURS, the moon our only guide.

Leaving the road, we followed a trail through the bush, deeper into the trees where shadows swallowed shadows. Though I heard no sounds of pursuit, I didn't dare slow our pace.

Hawke stayed pressed against me, his blood soaking through my blouse, his breathing growing more ragged with every mile.

When Shadowlark finally began to flag, her sides heaving, I let her slow to a walk. We'd reached a ridge overlooking a wide gully cloaked in darkness. In the distance, mountains rose like sleeping giants against the star-strewn sky. The horse meandered downhill until we came to a river with a pebbly shore, the water gleaming silver in the moonlight.

An overhang of granite jutted out over a sandy stretch, not quite a cave, but decent shelter. I slid from the saddle, then helped Hawke down, his body heavy and burning against mine. I took his hand and led him to the overhang, settling him against the rock wall. His skin felt like fire beneath my fingertips, his eyes glazed as he looked up at me.

"Miss Granger, I need to tell you something."

"Save your breath, Mr Hawke. We'll talk after I've set up camp."

I unsaddled Shadowlark and let her wander to the water's edge. She drank deeply, her black coat shimmering in the fading moonlight as the first hint of dawn crept into the sky.

I gathered sticks and bark to build a fire. The matches from the saddlebag sparked, catching the dry kindling. Soon a small flame danced between us, casting long shadows against the granite.

While river water boiled in our dented billycan, I crouched beside Hawke and peeled off his blood-soaked waistcoat and shirt. The bullet had gone straight through the fleshy part of his shoulder, leaving a clean hole at the back but exploding from the front in a mess of torn flesh and weeping blood.

I reached for the saddlebags, but Hawke caught my wrist.

"Leave me," he said hoarsely. "Take the horse and find your little one. I'll only slow you down."

I pulled away, wriggling out of my petticoat and tearing strips from the hem. "I need you, remember? Navigating by the stars, avoiding main roads? Dodging killers?"

He caught my eye, a smile lifting one corner of his mouth. "As good as it feels to hear you say that you need me, I'm sure you're more than capable of surviving alone."

"If I leave you here, you'll die."

"You'd be free of me."

I swallowed hard, pushing down a black tide of panic. "Just be quiet, will you? I'm trying to concentrate."

He sat still and shut his eyes, allowing me to bathe his wound. So much blood—dried and crusted, fresh and oozing. He might die anyway, no matter what I did. What was I supposed to do, anyway? I had no needle and thread to suture the torn flesh, no way to extract any bone shards the bullet might have splintered, or any fabric fragments from his shirt. No ointment to help the skin heal.

The best I could do was clean him up and pray.

I washed the blood from the ragged wound on the front part of his shoulder, then turned him towards the firelight so I could clean his back.

And froze.

The skin covering his muscular shoulders and back was ridged with long, ragged scars. Lashmarks.

"It's bad, isn't it?" He tried to look back, but I pressed my palm against the side of his face and turned him away.

"You were flogged," I said as evenly as I could, unable to keep the edge from my voice. I no longer feared him, yet the scars were a reminder of his less-than-wholesome past. A reminder of who he really was—beneath the gentler mask he sometimes wore. "Multiple times by the look. Can I ask why?"

"I'd rather not say, Miss Granger. For fear you'll think less of me."

I dipped the blood-soaked rag into the water and wrung it out, gently mopping the skin around the bullet wound. "Don't trouble yourself, Mr Hawke. My opinion of you can't really drop much lower."

"Good to know."

"What, then?"

He shifted, lowering his head. "I punched a guard, the first time."

"Oh … heavens. What did he do, forget to salt the mutton?"

"He killed a friend of mine. An Aboriginal man I'd grown close to. Shot him dead and claimed he'd been causing trouble, but it was a lie." He twisted his head and looked around at me, his eyes hard and fierce in the brightening light. "Can you imagine it, Miss Granger. Being condemned for something as insignificant as the colour of your skin? But then again, to the rich white men who now run this country, skin colour's not insignificant, is it? It's all about power. It gives them someone to blame—a clan, a family group—to punish for whatever wrongdoings the establishment needs a scapegoat for."

The ferocity in his voice, the dark ice in his eyes had frozen me in place.

I did not fear him, but I feared what he said. And the way he said it. I could feel his words vibrating through me, as if his anger and hurt were palpable things, like fire and rain, frost and snow. *The rich white men who run this country.* Men like my uncle and his privileged friends, born into entitlement, who were a law unto themselves.

I swallowed, blinking back my horror.

"And the other times you were flogged?"

He slumped, turning away from me. "I told another guard what I just told you. After that, I'd get a thrashing just for looking sideways at someone. I learned to keep my head down. And my opinions to myself."

I resumed cleaning, and for a long time, neither of us

spoke. My glibness before his outburst rang in my ears, and my cheeks burned with shame. *What did he do, forget to salt the mutton?* No, Solaine, you insensitive fool, the guard killed his friend.

I recalled the night in the cave when Hawke had bared his soul to me about his father's murder, his face hollow and raw. After the raid on the cedar cutters' camp, local landowners had slaughtered a group of Aboriginal people, claiming reprisal. Hawke said he'd spent his life trying to take back what they stole from him. From his father ... and from the Aboriginal people they wiped out. Only, nothing he ever did seemed enough.

It made me think of my father. *Before you ever judge someone,* he used to say, *ask yourself what you'd have done in their shoes.*

I wiped back a strand of hair with my forearm, then dunked my cloth again, wringing it out and dabbing around the seeping bullet wound.

If I'd been in Hawke's shoes, seen what he'd seen as a boy, the pointless slaughter and injustice, I might have ended up at Cockatoo Island, too.

A sigh shuddered out of me. "What a horrible mess."

Hawke flinched, the flesh along his ribs rippling.

"Leaves," he ground out. "You need tea tree leaves."

I shook out of my reverie. "What are you gabbing about?"

"There's a shrub the Aboriginal people use to heal. Tea tree, with small white flowers and thin leaves—"

"I know what a tea tree is."

"Crush the leaves into a paste and pack it into the wound. It'll help."

I left him and went in search of the plant, returning with handfuls of leaves and blossoms gathered in my skirt. I used two large flat stones from the river to crush them into a paste, then packed it carefully into the bloody mess of Hawke's shoulder, wrapping it with strips of my petticoat.

At first, he refused to close his eyes.

"Someone has to keep watch, Miss Granger."

"For the next little while, that'll be me." I brought out Deacon's revolver and placed it by his side. "The minute I sense danger, I'll wake you."

"Promise?"

I gave a long-suffering sigh. "Mr Hawke, you need sleep to heal. You need to heal so you can help me find the Chinese miners' camp. So close your eyes and stop earbashing me."

WHILE HAWKE SLEPT, I went down to the river's edge.

As the sun climbed higher, I peeled off my blood-soaked blouse and washed it in the shallows. The delicate silk was ruined, but I spread it on a sun-warmed rock to dry anyway. Then I washed my other garments, and Hawke's clothes as well, laying them all out to dry on the rocks beside my blouse.

Naked, I waded into the water until it was deep enough to dive under and swim to the other side.

The water was icy, but I used the little bar of soap to wash away every sticky trace of blood, every smear of grime and dust that I'd collected since leaving Elliotville almost two weeks ago.

Two weeks. Uncle Niall would be frantic with worry. Deacon would have told him that I'd gone to see Hawke in the lockup, and the troopers would be on high alert.

But two weeks. A long time for them to be looking and not finding.

I floated on my back, examining the forested ridge overlooking the river, the steep gully walls that seemed to shelter us from the outside world. Hawke wasn't the only one on the run now.

I was running, too.

Because if the troopers caught me and dragged me back to Elliotville without Charlotte, any chance I had of finding her would vanish. Forever. She'd be lost to me, and I had no intention of letting that happen. Reaching the miners' camp, facing what awaited us there, scouring the place for signs of her, following her trail—that was all that mattered to me now.

I glanced at the overhang where Hawke slept, a thread of smoke rising from the dying fire.

Hawke was right, I did need him. But not for the reasons he thought. Not for navigating by the stars or evading trouble on our way to the miners' camp, or even facing the bodies and bloodshed we might find once we arrived there.

Henry Hawke was the only person, other than me, who believed that finding Charlotte was not just a foolish false hope—but a definite possibility. Despite keeping me tethered to him, and despite the desperate things he'd done in his life before, he was the only one who believed as I did.

The ones we love sometimes find their way back to us, Miss Granger.

"Don't die, Henry," I whispered. "Please, don't die. I need you right now more than you'll ever know."

When the hot sun had dried our clothes, I quickly dressed, then folded Henry's shirt and waistcoat, walking up to the shady overhang and placing them beside him. He murmured in his sleep, his hand reaching blindly for me, his fingers curling briefly around mine. I tucked his arm back against his side, and soon he was snoring again.

Then I collected the snares from the saddlebags and went in search of food, leaving Henry to his troubled dreams.

BY THE TIME I returned to our camp with two plump rabbits, dusk was falling. I ducked under the overhang, inhaling the sharpness of eucalyptus and blood. Henry was burning with fever, murmuring incoherently, the bandage on his shoulder stained dark with fresh blood. I cleaned the wound again, applied more tea tree paste, and re-wrapped it.

I skinned and washed the rabbits as he'd taught me—a lifetime ago, it seemed now, though barely a week had passed—and set them to cook on some hot stones among the embers. The crackle and smell of roasting meat filled the night air, but Henry hardly stirred. I boiled some water and tore more strips off my petticoat.

"Let me look at that wound again," I said, nudging him awake. "It's still bleeding."

"It's fine, Miss Granger."

"Nothing about you is fine right now." I began unwrapping the bandage, wincing at the angry red flesh beneath. His face was grey, his pupils so large they nearly swallowed his eyes. I cleaned away the fresh blood, adding more of the pungent tea tree paste, and began to carefully bind his shoulder with the cleanest strips I had left.

I worked slowly in the dim light, taking my time.

There was something intimate about tending to his injury —the way he held perfectly still, the heat of his skin beneath my fingers, his gaze pinned to my face the whole time, trusting as a lamb. I'd never done anything like this before, had never been the one offering care rather than receiving it. The naked admiration in his eyes made warmth bloom in my chest.

"There." I tied off the bandage, tossing the soiled one into the fire. "That should hold."

We ate in silence, Henry barely picking at the portions I gave him. Dark shadows clung under his eyes, and sweat dampened his flushed skin. Other, older scars gleamed in the firelight—a jagged line across his ribs, a slash over his heart. Circling both wrists, the silvery threads of his manacle scars, and on his forearm, the dark blur of his sparrow tattoo.

My breath caught.

He was lean and muscular, his whiskery face shrouded in shadow, his big, scarred hands trembling slightly as he dragged fingers through his thick mane of black hair. He was somehow magnificent, a fallen god in all his rugged, ruined glory.

"I'd like to draw you," I said, then winced. I hadn't meant to speak it aloud, but it was out now and no way to take it back.

He looked vaguely startled. "Draw and quarter me, Miss Granger?"

I smiled at his absurd question, then found myself laughing. Buckling over, face in my hands, helpless. Perhaps it was shock setting in, the worry over Charlotte, the faint smell of blood that clung to the air like a warning. Like a threat of what lay ahead of us at the miners' camp. Tears began seeping through my fingers, and a sob shook my ribs like a bear rattling its cage.

Henry got to his feet and crouched in front of me, unfolding my arms so he could stare at my face. Carefully, he thumbed away my tears.

"You'll find her," he said hoarsely. "Keep your hope alive, miss. We'll find her together."

I blinked. Up close, he was even more devastating. More impossibly beautiful. His cheeks had hollowed, his beard dark against the pallor of his skin, the scar above his lip stark white. Shadows swarmed over him as firelight did its best to gild him in its dying glow.

Something had changed between us since that night in the cave, but I couldn't pinpoint what it was. A blurring of the lines. An easing from one state into another.

"Before," I whispered, "when we first arrived here. You said you wanted to tell me something?"

His eyes dropped shut for a moment, and when he opened them again, they seemed blacker, more aware, like an animal alert to sudden danger. His stare trailed to my mouth, and he leaned in, lightly thumbing the trail of my tears. My spine unwound, tipping my face up to meet his—

"Get some sleep, Miss Granger."

When he drew away, the emptiness he left behind

throbbed like a bruise. He settled onto the ground beside me and fell into a restless sleep soon after.

I sat gazing out at the night.

Keep your hope alive, miss.

I took out my scrap of linen and unwrapped the silver piglet charm, turning it over and over in my fingers. Despite what Mrs Landy had said about the miners' camp being massacred, and despite the passing of so many weeks since Charlotte was taken from me, I would cling to my hope, like Henry said.

We'll find her together.

34

SOLAINE

THE MORNING SUN scorched my face as I crouched by the river, scooping clear water into the billycan.

We had been here for two days, and Henry's fever was now raging through him like a wildfire. His skin was too hot, the wound inflamed and seeping thin watery blood. I had seen the fever take my mother. She had burned for days, her lucid moments growing fewer until finally she'd slipped away.

A splash made me look up. Where the river was deepest, shaded by rocks, a platypus poked up her flat nose and peered around, water streaming from her glossy fur, her eyes glinting. She dived under again, and a moment later appeared with her young, the three of them frolicking in the tranquil water.

I stayed very still, hoping the bash of my heart wouldn't scare them away. I pictured my daughter's little face lighting up to see them, her eyes wide as she held her breath in awe. I imagined bringing her here one day, showing her the beauty I was learning to see in this wild land we travelled through. Teaching her to weave a fish trap from twigs and grind a healing balm from leaves.

"You have to find her first."

I swallowed the ache of longing. We were less than two days' ride from the miners' camp where Mrs Landy had found my daughter's piglet charm. After weeks of fearing and not knowing, and now finally having a lead, I felt desperate to be on my way to her.

I glanced over my shoulder to the overhang where the fire smouldered. Where Henry Hawke lay in the shadows, restless in his fever. I changed his bandages morning and night, now boiling the stained strips in river water, hanging them on branches to dry in the searing sun so I could reuse them.

Why bother, Solaine? He's going to die. You know it, and he knows it, too. He's already told you to leave ... so why are you still lingering?

"Yes, why?"

The platypus family dived under at the sound of my voice and disappeared.

I carried the water up the slope to the overhang. Thin wisps of smoke from our fire trailed into the air, quickly dispersing. I placed the can into the hot coals and settled under the shady overhang.

Henry murmured, tossing restlessly.

Leave me, he'd said that first day. *Take the horse and find your daughter. I'll only slow you down.*

He was sleeping so deeply that for a moment I thought

he'd slipped away already. But then his eyes opened, his pupils dilating to swallow the blue as he regarded me.

"Go," he murmured. "Find her."

I nodded, and something separated inside me, a decision I had already made coming clear. My fingers were cold from the river, and at other times I'd have rested them on his brow to ease his heat, but now I curled them into fists at my side.

No point making this any more difficult than it needed to be.

I left some food and water and carried the saddle, saddlebags and rifle quietly to where Shadowlark grazed nearby on the banks. I saddled her and climbed up, then glanced back.

A thin trail of smoke lifted into the air above the overhang, but underneath it, the shadows were still and silent, already like a tomb.

Shadowlark whinnied as I urged her up the rocky embankment and back onto the trail. As we approached the wider road, she rolled her eyes back to stare at me accusingly.

"Quit that," I whispered. "I know what I'm doing."

She trotted on, her hooves pounding the compacted ground, her ears flicking back at every falling branch and fluttering leaf. As the sun climbed higher, her pace slowed to a dawdle, her big head swinging sideways as she looked behind.

"He's not following," I told her sternly. "So don't get your hopes up."

She snorted rudely, whipping her tail.

"We've barely been on the road an hour. What are you playing at?" I nudged her with my heels. "Anyway, Charlotte's more important. He said it himself."

Shadowlark blew dust from her nose and plodded on. I slumped in the saddle. Who was I trying to convince—the horse, or myself? I twisted around, searching the way I'd come. There was no sign of smoke or movement, just a thin plume of dust that trailed us like a sad, brown shadow.

I pictured Henry lying beneath the overhang, dreaming his terrifying dreams alone. Maybe right at this moment, he was reliving the horrible night he'd witnessed his father's murder. The shame and guilt he'd carried ever after, lashing back at injustice by turning to a life of crime.

Fate's just preparing us for things we secretly prayed for but never dreamed possible.

I remembered him on the grassy slope the night he'd faked the snake bite. Pulling me close to his chest, folding me in his arms. Trembling against me. The bite was a trick, but his tremors were real. And me, the gullible fool, thinking it an act of kindness, of mercy even, to press my lips to his in farewell—

"Oh, dear."

I slumped in the saddle, letting the reins slither from my fingers, dropping my face into my hands. My skin and clothes reeked of tea tree leaves, a sharply pleasant scent that had helped to calm my frayed nerves. Now it just reminded me of the vulnerable man I'd abandoned by the river.

Shadowlark stopped walking, softly blowing air through her nostrils.

Ahead, somewhere on the other side of the ridge and in a valley less than two days' ride from here, was the miners' camp where my daughter had been. Every moment I dallied, Charlotte's trail grew colder. Three weeks to the day had passed since the bushrangers took her. Three long, horrible weeks since she was ripped from my arms and taken away.

My fingers burrowed into my pocket, seeking the little piglet charm tucked safely at the bottom. Henry Hawke meant nothing to me. He had kidnapped me and held me prisoner. He was a criminal, a man already condemned to death. What did it matter if his end came sooner rather than later?

Charlotte needed me. My baby wisp, who was everything. My sweet little girl with her round eyes and plump, rosy cheeks, always giggling behind her hands. She needed me. She believed in me. She would be wondering why I was taking so long to find her.

All I had to do was keep riding to the crest of the ridge and follow the peak down into the valley below. Find the mining camp and ask the miners if they'd seen her—

On the road ahead, a blurred thumbprint smudged the horizon. I squinted. A dust cloud. My ribs contracted, my heart pulsing as realisation swirled around me.

Riders.

Coming this way.

We need to stay off the main roads, Henry had warned. *Avoid being seen at all costs.* He'd said it over and over, drumming it into my brain. Yet here I was in full view of whoever it was now riding towards me. And if I could see their dust cloud, then they could certainly see mine.

If you don't know for sure that someone's your friend, Miss Granger, you'd best assume they're your enemy.

I glanced around. Beside the road, a gully plunged away downhill, saplings growing from its sides. Further down, the trees were taller and more densely spaced, bushy tea trees and round-leafed geebungs pushing among them. I urged Shadowlark off the road and down the gully wall, into the denser trees until the thick growth hid us from view.

I waited, crouched low over the horse's neck, my pulse hammering as the clop of hooves approached. Male voices drifted on the hot air, growing clearer as they passed above me.

"I'm just sayin' he won't listen, yer mad bastard. Tell him what you like, but keep me out of it."

The other man grumbled, but they said no more. One of their horses snorted, and Shadowlark pricked her ears, but then the noise of them faded, and silence fell back over the road.

My throat clicked dryly as I swallowed.

They were heading in the direction of the river. Towards where I had left Henry defenceless under the overhang. Deacon's revolver was in the saddlebags, and the rifle lodged snugly in the saddle holster behind me. Why had I not thought to leave him a weapon?

In the mouth of the overhang, the fire was probably still smouldering, smoke drifting into the hot air, coiling against a sky so blue it ached against my eyes. Another rule I'd broken by letting the fire burn during the day. Would they follow the smoke and find him? Would they guess who he was, know he had a bounty on his head? Two thousand pounds was a fortune to most people, and Henry was a sitting duck.

Would they take him alive, or would they—?

"Damn it!"

I urged Shadowlark through the trees, but instead of heading back up along the road, I nudged her down the gully side, deeper into the scrub. Praying that somewhere below me ran the river, and if I rode along its banks far enough, it would take me back to him.

35

HENRY

My body burned in the darkness, my veins full of fire, the backs of my eyes flashing with dream fragments.

The wound on my shoulder throbbed so violently that it seemed to make the ground beneath me shudder and shake. Or maybe it was my bones trembling. Small, persistent quakes, as if someone was—

I blinked awake.

Was someone sobbing?

Probably just another dream. That was how they came, creeping in softly, then rising to a roar, charging through me like demons. Demons on horseback, their faces hidden behind masks, their machetes gleaming as they swooped, the blood raining down. Any effort I made to escape them only drove me deeper into the unholy darkness—

A small hand slid under my shirt, pressing against my feverish skin. Resting on my ribs like a cool leaf, making every bowstring in my aching body suddenly unwind. The

221

demons retreated. I smiled, reaching for the little hand, nestling my burning fingers over it.

The sobbing grew more ragged. I fought off the drug-like sleep, realising that someone lay with me in the darkness. Maybe it was an angel, helping me cross to the other side?

It couldn't be Miss Granger.

She had left some time ago in search of her daughter. I was glad she'd gone. Though it pained me deeply not to ride with her to the mining camp, protect her, it pained me more to keep her here against her will. The way I'd been keeping her these last few weeks, too concerned with my own escape over the border to properly consider how desperate she must have been over her little girl.

"Bloody mongrel," I murmured.

The sobbing stopped. The hand retreated. I tried to catch it, but it was gone.

"Henry?"

I snapped to my senses, rolling onto my back, capturing the angel around her waist. I held her tight with my good arm, terrified she'd fly away and leave me alone again.

"Henry, it's me."

I sat up, dragging her closer against me. "Miss Granger? I thought—?"

"I came back. I …" She uncoiled herself from my clutches and eased away, pressing her back against the stone wall, wiping her palms over her face.

I rolled onto my knees so I could face her, ignoring the bolt of pain in my shoulder, my heart plunging. "Did you find her? Is she—"

"I never made it to the camp." She huffed a laugh, husky and uncertain. "I think you've cast a spell on that silly mare.

She behaved quite badly till I turned her around. Seems I'll just have to wait until you die or recover, whichever comes first."

I found myself smiling as I reached for her hand, her fingers still cosy from where they'd nestled on my ribcage.

"You missed me."

She batted me away. "Don't be ridiculous. Like I said, the horse was impossible." She turned her head and called softly into the dark, "Did you hear that, you wilful beast—?"

Somewhere nearby, Shadowlark blew air from her nostrils.

My smile fell away. "Why were you sobbing?"

"I wasn't." She got to her feet, bracing her hand against the underbelly of the great rock that sheltered us, moonlight grazing her cheek as she glared into the dark. "You must have been dreaming."

"The heck I was." I got to my feet, meaning to stand beside her, explain how sorry I was for making her cry—for holding up her search for her little girl, for everything I'd done to vex her. But as I straightened my spine, the rock shelter tilted, the starry outside world started revolving like a carriage wheel, and then the ground flew up and punched me in the face.

When everything lurched to a stop, I felt her cool touch rest on my brow.

"Lord help me, Mr Hawke," she grumbled. "What possessed you to get to your feet? You're still in the grip of a fever."

I huffed out a frustrated sigh. "I'm a damn weakling, Miss Granger."

She helped me settle onto my back, her fingers alighting on my bandaged shoulder, patting it gently.

"You're an opportunistic arse," she said, adjusting her shawl beneath my head. "But you're anything but weak."

"Can't even stand."

"If I'd have taken that bullet instead of you, we wouldn't be having this conversation. Now get some rest. The quicker you heal, the sooner we can be on our way."

I growled softly. "If you'd taken the bullet, there'd be bodies strewn all the way back to Elliotville."

She went quiet, fussing over me, smoothing the damp strands of hair from my face. "Did I ever tell you how my mother died?"

My breath caught. "No, miss."

"She fell from her horse. She'd been riding since she was a small child, and her horses were the love of her life. At least, until she met my papa."

"I like her already."

A soft huff. "She was incredibly hearty. Never a day of illness in her life. She'd taken countless tumbles from the saddle, and not one broken bone, or even a sprain." Her fingers came to rest on my chest, her voice turning gentle. "Then one day, when I was ten, she took a fall and within a few weeks she was gone."

I found her fingers and gathered them to my chest, wanting to tell her how sorry I was, losing her mama so young and so quickly. But I knew the tears shining on her cheeks weren't for the past, but for what she feared she'd find in the future.

"Your little girl is stronger than you think, Miss Granger.

Remember the day she was almost trampled? Didn't shed a single tear. She's a brave one, all right."

She nodded, pulling her fingers from mine and dashing them across her cheeks, then mopping her face on her sleeve.

"Get some sleep, Henry."

She was a shadow against the night sky, the starlight silvering her dark hair. She reminded me of someone else, long ago. Someone who'd been kind to me. The quiet voice and gentle hands, the way she fussed and comforted. The long, glossy hair and bewitching face.

"If you're not here when I wake," I told her, as the darkness began to settle over me again, "I'll understand."

SOLAINE

A T D A W N , I hurried down to the river.

Untying the rope from a slim casuarina trunk, I hauled my fish trap onto the shore, smiling to see a large speckled trout flopping around inside. I lit a fire, cleaned the fish as I waited for the flames to die down, then placed in on a flat stone among the coals to roast.

While we ate, Henry's words lingered in my mind. *Your little girl is stronger than you think.* He was right about Charlotte. She'd regained her wits immediately that day, too intrigued by her rescuer to fuss over a runaway horse. The memory made me smile. Gave me something to cling to. Galvanised me to get Henry well as quickly as possible, so we could set out together for the miners' camp.

After breakfast, I took the gun and walked a little way beyond our camp, climbing the grassy hillock towards the track. The sky was clear, the sun a glowing ball at the edge of it, streaking the hills with gold. No sign of dust plumes or fire smoke other than ours. No sign of the men I'd hidden from yesterday on the road.

I rubbed my arms.

Lorikeets chirped in a paperbark tree, gorging on nectar from the froth of creamy white blossoms. Butterflies swarmed over the long grass, and a water dragon basked on a nearby boulder.

"Such a pretty day." I pressed my palms over my lower ribs to settle the sudden ache there. If only my little wisp was here to enjoy it with me, then it might be perfect.

I walked over to the paperbark tree, where a flock of lorikeets flapped and squealed. I tore off some strips of the soft, pale bark, then hurried back to our camp. Henry was murmuring in his sleep, an unconscious lump in the shadows. I touched his face, pleased to feel his fever finally retreating.

From the coals of our fire, I chose a wedge of charcoal and sat outside under a shady tree, whittling the coal to a point. Then I shut my eyes, tipping back my head to summon my daughter's face. I could see her so clearly, my joyful wisp at the meadow, sitting on the picnic rug beside me, her round cheeks pink from the sun.

As the charcoal point scratched over the delicate bark, I captured Charlotte's chubby cheeks and domed forehead, the fine tentacles of her dark hair. I re-sharpened my charcoal and worked the details—her round eyes, the curved brows, her rosebud mouth—smudging the lines with my finger.

At the end of an hour, I sat back.

My daughter's sweet face gazed at me from the ragged scrap of bark. Seeing her again hurt more than I'd expected. I trailed my fingertip over the sooty lines, my soul aching. *The ones we love sometimes find their way back to us, Miss Granger.* But what if she couldn't find her way back? What if she was already gone?

I returned to the overhang and tossed the drawing into the fire. It flamed brightly, a puff of luminescence in the dappled shadows that carried a column of tiny fire sparks up into the sky.

"Find your way back to me, Charlotte."

I stared after the sparks, watching as they drifted against the vast blueness for a while before finally, one by one, winking out.

LATER, I walked down to the water's edge and checked my fish trap. Inside were two small fish that would barely fill the hollow emptiness in my stomach, let alone feed a hungry man as well.

We'd have damper tonight with the last of the flour, and sweet tea for dessert. Not exactly the fine fare Uncle Niall would be feasting on—pheasant with roasted potatoes, steamed peas and carrots, followed by a helping of Daisy's jam roly poly, or custard with hot blackcurrant jam.

My stomach growled.

Burning my drawing had left me feeling bereft, but as I stood there, listening to the river's babbling voice and feeling the cool breeze on my arms, something lifted.

The weight.

The constant, crushing weight of my fear. Like the fire

sparks, it seemed to fly upwards, releasing me. It would return, as it always did, but for now, the peace of this place washed over me, cocooning me in the moment.

Butterflies twirled over the wildflowers, the sky so vast and blue it was like gazing up at eternity. Later, when the stars came out, the sky would resemble a black lake full of bright little eyes, peering down on the sleeping world below.

Out here, so far from everything, the night noises and the stars and darkness all sang a song that my heart listened eagerly to. In it, I heard echoes of my mother's voice, and Papa's laugh, and Billy's whispered promises. *Being together means we'll be free, Solaine. Free to do as we please, make our own way without fear of your uncle's judgment and disapproval.* At the time, I had nodded in agreement, but I hadn't really understood.

Until now.

All around me, this wild natural world sang of freedom. And I was slowly, finally learning to sing along.

"Not even Daisy's jam roly poly can compete with that."

As I went about my routines, changing Henry's bandages and setting tomorrow's snares, positioning my fish trap in the rapids, the day slipped away. Henry refused to wake up, so I ate alone in the firelight and saved his portion for later. Then I sat beside him in the warm darkness under the overhang, staring into the night.

If only Charlotte was here, safe beside me, I'd want for nothing more. A hairbrush, perhaps. But this moment, the lake of stars watching from above, the whispering, crackling bushland cutting us off from the world outside, seemed as perfect as any I had ever known—

A soft murmur drew my attention. Henry's fingers were

twitching, as if trying to grasp something just beyond reach. I crawled over and sat beside him.

"Henry—?"

I moved closer. He was shifting restlessly, caught in one of his nightmares. I took his hand. It was too warm, still burning with fever, his strong fingers suddenly tightening around mine. His eyes flew open, staring at me yet somehow through me, as if seeing someone else's face before him.

"Miss Lottie?"

I froze, my heart lurching to a stop, my breath hitching. The world tilted beneath me. I tried to pull away, but he kept me trapped by his side.

"Henry," I breathed. "It's me."

He blinked, emerging from the dream, his gaze gradually focusing on my face. The tension melted from his body, but his fingers remained tight around mine.

"Miss Granger?"

"You were dreaming."

He nodded, struggling into a sitting position with his good arm, scrubbing his palm over his face. "But a good dream this time," he said softly, smiling. "I was a kid again. Back at the farmhouse, where Old Cap lived with his wife and little daughter. My safe place."

An icy chill washed over me. "You mentioned someone. Miss Lottie?" The name caught in my throat, tears filling my eyes. "Was she the lady who was kind to you?"

"Yes."

"And your friend, Old Cap." I swallowed the sudden lump in my throat. "Why did you call him that?"

"He was a bushranger." Henry touched the dressing on his shoulder, his eyes finding mine in the flickering emberlight. "Known as Captain Twilight. Slipping out of the twilight like a ghost when the unsuspecting mail coach or rich merchant least expected it." He smiled, glancing at my hand still encased in his. "Maybe you've heard of him?"

I slid my trembling fingers from his grasp, nodding, my throat too tight to speak.

Henry sat up further, wincing. "He used to say that he wasn't a bushranger at all, but a tax collector. Imposing his own tariffs on the wealthy to help the disadvantaged."

"Oh?"

"He had a saddlery in town, and didn't need the money for himself. So he gave it all away. I went with him sometimes, loaded up with supplies and cash for struggling widows and families around the district." He shook his head, a smile lighting his eyes. "He saved me from the riverbank after my father was murdered. Took me back to his home and made me part of his family."

I gulped back a sob. "His name?"

Henry swiped a hand over his face, smiling shakily in the dying firelight. "His real name was James Beaumont. Jim to his mates. Best man I've ever met."

James Beaumont.

The ground under me pitched sideways. My breath caught in my throat. Hearing the name spoken aloud jarred me loose from the silence Uncle Niall had enforced for the past ten years. I felt as though the ground had opened beneath me, pulling me into an abyss where nothing made sense.

Where everything suddenly, finally made perfect sense.

"James Beaumont was my father."

SOLAINE

"OLD CAP WAS YOUR FATHER?" Henry stared at me, utterly still. The only sounds were the crackling flames and the distant murmur of the river below. He shook his head, a faint smile ghosting his lips. "You're his little sparrow?"

"And you're the boy who ran away and broke his heart."

As we stared at each other in the light of the flickering flames, glimmers of my memory trickled back.

Not the twisted versions Uncle Niall had fed me, but the real ones. Summer days splashing in the creek. Evenings on the verandah with Papa's pipe smoke curling in the air, and Mama's gentle voice reading aloud. And me drawing pictures, showing them to the dark-haired boy who sat beside me, and him smiling despite the haunted look that never left his eyes.

"Henry, why did you leave us?"

"I had to go," he said quietly. "God help me, I didn't want to. But my dreams—they were so real back then. Night after night, I saw those masked men coming for your family. Cutting them down like they'd cut down my pa."

"But you always had the dreams."

His throat worked, and finally he nodded. "The month before I left, there was another massacre. An Aboriginal tribe near Walcha was attacked in the night by white squatters. Retribution for some wrong or other, they claimed. Jim was upset. He tried to protect me from the stories. But I'd already seen the devastation first-hand with my pa. Somehow, I felt those men were looking for me. The kid who escaped. And they were getting closer. That's when I realised I was putting you all in danger just by breathing the same air. I thought ... I thought if I disappeared, you'd be safe."

"You left to protect us?"

He sighed. "I ran away from my nightmares. Guess I'm still running. Always the coward."

I leaned closer, searching the shadows swarming over his beautiful, ravaged face. My heart aching for the troubled boy he'd once been.

"You're a better man than you think, Henry Hawke."

He looked up at me through his brows, a reluctant smile curving his lips. "Huh, well. Don't know about that."

"I do. But tell me, where did you go?"

"South towards Sydney. Started holding up the mail coaches from Melbourne." He stared at his scarred hands as if they belonged to a stranger. "Planned to save enough to buy land, raise horses. Bury the past and come back to Old Cap clean, show him his faith wasn't wasted."

"He already loved you." My voice broke. "He used to say you were the son he always wanted. That someday, somehow, you'd find your way back to us."

Henry's head dropped, but not before I caught the glimmer in his eyes. He stayed that way for a long time, and when he finally looked up, his face was stripped bare, all his armour gone. He reached forward, catching my hands in his fevered grip, his eyes wild.

"But I was too late. The bastards had already got him."

Something shattered in my chest, the careful wall I'd built around my heart crumbling. Uncle Niall's poisonous words echoed in my head. *Your father was a monster, Solaine. He ruined your mother, dragged her into his filthy world. It was his fault she died.*

"Tell me again," I whispered, the words scraping my throat like thorns. "What was it really like? With them?"

He inhaled deeply, his brow creasing. "You don't remember?"

"My uncle filled my head with poison. Tangling up my memories till I couldn't tell truth from lies." I shifted closer, drawn by the fever-heat radiating from him. "Please, Henry. Help me remember."

His grip tightened on my fingers, and he nodded. "Miss Lottie used to draw pictures. Birds and flowers. Horses dancing across the paper. She taught me to see colours and details I never noticed before." His thumb traced my knuckles with infinite gentleness. "She was the kindest soul I've ever known. But fierce too, like a lioness. No wonder Old Cap worshipped the ground she walked on."

"And me?" I breathed. "What was I like?"

"You, Miss Granger?"

"Please, call me by my name."

"Little sparrow?" he teased.

I shook my head. "My other name."

A smile softened his rugged features, and he bit his lip, his edges gilded by the firelight. "You were always chattering, flitting from one thing to another like a bird that couldn't stay still. Curious about everything. 'Henry,' you'd say, 'Look at this praying mantis, why's it look like a stick?' That's why I called you a little sparrow, and it stuck." He rumbled a soft laugh. "You followed me around like a shadow, asking every question under the sun."

"I remember you now. At least, I'm starting to. A tall boy with black hair and intelligent eyes. Beautiful eyes. You helped in the stables, startling at the slightest noise. I used to creep up on you sometimes—"

"And shriek, you naughty thing."

"It was so funny watching you grab your chest and pretend to fall over."

"I *did* fall over!"

I laughed softly as the past flowed back, old memories breaking through the clouds like sunbeams. But then my smile fell away. "You had nightmares, even back then. You were sad sometimes, and secretive, but we all ..." I grazed my fingers over his knuckles, adding quietly, "We all adored you."

Henry stiffened, then his big shoulders slumped as if under a sudden deadweight. His face hollowed, turning raw and unguarded, his eyes dark in the firelight.

"You and your family," he said hoarsely, "you were different to most people. You saw me. Not the scared, broken kid I was, but someone worth caring about. For the first time in my life, I felt awake. Alive." He swallowed hard. "Loved."

The sound that escaped me was half sob, half desperate gasp. Henry pulled me against him with sudden fierceness, and then I was pressed to his chest, his arms crushing me close, his lips moving in my hair.

"Solaine."

Just that. My name. Over and over, a whisper that wrapped around us, binding us to the flickering firelight and the river rushing past below, the stars blazing above. And that long-ago time we'd thought lost forever, but that had somehow just found us again.

38

SOLAINE

THAT NIGHT, I abandoned my place on the other side of the fire to lie beside him, the embers of the fire crackling softly, its red glow warding back the night. Henry's breathing slowed and fell into a steady rhythm.

Unable to sleep, I leaned up on one elbow to watch him. His lashes made black half-moons on his cheeks, his whiskers softening the jaw that was clenched as tight as my own.

Nightmares still plagued him.

Every night they came, dragging him back in time to that muddy, starlit riverbank where he watched his father die. I had watched my father, too. But I'd buried my demons so deep under the surface that they rarely came up for air. I could feel them, though. Writhing and shrieking like lost souls, wanting so badly to rush up and devour me, but I was far too cowardly to let them.

Henry was the brave one.

Facing them. His monsters.

Battling them night after night, as if confronting the old wounds would somehow cleanse him, make him whole again. As if he might somehow win.

Maybe one day he would.

Meanwhile, mine were suffocating down in the dark, stewing in my denial, waiting for a chink to appear so they could rush out all at once and consume me. Most of the time, they stayed buried, but moments like this, in the darkness with nothing else to cling to, they raged upwards, and the membrane holding them back seemed paper-thin. Worst of all was the guilt.

"She might die," I murmured to the stars twinkling beyond our shelter. "She might already be dead. And it's all my fault."

Henry stirred at the sound of my voice. His eyes opened, and he studied my face, frowning at something he saw there. He lifted his hand, settling his big palm on my cheek, turning my head to face him. His thumb smudging the dampness under my eyes.

"We'll find her, Miss Granger. I promise."

I swallowed, my throat clicking. "If only I shared your certainty."

His gaze travelled over my face, lingering on my mouth as his thumb traced my jaw, his body shifting to face me. "I have enough for both of us."

I leaned into his hand, clinging to his words, aching for them to be true. His eyes were clear in the ember light as they found mine again, and I let myself sink into them.

Weeks ago, I'd hated him. He had bound my wrists and taken me prisoner, dragging me away from my life in

Elliotville. Away from all hope of finding my daughter. With his scarred hands and hard eyes, he represented everything I believed was wrong with the world. Everything I feared. Men like him had murdered Billy and led my father astray. They had taken my child.

I eased out a shuddering breath.

When had all that changed?

"Sleep, now," he whispered. His hand slid to my throat, still watching me, his thumb still stroking. Soothing me, the way I'd seen him soothe Shadowlark.

And it worked. My tense jaw muscles loosened, my neck growing warm under his palm. His warmth spread to my shoulder, down along my side, pooling across my torso and into my abdomen, lower, until my whole body felt ablaze.

His eyes flickered, and he removed his hand.

I rolled on my back again, turning my head to watch the stars glitter. Brilliant shards that seemed so close I could reach out and run my fingers through them like minnows in a winter stream.

'Goodnight, Henry.' My whisper trembled on the smoky air.

He muttered something unintelligible and slumped away from me, closing his eyes. After a while, his breath grew steady again.

You don't fool me, Henry Hawke. I know you're listening to every insect chirp and creaking branch. To every breath I take. I inched closer, his feverish heat drawing me like a moth towards the flame that could so easily consume it. Destroy it. A moth too foolish to know when it might already be too late to fly away.

39

SOLAINE

THE SCRAPE of boots on stone woke me, and I sat upright, reaching for the revolver. The fire had burned down to glowing embers, and pale dawn light filtered through the rocky overhang.

Henry was ducking through the mouth of our shelter. He was already dressed, the heavy saddlebags cradled in his good arm.

I sprang up and followed him down to where Shadowlark grazed.

"What are you doing?"

He turned, and something had changed overnight. The wariness that usually shuttered his expression had softened, replaced by something I couldn't quite name.

"Cold Mountain Creek is still two days away. The sooner we leave, the quicker we can find your little girl."

I helped him lift the saddlebags behind the saddle and strap them on. He moved stiffly, his shoulders hunched, favouring his left side where the bullet had torn through him a week ago.

I stood back, pushing my hair from my face. "Henry, you can barely stand."

His jaw was clenched, and beneath the stubble, his skin was waxy pale. He stared over at me, his face softening. "Your girl's been missing long enough. It's time we found her."

A tremor went through me, and I dipped my head to hide the burn of sudden tears. He was risking everything to help me. Not to mention the pain it would cost him to ride today and the day after. All so I wouldn't have to face the camp—and whatever I found there—alone.

I nodded and hurried back to the overhang, collecting the last of our things. I pulled another trout from the river and wrapped it in layers of paperbark, then broke apart the trap and flung it into the trees. I kicked dirt over the coals of our campfire, covering any evidence we'd been here.

We rode in silence for most of the morning. Henry pushed the horse until I made him stop and let her rest. We sat under a shady tree, and I changed his bandages while he asked questions about my life—Charlotte, and the years after Papa's death. I found myself telling him things I'd never spoken aloud, small memories that Uncle Niall's lies hadn't quite managed to destroy.

We walked for the rest of the day, Shadowlark plodding behind us through the thick trees, Henry navigating by the sun as it sank towards the west. By evening, we'd made good distance despite Henry's condition. He was silent by then, answering my queries with a nod or a grunt, his skin slick with sweat, his face an unhealthy grey.

We camped beside a creek, the sound of running water a sweet relief after the day's dusty travel. Henry unsaddled the horse before I could stop him, though I saw him lean heavily against Shadowlark's sweaty flanks when he thought I wasn't looking.

"Stubborn fool," I muttered, dumping an armload of twigs for the fire.

"I heard that."

"Good. Maybe it'll sink in."

He smiled—a real smile, not the careful expression he usually wore. "You always did have a sharp tongue, little sparrow."

The nickname sent warmth spiralling through me. "And you were always too proud for your own good."

When the fire was dying down, I placed the bark-wrapped trout on the embers to roast. We ate as night settled, the firelight dancing between us, cicadas chirping in the bushes. As the darkness deepened, I settled back against a tree, smoothing the thin blanket under me.

"Tell me more about them, Henry."

Henry was watching me. "Did your pa ever tell you how he met Miss Lottie?"

I shook my head. "He used to say she cast a spell on him. I knew she left her family to be with him. But neither of them told me how they met."

"Old Cap bailed her up one fine morning. At gunpoint."

"Oh, lord."

Henry smiled, shaking his head. "Not the most romantic start. He knew her family was the richest in the district. And he knew she rode alone every morning, out along the old station road. He thought she'd be easy pickings for a gold watch or purse full of coin."

I bit my lips around a smile. "Mama, easy pickings? My poor papa, I feel sorry for him already."

Henry laughed softly. "She looked down her nose at him and said, 'Why, you insufferable scoundrel, put away your weapon and take off that ridiculous mask. I recognise your horse, Jim Beaumont, and if you balk a moment longer in asking me to step out with you this evening, then I'll make sure you hang.'"

I blinked, gasping out a laugh. "Oh Henry, you wicked thing. She never said that!"

Henry placed his hand over his heart. "I swear on my life, Miss Granger. Old Cap obediently tore off his mask and asked her to step out, and three months later they were wed."

I slumped back against the tree, giggling at the perfect way Henry had captured Mama's tone, and at the outlandish story that—knowing my mother—I utterly believed. I could picture them so clearly. My handsome Papa with his merry eyes, bewitched by my beautiful, imperious mother, whose outward pomp concealed the kindest, most glorious heart of anyone I knew.

My shoulders shook, even as my laughter died away. My hands crept up, as Charlotte's so often did, hiding my face. My fingers trembled as I pressed them against my eyes, trying to stop the sudden gush of tears escaping.

"Miss Granger?"

"I'm all right, Henry. I just …" I was twelve again, back in the courthouse yard. I could see my father standing on the gallows platform. The sun in my eyes, the rope creaking, and Uncle's hand firm on my shoulder, but still I could see him—

A sob tore out of my throat. "I watched him die."

Henry went still. Only his chest was rising and falling as he stared at me. When he moved, it was in a single fluid action, like a wildcat springing for its prey. He landed in front of me, reaching for my face, his fingers calloused and warm as he traced them along my cheek.

"You were there?"

I nodded, not trusting myself to speak.

Henry searched my eyes, his thumb brushing away my tears. "Ten years ago, you were … twelve? Then how in God's name were you allowed to watch—?"

"Not allowed." The words came out flat, emotionless. It was the only way I could say them. "Made to. Uncle Niall said I needed to understand how bad my father was. What my mother's recklessness had led to."

I heard Henry's sharp intake of breath, but I couldn't look at him.

"He dragged me to the courthouse yard. Stood behind me, gripping my shoulders. His fingers were like steel claws, burrowing into my flesh, hurting me. Forcing me to stand there. Every time I flinched, they dug deeper, and the next day, my shoulders were black and blue—" My voice cracked. "Papa saw me. Our eyes met just before … He tried to smile. Even then, facing death, he tried to reassure me."

"Jesus." Henry's voice was strangled. "What kind of man forces a child to witness her father's death?"

"The kind who wanted to be sure I'd never make my mother's mistake."

"What mistake?"

"Loving someone beneath her. An outlaw." I finally looked up, meeting his horrified gaze. "He made me watch them put the noose around Papa's neck. Made me watch him fall. Made me watch him ..." I couldn't finish.

Henry pulled me hard against his chest, trapping me in his arms, holding me so close I could feel every ripple of muscle, every pound of his heart. I went rigid at first, then crumpled into him as the grief I'd buried for so long finally broke free.

"I'm sorry," he whispered into my hair.

Protected by his arms, surrounded by the scent of tea tree leaves and fire smoke lifting off his clothes, I let myself come undone. My sobs shook us both, great heaving wrenches that surged up from a deep place, buried for so long under my uncle's lies. Henry held me through it all, his arms strong and steady around me, his voice murmuring wordless comfort.

When the worst of it passed, I found myself curled against his side, my head on his shoulder, his fingers stroking through my hair.

"Your uncle was wrong," Henry said quietly. "Your mother didn't make a mistake. She loved a good man. A man whose only crime was trying to balance the wrongs of an unfair society."

I closed my eyes, breathing in his warmth, his solidity. "I hated my father for so long. I believed Uncle Niall when he said Papa was a bad man, responsible for my mother's death."

Henry's hand stilled in my hair. "And now?"

I pressed closer, feeling his heartbeat beneath my cheek, strong and reassuring. "I was mistaken. About so many things. But now I'm remembering, and it's like my family is returning to me. And I have you to thank for it."

His arms strengthened around me, and he pressed his lips to the top of my head. The fire crackled softly, and the moon shifted across the sky, the stars burning bright and watching down.

As I shut my eyes, a sigh shuddered out of me.

All the lies, all my uncle's years of brainwashing, had failed. Here I was, held tight in the arms of a wanted man, a man with a price on his head. A man who was, without doubt, an even more dangerous criminal than my father.

And heaven forgive me, I was falling recklessly, completely, unable to stop myself even if I wanted to.

HENRY

I WAITED till her breathing became steady, then shifted my weight, easing the pressure from my shoulder. A bead of sweat trickled down the side of my face, but I didn't move to wipe it away.

Solaine slept soundly against me, her solid warmth filling me with a longing fiercer than anything I'd ever experienced before. After the cruelty she'd spoken of tonight, my old urges had risen in me, the way they had after Pa's murder. The urge to make someone pay for the suffering they'd caused, to wreak justice on an unjust world.

Pray you never meet me, Niall Granger. Because if you do, I'll wring your neck with my bare hands.

My hold tightened around her. Old Cap's little sparrow. Now grown up with a child of her own, and somehow still fighting and fending for herself in a world that had betrayed her in the worst possible way.

I thought of Cap's abandoned cottage back in Elliotville,

with its overgrown yard and buckled cladding, the tumbling verandah. I had shared so many happy times with the Beaumonts on that wide, shady verandah, the four of us laughing and bantering, or quietly enjoying a meal together. Feeling like the family I'd never had before.

Back then, I'd thought them better off without me. But now, seeing how fate had delivered blow after blow, first Miss Lottie, and then Old Cap, and Solaine enduring her grief alone—it killed me to think how different things might have been if I'd stayed.

"I'm here now," I murmured into her hair.

She shifted her weight, warm against my side.

Longing gripped me, not for the past, but for the future I could already picture unfolding ahead of us. Solaine and little Charlotte, their faces glowing in the firelight, happy and laughing beside me. Spending our nights in the peaceful dark, a campfire crackling softly nearby. The three of us, a family.

"We have to find her first."

Urgency flooded through me, and if Solaine hadn't been sleeping so deeply, if she hadn't just told me a story so heartbreaking I knew rest was her only escape from it, I'd have leapt up that very instant and ridden into the night in search of the girl.

Pray God she's still alive.

Nothing else mattered, now.

Even if helping Solaine dragged me into the path of the law and back to the gallows, I didn't care. Doing this one good thing, this last humane act, an act of love, might finally give my wretched life meaning.

41

SOLAINE

During the night, I woke, my head at an odd angle, my neck twinging. I tucked my face down, snuggling deeper into the warmth, the scent of woodsmoke and horses enveloping me.

Arms tightened around me. *Henry*.

My eyes popped wide, panic pooling in my belly, my body holding still as last night's confession tumbled back into my bleary brain. My nerve endings felt tender, as though I'd torn them out and trampled them under me, exposing the rawest part of myself. Spilling my pain, admitting the lies Niall told me. Admitting how gullible I'd been to believe him.

And then hearing Henry's version of the truth. *Your mother loved a good man … a man whose only crime was trying to balance the wrongs of an unfair society.*

Henry would say that. Of course he would.

He had fashioned himself after my father. He saw crime as a rebellion, an act of revolution against a society he believed was unjust. That *was* unjust. But robbing people, even killing them—was it really as noble as Henry made it out to be?

Of course not.

My father might have been a good man and a loving husband. A man who'd once rescued a frightened young boy from the riverbank. But that didn't make the life he'd chosen right. It didn't excuse the actions he'd chosen to take. Actions that had torn him away from his child, forcing her into the care of someone like Uncle Niall, who had his own cruel agenda and purpose. *So typical of you, Solaine,* my uncle had said. *You're so like your wretched mother—wilful and strong on the surface, but the moment life gets tough, you crumble.*

I closed my eyes again, sliding back in time to the court-house yard. My uncle's hand gripped my shoulder, my jaw clenched so hard my teeth ached as I rolled my eyes away, looking anywhere but the gallows. The sun had made my head ache, blinding me, but my uncle's bony fingers kept digging into my flesh, forcing me to watch. The noose slid over my father's head, but as he turned his face towards me, it wasn't my father, but—

"Henry!" I jolted upright.

I was alone on the blanket with my back to the tree.

Fragile dawn light was hazing through the treetops. Bird-song rang around me, and the fresh scent of early morning humidity sweetened the air.

Henry crouched in front of me, a mug of steaming tea in his hands. He passed the mug to me, his smile teasing.

"Dreaming about me again, Miss Granger?"

I took it and drank deeply until the tea was gone. "More of a nightmare," I said, swirling the dregs, tipping my head to squint at him. "Are you still so determined to come with me to the miners' camp?"

He frowned. "More than ever."

I looked at him in the morning light, anxiety tightening my chest. "If the camp was ransacked like Mrs Landy said, the police might be coming and going. What if they show up while we're there?"

He dragged his fingers through his hair, his gaze unwavering on my face. "The traps'll be long gone by now." He patted the gun tucked in the front of his belt, quietly confident. "I promised to be there with you, whatever the risks. And I will be."

I sighed, glad of his loyalty but terrified too. "I was afraid you'd say that. You know …" I sucked my bottom lip, tasting the tea's sweetly bitter residue. "Just because you loved my father doesn't make you obligated to me. There's still time for you to leave. To head north and make it over the border. Save yourself."

He scratched his whiskers, the blue of his eyes hardening in the fragile dawn light.

"What sort of man do you think I am, Miss Granger? A lowlife who'd just abandon you to save my own neck? I made a promise, and nothing will stop me from keeping it. Not even you."

My dream flashed back—the noose around his neck, the sun in his eyes turning them pale and fierce as they locked with mine. The grip on my shoulder, forcing me to watch him die. The old fear uncoiling inside me, my heart stuttering wildly, as if I was seeing the future instead of the past.

"You seem to have this misguided sense of honour,

Henry." I fought to keep my voice steady. "As if you're some kind of hero, when in fact you're the villain."

Henry scowled and took my empty cup, throwing the dregs over the smoking coals with a swift, irritated motion.

"I know what I am."

I climbed to my feet, raking my hands through my tangled hair and pinning it lopsidedly to my nape, needing something to do with my trembling fingers.

"I don't think you do."

He ignored me, kicking dirt over the remaining embers and turning his back to me. He had already tidied the camp and packed the saddlebag while I slept. Without another word, he picked up the saddle and bags, and stalked towards the horse.

I trailed after him. "I understand why you chose this life and why you became the man you are. But it eludes me how one moment I'm an insurance policy … and the next you're risking your life to help me. And don't say it's your connection to my father, because your offer to help came before you knew that."

He eased the saddle over Shadowlark's back and buckled it on, then turned to face me. He stared at me for the longest time, his face unreadable. Then he closed the distance between us in two long strides and gripped my shoulders, his touch searing through the thin fabric of my blouse.

I could see every detail of him in the frail sunlight—the dark stubble, the shadows carved into his cheeks, the tension along his jaw.

"You want to know why I'm helping you?" The roughness in his voice seemed to vibrate through my entire body.

I nodded, wide-eyed, unable to move.

He leaned in, closing the gap between us so we were almost touching, his gaze still locked on my face.

My limbs began to tingle from the awareness swirling through me, a flush heating my skin. My head tilted back of its own accord, my lips parting. We stood too close, and his proximity was making me ... *feel*. Shaky. Unbridled. Fiercely alive.

My fingers twitched. I had to touch him. I needed to ... but that was wrong, so horribly wrong, and I clenched my fingers into fists. As if that would stop my heart racing so wildly. As if it would let me tear my gaze off him and look away.

There had only ever been one love in my life, and that was Billy ... but he'd never made me flush this way. Had never set me ablaze. Not like this. He'd never turned my knees to water, my bones to jelly. Had never filled my veins with such unbearable, sweet heat.

I leaned towards the source of that warmth, savouring Henry's scent—horses and fire smoke, saddle oil, and something uniquely him that made my heart thump almost painfully.

His gaze dropped to my lips, lingering there with such naked hunger that I felt devoured before he'd even touched me.

I tangled my fingers in the front of his shirt and drew him down towards me. That was all the encouragement he needed. He swooped on me, crushing his lips down onto mine, dragging me hard against his chest. His kiss wasn't gentle—it was desperate, hungry. His fingers threaded through my hair, dislodging the pins I'd just placed, cupping the back of my head, pulling me tighter against his body and deepening the kiss.

The world disappeared—there was only his mouth on mine, his hands in my hair, the pounding of my heart against his. Everything I'd tried to deny rushed to the surface, leaving me trembling and clinging to him as though he was the only solid thing in a world turned upside down.

When he abruptly stepped away, I was breathless. His eyes had turned hard, but I could see the rapid rise and fall of his chest, the slight tremor in his hands.

"Does that answer your question, Miss Granger?"

My fingers crept up to my bruised lips, covering them as I met his cold stare. But then I dropped my hand and squared my shoulders, glaring back at him.

"I told you to call me Solaine."

His stare was steady, but something shuttered in his eyes, and I sensed him retreat into himself. Without another word, he sprang up onto the horse, glaring ahead as he waited for me to join him.

I climbed shakily into the saddle behind him and slid my arms around his waist, noticing the taut muscles beneath my fingers. Remembering his lips on mine, his breath in my mouth, the crush of his arms pinning me against him.

My mind whirled. *Does that answer your question, Miss Granger?* I huffed in irritation. What good was an answer when it raised so many more questions?

He was doing this for me. He wanted me, but what did that mean? Was I a prize to him, a conquest? Or did he have intentions for afterwards … after we reached the camp, after we knew the truth about Charlotte?

Intentions I could not possibly honour?

He steered the horse back onto the trail with a click of his tongue, and Shadowlark resumed her canter through the trees.

Daylight peeped over the distant hills as we rode northwest towards the miners' camp. The taste of him lingered on my lips, filling me with the knowledge that everything between us had—for better or worse—irrevocably changed.

42

SOLAINE

Morning sunlight glowed through the trees, casting dappled shadows across the back road we'd been following since dawn. My skin tingled, feeling sunburned, but it had nothing to do with the day's rising heat.

And everything to do with Henry.

I touched my lips, the faint bruised feeling proof that our kiss was real, that I hadn't just dreamed it.

No, what I had dreamed was Henry with a noose around his neck—doomed to the same ending as my father. And like my father, he'd eventually be torn away from anyone foolish enough to love him, leaving devastation in his wake.

Our kiss meant nothing. I couldn't afford to let it mean anything. As tempting as it was to lean on him and draw strength from him, as I'd been doing, I couldn't risk what our growing closeness might do to my heart.

I eased back in the saddle, studying his profile as he surveyed the landscape, tension etching his brow.

A few weeks ago, he'd seemed like the worst kind of monster to me. An escaped convict, a bushranger and criminal, no better than the men who'd killed Billy and taken Charlotte. He'd stolen me away in the night, shackling me with his belt, forcing me to spend endless hours in the saddle when I should have been looking for my daughter. *Yes, and now he's riding out of his way into danger's path. ... for you. Because he cares. Cares enough to help you when everyone else has given up.*

A trail of sweat gleamed on the side of his face, gluing a strand of dark hair to his cheek. His whiskers had almost thickened into a beard, making him seem fierce, maybe even dangerous, had it not been for that wide, luscious mouth ... a mouth that made my pulse pound harder as I remembered how sweet it felt pressed to mine—

"Damn," I muttered under my breath. "How did I let this happen?"

Henry dipped his head and turned slightly, his lips twitching. "What was that, Miss Granger?"

"Nothing," I said sourly, fanning my neck with my hand.

Was this rough man really the boy I'd idolised as a child? The boy who once tricked me into eating a worm, and then ate one too, so I wouldn't feel so bad? The boy who listened to my chatter and made up silly stories to make me laugh?

It hurt to remember. Remember that we'd lost him, that he'd run away to save us. It hurt even more to think that even back then, my small family was already doomed ...

He shifted in the saddle.

Watchful all of a sudden, unusually alert, his hand moving near the gun tucked in his belt. When he slowed

Shadowlark to a halt, I sat forward, craning to see over his shoulder.

"What is it?"

He turned, pressing a finger to his lips.

"Someone's been here," he murmured, nodding towards a small clearing just off the road. "I've been smelling smoke all morning, but it's stronger here."

He nudged Shadowlark off the road and along the track towards the clearing. Moments later, an abandoned campsite came into view. A fire ring with dead ashes, a few discarded items scattered about, as if the occupants had fled in a hurry. My heart quickened.

"Bushrangers?" I whispered. "Bounty hunters?"

"Or maybe just travellers." He dismounted, his hand still hovering near his gun as he surveyed the abandoned site. "Looks like they left in a hurry." He knelt beside the fire, sifting his fingers through the ashes. "Cold. At least a day old."

He helped me out of the saddle and left Shadowlark to graze, wandering past the campfire and downhill a little way to a small sunlit creek. "There are fresh horse tracks over here."

I circled the remains of the fire, stretching the stiffness out of my legs. We hadn't seen anyone on the road, so whoever had camped here was probably travelling ahead of us. I glanced over at Henry. He was alert, but seemed confident the campers were no threat.

Sunlight flared near a fallen log, and I wandered over to investigate. A full bottle of brandy sat propped against the log, its cork still perfectly sealed by wax. Whoever had been here had expensive tastes.

"Henry," I called softly, holding up the bottle. "You're not going to believe—"

As I turned, a flash of faded green caught my eye beneath a fallen branch. I held very still, fearing another snake, but then frowned. Just a piece of fabric, but it started my alarm bells ringing.

Stalking over, I snatched it up.

A sash. Faded green cotton, frayed at the edges, but unmistakable.

Henry crossed the clearing in three long strides, his eyes lighting up as he saw the bottle. He took it from my hand, then stopped.

"Miss Granger?"

My fingers trembled slightly as I held up the strip of fabric. "I've seen this before. One of the men who took Charlotte was wearing it—or one exactly like it. Do you think …" My voice sounded strange to my own ears, thin and breathless. I swallowed. "He wore it around his waist like a belt. I remember it clearly."

Henry's expression sharpened. He took the sash from my hands, examining it with narrowed eyes, his brows furrowing.

"I've seen it before, too."

"What do you mean?"

He looked up, dark fury flashing across his face. "The day I left Elliotville. Not long after I saw you in the street."

"I don't understand."

His jaw tightened. "I was heading west of town. Years ago, I hid a weapon in a tree trunk, so I was riding out to collect it. I saw horses on the road ahead of me and hid in the trees, thinking they were traps. But it was a group of rough men. One was wearing a green sash exactly like this, with an eagle feather stuck in his hat."

"A grey-haired man?"

Henry scratched his stubble. "He struck me as older, so maybe. Yeah."

My breath caught. "It's him, Henry. He was here. The man who took—" I broke off, my mind racing. "Why didn't you tell me this before?"

"I never made the connection." His voice had turned defensive. "I didn't know it was related to Charlotte."

I snatched the sash back from him. "What else did you see? Tell me everything."

Henry rubbed the back of his neck, the scarred fingers of his other hand strangling the brandy bottle. "There were three of them. Then a fourth man came along. Not part of their gang—he was dressed like gentry. I saw him hand over money. Paying them for some job."

Cold dread pooled in my stomach. "Who was he?"

"Don't know. I didn't see him clearly. But he was well-dressed. Expensive coat, fine horse. Someone of means."

I turned away, trying to make sense of it all. Who would pay bushrangers to take Charlotte? And if they were paid, why had no ransom note ever arrived?

"This doesn't make sense," I whispered, dread turning my limbs to ice. "If someone paid to have her taken, then it wasn't for money. Who would take a child and never demand payment?"

"You said your uncle was a powerful man?"

I nodded, twisting the sash in my fingers. All I could think about was Charlotte being ripped from my arms, the terror in her eyes, crying out as the man bundled her away—

"Miss Granger." Henry placed the bottle on the ground and stepped up to me, smoothing his hands along my arms. "Does your uncle have any enemies?"

I blinked. "Enemies?"

"Anyone who'd like to hurt him. Hurt his family."

"He—" The realisation struck me like a blow to the chest. Uncle Niall had a tight group of close friends, wealthy landowners or government officials like him. Most of the people he brushed shoulders with were cool acquaintances. But how many more were lower down the ladder, people Niall had ruled against, convicted of crimes? Confiscated property from?

"He said I'd been careless," I breathed, my throat tight. "He said she was taken because I refused to follow the rules. His rules. He said—" I swallowed the lump in my throat. "It was never about me, was it? It was about Uncle Niall. Someone seeking revenge against him."

I pushed away from Henry, the sash trailing behind me as I stalked into the trees. Away from the camp. Away from the horrible truth that was dawning.

"Miss Granger, wait." Henry caught up with me. "We don't know that any of this is true."

I ignored him, picking my way deeper into the trees, my skirts catching on thorns as I walked without seeing.

"But to take it out on a child?" My voice cracked. I looked down at the faded green sash in my hands, and for the first time since Charlotte had been taken, I allowed myself to consider the terrible possibility that had always been lurking in the back of my mind. "What if ... what if she's not—"

"Don't," Henry said sharply. He caught me around the waist and swung me to face him. Cupping my face in his palms, forcing me to look at him. "Don't even think it. We're going to find her."

But I saw the flicker in his eyes, saw my own doubts mirrored there. For weeks, I'd clung to hope, to the belief that Charlotte was alive somewhere and waiting for me. Now, that hope felt fragile, like something that might shatter at the slightest touch.

"We need to keep moving," he said, his voice gentler now. "We're approaching Cold Mountain Creek. The miners' camp can't be far. If anything, finding the sash gives weight to Mrs Landy's claim that she found Charlotte's charm at the camp. Your daughter might be closer than you think."

I nodded and wound the sash around my waist, knotting it to the side the way the bushranger had done. As Henry helped me back onto Shadowlark, his hand lingered on mine, his eyes searching my face.

"Thank you," I said shakily. "I'd never have made it this far without you."

"I'll find her for you, Miss Granger," he said, his voice low and fierce. "I swear it."

I nodded, but not even the strength of his words could warm away the chill that had taken root inside me. My uncle's words replayed in my mind, taking on new meaning. *You coddled the girl, Solaine. Made her wilful and headstrong. Do you really think she'll survive long in the company of bushrangers?*

A sob barked out of me, my heart so full of fear that I could feel it pumping through the rest of my body like poison. Not bushrangers—but someone of means who wanted revenge against my uncle. Someone dangerous.

Henry's hand reached around and caught my fingers,

squeezing gently. I gripped back, wilting forward to press my face between his shoulder blades, seeking comfort.

But as we rode along the back road towards the miners' camp, the sun climbing higher in the sky, beating down on us without mercy, I couldn't shake the terrible feeling that we were already too late.

43

HENRY

LATE AFTERNOON SUNLIGHT dappled the clearing, turning the river below us to liquid amber. We'd stopped early to make camp, both of us needing to wash away the dust before facing whatever waited for us at the miners' camp tomorrow.

I'd already taken a dip in the river, scrubbing off the worst of the grime and washing my hair. Then I'd speared two decent-sized trout for our supper. I scaled and cleaned the fish downstream and headed back to the grassy patch we'd claimed for the night, passing Miss Granger on the way.

She walked past me towards the water, her eyes lowered, the golden sunlight spilling over her like shimmering coins. Pausing, she slid the sash from around her waist and hooked it on a tree branch, then disappeared into the shadows.

The green material fluttered in the breeze like a wide, flat snake, the cursed thing taunting me.

It's not the sash that's cursed—it's you.

If only I'd followed the men that day on the drovers road. Not the toff. He'd made himself scarce in a hurry. But the other three. The ones who'd taken Miss Granger's little girl. I wouldn't have needed my firearm. I'd have taken the mongrels on empty-handed, starting with the blaggard in the green sash and then mopping up the two brainless youths.

If only I'd been thinking of someone other than myself. Miss Granger could be at home with her child, the lines of worry gone from her face, her baby safe in her arms.

And you'd be worm food.

I turned away, trying not to think about the damned sash. About how badly it had rattled her. Or that a wretched part of me deep down was secretly glad we'd met. Not the unhappy circumstances, but certainly the meeting. In a few short weeks, she'd given my life a purpose I hadn't even known it was missing.

I built a fire, and while it crackled, I scouted around and found a cut-leaf mint bush in a sunny patch. Its leaves released a fragrant peppery scent as I tore off some sprigs and laid them on flat stones in the embers, feeling the heat radiate as I placed the fish on top.

I sat back on my heels, eyeing the track to the river.

Frowning at the fluttering green sash.

Miss Granger had known what I was when she met me that day on the street. I'd seen it in her eyes, her alarm when she noticed my manacle scars. The glimpse of my tattoo. She had looked into my eyes with her dark amber gaze and deemed me untouchable.

Beneath her.

Yet her pupils had bloomed with something else, a sort of recognition. Her gaze lingering longer than was proper, her cheeks flushing pink. Then this morning, when we kissed, the way she melted against me, trembling and clinging like I actually mattered.

"Lord, man. Get a grip—"

"Chatting away to yourself again, Henry?"

I glared around, my witty comeback dying on my lips when I saw her. She had removed her corset and washed her skirt and blouse, which she carried against herself, soaking her thin petticoat and chemise, the flimsy material clinging to her curves, her long hair falling around her shoulders.

I blinked, trying not to stare. Failing.

Watching silently as she settled by the fire on the blanket I'd laid out for her, toasting her palms, her gaze flicking to me for a heartbeat, and then back to the fire and the fish sizzling over the embers.

"They smell delicious," she said, almost to herself. "I'm quite famished."

I unbuckled the saddlebags, taking out our tin plates and the unopened bottle of brandy. Watching her lean closer to the heat as she dried her hair, the wet strands darkening the shoulders of her chemise.

My fingers still tingled from the chill of the river, but the rest of me was warm. Too warm, whenever I looked at her. Whenever I thought about how soft her lips were against mine this morning, the strength in her arms as she'd wound them around my neck—

"I think we've earned ourselves a tipple," I said lightly, breaking off the wax and uncorking the bottle with my knife. "Fancy a drop?"

Her eyes brightened. "I'd forgotten about that."

I sat opposite, placing the brandy bottle on the ground between us, then filled our plates with the fish.

"Thank you," she murmured, taking the plate, breaking the fish open with a twig to cool it. Steam puffed up, and she inhaled it with a sigh. The sunlight caught in her damp hair, turning the brown to gold around the edges. Like a halo. Like she was something otherworldly, that I had no business pining for.

We ate in silence for a while, the river gurgling beside us, birds calling overhead. Shadowlark cropping grass further along the bank.

It was peaceful. The kind of place a man might dream of settling, in another life. I glanced across the fire. Solaine was prodding at her food, nibbling little bites, nothing of the healthy appetite she usually showed. I could tell that her thoughts were far away, as they mostly were, with her daughter.

"Tell me about Charlotte's father," I said finally, hoping to distract her. "You mentioned him once, but not how you met."

Her fingers stilled on the fish. "Billy? He was an artist. Uncle Niall hired him to teach me to paint, thinking it would bring me out of my shell. And it did. Billy was kind, gentle-natured." A small smile touched her lips, but it was sad. "He'd bring me wildflowers he picked on his way to the house. Uncle Niall didn't approve of him courting me— Billy's family were all lumber men from Dorrigo, not the right social class—but Uncle finally gave his blessing when I turned sixteen."

"And then?"

Her smile faded. "We had one delightful year together.

Charlotte was born, and the following winter, Billy was killed. Bushrangers." She looked across at me, bitter accusation in her eyes. "They stopped him on the road from Dorrigo one freezing afternoon. Shot him when he wouldn't hand over his mother's broach he was bringing back for me."

My heart sank like a stone.

No wonder she'd looked at me with such hatred when she knew what I was. No wonder she'd fought me so fiercely in those early days.

"I'm sorry," I said.

She nodded, her gaze dropping back to her half-eaten meal. "So am I."

"You didn't keep your married name?"

Her shoulder twitched. "Uncle convinced me to change it back to Granger, so that Charlotte would inherit my share of the Granger fortune if something happened to me. Or that I would still inherit if something happened to him. It made sense on paper, or at least back then it did. Yet I still suspect he had other motives. More selfish ones."

"What motives?"

"Preserving the Granger name. Bringing me back under his thumb, I don't know." She swiped her face, looking up at me, forcing a smile. "At the time, I didn't give a fig about his motives. He was kind to me and Charlotte, in his way. And I did as he asked, just grateful for his support. Burying my grief deeply enough so I could care for my baby."

The pain in her eyes nearly crushed me.

A grieving young mother with a babe, an uncle with his own selfish agenda. Her future in tatters because of some desperate men with no conscience.

I wanted to tell her I wasn't like the men who'd killed her

husband, that I'd never taken a life—but that would be a lie. I'd shot a man during a holdup outside of Newcastle. He hadn't died, but I'd meant to kill him. What made me any different from the men who'd widowed her?

"What about you?" she asked suddenly. "What was your life like before ... before your father was murdered?"

The question caught me off guard. Most people only cared about the outlaw I'd become, not the boy I'd been before. Before the nightmares began. Before I started punishing the world.

"Ma worked in the wash-house at a big wool property near Armidale," I said, setting aside my plate. "She was frail, her hands always chafed. A quiet woman, apart from her constant cough. She's ghostlike in my memory now. I barely remember her. Fever took her one winter when I was young."

Miss Granger reached for the brandy bottle. "And your father?"

"Pa was quiet too. I think he never recovered from losing her. After she died, we left the property. He moved us around a lot, following work cutting cedar in the northern forests."

She took a sip, wincing, and then passed the bottle to me.

"You never wanted to cut cedar yourself?"

I took the bottle but didn't drink right away. "At first, I did. It was hard work, but I enjoyed it. Working alongside Pa and the other cutters made me feel like I belonged. I used to love the smell of cedar sap on my hands." I poked at the fire with a stick, watching the sparks rise. "Afterwards ... I couldn't bear it."

"What will you do?" she asked softly. "When you cross the border?"

I lifted the bottle, resting the rim against my mouth,

picturing her lips touching the glass only moments before. When I drank, I savoured the burn, shutting my eyes, letting the warmth seep through me.

"Been thinking I'd like to make saddles." I glanced at her, gauging her reaction. "Like Old Cap. He taught me how during my time with him. Let me work alongside him in the saddlery sometimes."

She smiled wistfully, her eyes gleaming in the firelight. "If only you had stayed with us. Your life might have taken a different path. Maybe mine as well."

I looked away. Saddlery wasn't the only thing her father had taught me. Old Cap made sure I knew how to oil and clean a pistol. How to shoot it. And how to slip through the tree shadows in silence along a deserted road to lie in wait.

I drank again and wiped the rim with my sleeve, then reached across and placed the bottle beside her. Her hand moved towards it, but instead she picked up something from the ground.

"Pass me your knife, would you?"

I passed it over. "What have you got there?" She held it up, and I smiled. "Found yourself a nice little silver wattle burl. They're pretty rare. Pa used to say they bring good luck."

She started working the knife into the burl, like she was peeling a potato. While she worked, I helped myself to the brandy bottle, watching her fingers nimbly maneuvering the blade to carve into the burl's surface, her forehead creased in concentration.

Her fingers were soft and pale—a lady's hands, unmarked by the kind of hard labour that had killed my ma. Yet they moved swiftly, with a skill and purpose that mesmerised me.

"You really know how to handle a knife," I observed, the brandy heat pulsing through my veins. I took another sip. "Who taught you?"

"A boy I knew once."

I smiled, the memory settling over me like a warm blanket. She would have been about ten, her hair spilling over her shoulders like it was now, her eyes wide as she stared at the pocket knife I was scraping over a knot of cedar I'd found in the forest. I had carved her a bird, and she'd taken it from me, wide-eyed. *Oh, it's lovely,* she said, peering up through her lashes. *Will you show me how?*

She reached across the fire, the burl caged in her fist.

"It's for you, Henry. It's Shadowlark."

I smiled crookedly, suddenly feeling the effects of the liquor, my head light, my heart lurching all over the place like a tipsy kangaroo.

"For me?"

She nodded.

I took the little carving, turning it over in my palm. She'd made the likeness of a horse's head, the eyes and nostrils perfectly detailed, letting the burl's natural swells and hollows suggest the head and flowing mane.

Something tightened in my chest—a feeling I couldn't name, didn't want to name. No one had given me a gift in years. Not since I'd lived with Old Cap. And never anything so exquisite.

"Huh," I said by way of a thank you, my voice rougher than I meant. I traced my thumb over the carving, feeling the smooth places where her fingers had worked the wood. "It's my best treasure—aside from Shadowlark herself." *And you, I* didn't add, though the admission sat on my tongue like a bitter pill I didn't have the heart to swallow.

Instead, I took another gulp of brandy, turning the carving over and over again in my hands.

Miss Granger smiled, and for a moment, I let myself believe ... that we'd find Charlotte at the camp. That Miss Granger might someday look at me and see not the outlaw who took her hostage, but a man worthy of her regard. That there might be a future for us beyond the miners' camp, beyond the search, beyond the lies and crimes that had defined my life.

But as the sun sank lower, casting long shadows across our clearing, my old doubts crept back in.

I was on the run, a wanted man with blood on my hands. She was a lady, widowed because of men like me, desperately searching for her child—a child who was missing because of men like me. Rough men, lawless and untamable. Outlawed. Even if she could forgive what I'd done, what future could I possibly offer her? What right did I have to even imagine one?

I slipped the carving into my jacket, close to my heart, knowing it might be the only piece of her I'd ever be allowed to keep.

44

SOLAINE

THE MINGLING aromas of brandy and roasted fish, wood smoke and river water trailed in the air. I shut my eyes, inhaling it all with a smile. Once, I'd have preferred to fill my lungs with expensive perfume imported from Paris, or lavender hair tonic or some such.

When had that changed?

Night stole softly around us, falling like a whisper, the stars appearing one by one, twinkling in a black velvet sky. The casuarina trees whispered to each other, their slender branches swaying in the air. Beside us, the river raced over rocks, its voice a constant murmur beneath our quiet conversation.

Henry had stoked the fire and placed our billycan over the glowing coals, the flickering radiance casting a golden glow across our faces. We sat close, shoulders nearly touching, the warmth between us having nothing to do with the flames, and even less to do with the half-empty brandy bottle beside us.

Henry tossed a twig into the embers. "What will you do after we find Charlotte? Return to your uncle in Elliotville?"

"Probably." I traced patterns in the dirt with a stick, avoiding his gaze. Grateful that finding her was—at least in his view—a possibility and not just wishful thinking. "Maybe."

"You seem uncertain."

"My uncle's house ... it's not *my* house. Uncle Niall means well, but his strictness and disapproval weigh on me sometimes. He told Charlotte that it's unbecoming for a little girl to be too happy."

"Unbecoming?" Henry looked aghast. "But children are *supposed* to be happy. Lord knows they grow up too quickly, and then they're bound to be miserable."

"That's exactly what I said!"

Henry blew a breath at the sky, shaking his head. "Forgive me, Miss Granger, but your uncle's a dunderhead."

I bit my lips around a smile. "I had dreams," I admitted. "Silly ones, my uncle says. And now, after all this—" I waved my hand at the dark bush surrounding us. "Losing Charlotte has made me see he was right. I'd never make it on my own."

Henry's brow creased. "What dreams?"

I sucked my lip, savouring the brandy's oaky, spicy aftertaste. "To have a horse farm. A place to breed good stock, but also ..." I hesitated, remembering Uncle Niall's derision. "A sanctuary, of sorts. For old horses who can no longer work."

Henry's smile was soft in the firelight as he nodded. "Somewhere quiet, with room for them to run. A garden to grow all the carrots you're going to need. And a stable hand."

"A stable hand?" My brows shot up and I laughed. "Offering your services, are you?"

He made a show of patting his pockets. "I've got my letter of introduction here somewhere ..."

My lips quirked at the corners. "You realise that to employ you, I'd be forced to relocate my farm over the Queensland border?"

"I hear the grass up there is very lush."

"And the ticks, no doubt."

He puffed up his chest. "Catching the little blighters happens to be a specialty of mine."

"Specialty, really?"

He called into the darkness. "Shadowlark, help a man out, would you?"

The horse gave a sharp snort and shifted further along the river away from us, her hooves crunching through the dry grass.

"I'm sorry, sir," I said, laughing. "She seems unwilling to back up your claim."

Henry laughed too and flopped back on the blanket, his sigh sounding defeated. "After all I've done for the treacherous nag."

I flopped back too, my tense muscles loosening, my dark mood finally lifting. Finding the green sash this morning had plunged me into despair, but maybe Henry was right. *Finding the sash gives weight to Mrs Landy's claim that Charlotte was at the camp. Your daughter might be closer than you think.*

"It's a good dream, Miss Granger." Henry's hand found mine in the darkness, his rough palm warm against my skin as he gave a gentle squeeze. "I think you'll have your farm one day. You and little Charlotte and a whole herd of beautiful horses."

"I hope so." I traced my thumb over his manacle scars. "It feels good to talk about it. To imagine it's real."

And yet, in that moment, with the stars watching and the river murmuring, and cicadas singing in the grass around us, the future seemed very far away. Even tomorrow was distant as the moon.

I moved my fingers, lacing them through Henry's. It was a small touch, innocent even, but it sent warm shivers coursing through me.

He shivered too. "You know, Miss Granger." His eyes were steady on my face, a faint smile ghosting across his lips. "Being with you is the only time I've ever felt peace."

I leaned up on one elbow, watching him. Firelight flickered across his face, picking out the hollows and ridges, his whiskery jaw and wide mouth. Where our bodies touched, mine seemed to be burning with a delicious ache that drew me closer.

He was dangerous, an escaped outlaw. He was everything I'd learned to hate and fear. But right now, with the two of us cocooned in the gentle glow of embers and starlight, and the world hidden somewhere far beyond us in the dark, he was everything I wanted.

And by the look in his eyes, he wanted me, too.

"Henry," I whispered, lifting my hand to his face, tracing the line of his jaw with trembling fingers. "You insufferable scoundrel ... if you don't kiss me right now, I swear I'll scream."

His breath caught, his eyes darkening as they held mine.

"Solaine."

The hoarse way he spoke my name, the rawness in his voice, sent more shivers flying over me. I understood suddenly that he'd been keeping his distance before, calling me Miss Granger, not crossing the line into territory that was —for him, at least—uncomfortably familiar.

Now, that space between us vanished. His lips found mine, cautious at first, then hungry. His tongue swept against my lips, and I opened to him with a soft gasp that seemed to ignite something primal within him. He rolled us so he was under me, one palm cupping the back of my head, his other skimming down my side, tightening around my waist.

My fingers slid into his hair, drawing him closer. The world narrowed to the taste of him, the scent of him— woodsmoke and brandy, and the clean trace of river water.

"I want more of you," I gasped against his lips, my fingers fumbling for the buttons on his shirt. "All of you."

"Solaine," he breathed. "Are you certain?"

In answer, I took his hand and placed it over my heart, letting him feel its wild beating. "I've never been more certain of anything."

He moaned softly and pulled off his shirt, gathering me against his bare skin. He rolled us again so that I was on my back with him straddling me, his mouth finding mine again with new urgency. My fingers smoothed his shoulders, feather-light over his bandages, then trailing across the scars on his back.

I wanted to weep over those awful scars. Kiss them. Use my lips to scour away the past that had scarred him, replacing it with newer, sweeter memories. Ones that didn't hurt. That didn't wake him yelling in the night.

"Solaine." His lips traced over my jaw, down the sensitive arch of my throat, lingering at the pulse point where my blood raced beneath the skin. "I never thought," he murmured, "never dreamed you could want me this way."

"Tonight I do," I whispered, lifting my arms so he could remove my chemise. "With all my heart."

"Then tonight will have to last us forever."

The world beyond our small circle of firelight ceased to exist. There were only his hands, sure and gentle as they smoothed over my curves, his lips trailing fire across my skin. Soon, all our clothes lay scattered under us on the soft grass.

Henry drew back, his gaze travelling over me in the ember light.

"You take away my breath," he murmured, his fingers lacing through my hair, his eyes searching mine in the darkness, his breath on my lips. "From the moment I saw you, standing on the street that day, you cast a spell on me. A spell that nothing will ever break."

I stilled for a moment, my heart racing so hard it seemed to vibrate through both of our bodies.

No spell was unbreakable. A noose, a bullet, and the spell would come undone. And no amount of wishing could ever change that.

My breath hitched, and I swallowed a sob. Reaching for him, I pulled him down to me, skin against skin at last.

"Tonight I'm yours," I whispered fiercely into the hollow of his throat. "And you are mine. If this is all we ever get, then I pray it'll be enough."

45

SOLAINE

THE NIGHT DEEPENED AROUND US, the stars glittering like diamonds scattered across the sky. I lay in Henry's arms, my head resting on his chest, listening to the quiet thump of his heartbeat.

His fingers traced lazy patterns on my bare shoulder, tickling one moment, sending shivers over me the next. The fire coals were barely glowing now, but the night was warm, and Henry's body beside me even warmer.

"Solaine," he said, his voice a low rumble beneath my ear. "I've been thinking."

I lifted my head to look at him, his features half-shadowed in the dying firelight. "About me?" I teased, trying to ignore the sudden fluttering inside my heart. "Good things, I hope?"

"Always." He didn't smile. Instead, his eyes held mine, serious and intent. "When we find Charlotte ..." He paused, as if gathering courage. "Why don't the two of you come with me to Queensland?"

I stared at him, a thrill of heat rushing through me, but as his meaning fully dawned, my veins turned to ice.

"We could make a new life together," he continued, the words coming faster now, as if he feared I might stop him. "You could have your horse farm, and I'd help you run it. We'd be far from anyone who knows us. We could put all this behind us and start over."

I sat up slowly, pulling the blanket around my shoulders. The night air felt colder against my skin, or maybe it was the chill of the world closing back in around us.

"Henry ..." I stalled, swallowing. "I—"

He reached for my hand, his fingers warm against mine. "You don't have to say anything now. Just think it over. You said yourself nothing is waiting for you back in Elliotville but your uncle's strictness and disapproval."

"My uncle will pay for Charlotte's future," I said softly. "He might be a hard man to fathom sometimes—but he's an important figure in Elliotville with good connections. I can't just throw all that away."

"But what about your farm?"

"It's just a fairytale. That's all it can ever be."

Henry's face fell, though he tried to hide it behind a smile. "I expected as much."

"Then why ask?" The words came out sharper than I intended.

His thumb traced circles on the back of my hand, his gaze dropping to our intertwined fingers. "You can't blame a man for dreaming."

I drew away from him and rose, slipping into my petticoat

and chemise. I padded barefoot to the edge of our small camp.

The river rushed past, moonlight gleaming on its surface like shattered glass. I thought of Charlotte—her small face, her trusting eyes. What kind of life would she have, always running, the three of us constantly looking over our shoulders?

"I have to think of Charlotte," I said, still facing the river. "What kind of mother would I be if I put my own feelings before her well-being? I can't just give up everything and run off with a—" I stopped myself, the words sticking in my throat.

"An outlaw?" Henry finished for me, his voice flat. "A convict? A bushranger?"

I turned back to him. He had leapt up and pulled on his trousers but remained shirtless, the firelight casting long shadows across his chest, his face in shadow.

"I didn't say that."

"You didn't have to." He ran a hand through his hair. "You think I don't know what I am? What I've done? Confound it, Solaine. I took you hostage. I threatened your life to save my own skin. The more I know you, the more I hate myself for what I am. Because I know I'll never be the man you need."

My eyelids fluttered closed, hating the pain in his voice. Pain I'd inflicted.

"And yet now you're risking that same skin to help me find my daughter." I took a step towards him, torn between the urge to go to him and the need to maintain distance. "It's not that simple."

"It *is* that simple." He closed the distance between us, his hands gentle as they cupped my face. "I know what I feel. And I think you feel it too."

"It's not enough, Henry." I pulled away from his touch. "What kind of life would we have? Always running, always hiding. What kind of childhood would that be for Charlotte?"

"A free one," he said. "Far from your uncle's lies and judgments. She'd have horses. Open skies." He paused. "She'd have me. I'll never take Billy's place, but I could be there for her. In the best way I know how to be."

I blinked, my dream life with Billy rushing back—the cottage with its wooden bed and feather mattress, nights curled together in the dark. Coddling baby Charlotte, tending our garden, having meals around the table. Only now, instead of Billy, I pictured Henry at our side, his solid presence keeping the shadows at bay, the three of us a family ...

The dream shattered against the hard edge of reality.

A reality where Henry was a wanted man. Where every knock at the door might be the law, come to take him from us. The way they'd taken my father. And if the traps didn't come for Henry, would he always be there for us? Or would he run the moment his nightmares grew too real?

I couldn't risk it. Couldn't risk Charlotte's heart that way.

Or mine.

"I can't," I whispered, the words catching in my throat. "I'm sorry, Henry. I just can't."

His face shuttered, all emotion locking away behind a mask of careful indifference.

"I understand." His voice was flat, empty. He turned away, reaching for his shirt. Not looking at me as he rebuilt the fire, adding branches with precise, controlled movements. "I shouldn't have asked. You're right to protect Charlotte. She deserves better than the likes of me."

I wanted to tell him he was wrong. That he was a good man, despite his past. That in another life, another world, I would choose him without hesitation.

But the words died on my lips. Because he was right—I needed to protect Charlotte. And if that meant protecting my own heart as well, burying these new, fragile feelings before they could take root and grow, then that's what I would do.

I retreated to my side of the fire, pulling on the rest of my clothes with numb fingers. When I finally lay down, Henry was a shadow on the other side of the flames, his back to me, a gulf between us that seemed wider than the river beside us.

Tomorrow we would reach the miners' camp. Tomorrow, perhaps, we would find a trail to Charlotte. And when we did, these stolen moments—these impossible dreams— would fade like mist in the morning sun.

I closed my eyes, but sleep eluded me.

In the darkness behind my eyelids, I saw only Henry's face, heard only his words. *You can't blame a man for dreaming.*

No, I couldn't. But I could blame myself for letting my heart forget, even for a moment, all the reasons those dreams could never be real.

46

SOLAINE

DAWN BROKE in pale streaks across the sky, turning the river to molten silver. I moved quietly through our camp, gathering our belongings while Henry saddled Shadowlark and extinguished the last embers of our fire.

He remained closed off to me, keeping a careful distance and avoiding my eyes.

I avoided him, too.

Last night had brought us closer together in so many ways—but it had also divided us. He had offered an impossible future, a dream life that was as impractical as it was tempting. Running away to the wilds of Queensland with a wanted man seemed like one of the fairytales I spun for Charlotte. But I already knew how it ended.

A noose for Henry.

And a lifetime of heartbreak for me.

We left the river behind and rode northwest. Tall eucalypt

trees emerged from the shadows, their pale trunks glowing as the sun rose higher.

Today we would reach the Chinese miners' camp—and know, for better or worse, what news it held of Charlotte. I would need all my courage just to face it. It was enough knowing I wouldn't have to face it alone.

By midday, the heat was suffocating, my blouse glued to my back as I squinted into the glare. Henry sagged in the saddle too, his gaze locked on the horizon.

Only Shadowlark seemed pleased to be on the move again, tossing her mane and prancing like a show pony, lighter in heart than either of us felt.

Henry predicted we'd reach the camp by mid-afternoon. As much as I was impatient to scour the place for signs of my daughter, I dreaded it too. The convict woman, Mrs Landy, had described a devastating scene. *There was trouble at the camp, the kind that ends with bodies in the ground.*

I felt for the hard knot of the silver piglet charm in my pocket, trying to draw comfort from it. *Found this by the river,* Mrs Landy had said. *No child attached to it that I saw.*

My stomach clenched.

What if Charlotte had been there when the camp was attacked? What if her little body was among those buried in the aftermath? How could I live the rest of my life without her? And how would I ever know who had brought her so far from Elliotville and why?

A shudder went through me.

You won't know. Ever. And the not knowing will slowly kill you. You'll dream about her cries, the terror she must have felt, the devastation of her final moments. And you'll know that it was all because of you—

"Solaine, look." Henry clicked his tongue, tightening the reins. Shadowlark whinnied, slowing her pace as we climbed a rocky ridge.

The valley stretching below us was brown and dry at this time of year, the dark traprock soil stretching across several hundred acres of scrubby land, bare in places. A river cut along one edge, flowing south into the hills, pockets of green growing lushly along its banks.

I tensed, seeing why he'd stopped.

A trail of smoke lifted into the air, coiling lazily before disappearing into the scorching blue sky.

"A campfire?" I asked.

"No," he said quietly. Then, "I don't know. Hard to tell from here."

My heart plunged. If not a campfire, then what?

As we rode further along the ridge, the camp came into view. The trail of smoke rose above a scattering of what looked like tents and simple dwellings, with clear dirt trails meandering between them, a wider track leading to the river.

There was no movement.

No breeze to stir the leaves. No sign of life, just a solitary crow circling overhead in wide, swooping laps, as though avoiding the ragged column of smoke.

What if we were seeing smoke from a funeral pyre? Mrs Landy claimed she'd seen blood and bodies everywhere, and the horror of what we might find down there struck me hard. My gut knotted so painfully that I slumped forward against Henry's back, the world reeling giddily around me.

I closed my eyes.

In the past weeks, I'd become used to being near Henry this way—stealing moments of rest against him, inhaling the warm smokiness that clung to his clothes and skin, my lungs expanding and deflating with the same rhythm as his. Despite the heat and wretched dust, his familiar solidness calmed my senses, made me able to breathe more easily again.

His fingers brushed my knuckles briefly, as if sensing my fear, his large fingers lingering for a heartbeat before returning to the reins.

"Ready?" he asked quietly.

I nodded, my throat too tight to speak, and we began our descent. My daughter's face came to me. The way she was on the day of the picnic, chattering to Deacon, her hair shining and her chubby cheeks pink from the sun. *Please let her be alive*, I silently prayed. *Let us find something that leads us to her.*

Shadowlark was surefooted as a brumby on the slope, her slender legs grey with dust and sweat as she picked her way between close-growing saplings and loose stones. She skated once, her hooves skidding on the gravel, and the motion made me sit up.

We reached the foot of the slope, the valley scooping gently away before us, trees now hiding the camp from view. The saplings grew sparsely here, their leathery leaves clinging to twisted branches, the sun burning hotter without the shelter of the ridge.

Henry guided the horse along a narrow trail that hugged the foot of the hill, and as the ground evened out, he clicked his tongue, lightly tugging Shadowlark to a stop.

I frowned. "Why are we—?"

He twisted around, his gaze travelling over me. "I can feel you trembling."

Cold dread burrowed into me, turning my bones to ice.

Again, I thought of Mrs Landy's warning. *The place was ... blood everywhere ... and bodies, some still warm.*

"What if we find her ... *body*?" I murmured, fisting my fingers in Henry's shirt to stop them shaking. "What if she's already—" I cut off, unable to say it, a knot of terror constricting my throat.

Henry nodded, the crease between his brows deepening. "I know you're scared, Solaine. But what if she's alive?"

"But—"

"Don't bury her before you know for sure." His voice had an edge, like the night we'd fled from the cedar getters' hut, his words hammering into me. But his eyes were gentle, his voice calm. "Whatever we find is better than never knowing."

I flinched, sitting taller in the saddle, breaking contact with him. He was right. My thoughts were undermining my courage, and I needed to stay strong. For Charlotte.

For whatever was coming.

"I'm ready," I whispered.

Henry urged the horse forward again, his hand resting on the gun tucked in his belt. Shadowlark's hooves crunched over stony ground, and as we emerged through the trees, the camp appeared ahead.

Makeshift dwellings and bark huts lay in ruins, tents trampled into the mud. Cooking pots, buckets, and sluicing boxes were strewn about, the smoke of a solitary campfire coiling into the vast blue sky. Not a pyre—just the smoking embers of a few logs with a billycan and the remains of a meal nearby.

On the edge of the camp, a chestnut pony grazed beside a small wooden cart. The pony looked up as we passed, flanks twitching as its liquid black eyes followed our progress.

"Look." Henry pointed to a small group huddled further along the base of the ridge, around an outcrop of rocky boulders.

A Chinese woman stood protectively amid four little fair-haired girls. When she saw us, she ran towards us, waving her arms.

"Help, please!"

We dismounted, making hasty introductions as she led us back to the boulders. A deep mine shaft had been dug into the hillside behind the outcrop. The narrow entryway was partially caved in, earth mounding around the split timber support beams, the lintel crushed under a rockslide of stones and debris.

"One of my girls ran in there," Mrs Song told us breathlessly, her English broken and lilting. "Roof cave in yesterday. We try to dig her out, but it only collapse more. Please—" She wrung her hands, her grimy face tracked with tears. "She only little. Down there all night, we hear her crying. But today nothing."

Someone had propped a small shovel by the entryway, and Henry picked it up, glancing back at Mrs Song. "What happened to the camp?" he demanded. "Do you know who did this?"

Mrs Song shoved a black strand of hair from her face, her eyes wide and frightened.

"White men come with guns. Other miners. They say we take their gold, but it not true." She pointed towards the river winding between casuarina trees. "We work the tailings they leave behind. They don't want any more, they throw away. We find much gold in it, and that make them angry."

Henry's knuckles tightened on the shovel. "So they drove the Chinese miners away and stole their gold?"

Mrs Song nodded, wiping a shaky hand over her eyes. "They kill two men. The other Chinese miners run away, but I stay to bury." She blinked, gesturing to a spot further along the ridge. "I bury up there, my relative. Yesterday traps come. Police. Ask questions. Stay only for short time. But my girl get scared. Hide in tunnel. We only notice her missing after traps ride away."

"Is she your daughter?" I asked.

Mrs Song went very still. She looked up at me, her coal-black eyes softening, the tension in her face falling away.

"My daughter die, miss. Long time ago. These are orphan girls, no parent. Parent die in mine collapse or typhus. I their mama now."

My lips parted. I was so desperate to ask her about Charlotte, to explain about the silver charm that had led us here, about the bushrangers who'd ripped her away from me—but I stopped.

God help me, her eyes. The tears glistening on her skin. The crags and scars of a face that had once been heartbreakingly beautiful but was now etched by years of hardship and pain.

"We'll do our best," I promised her. "I only pray your little one is still alive."

Henry crouched in the mouth of the tunnel. He spoke urgently to the two little girls who'd trailed after him, gaping up like mice at a large, dangerous cat. When he spoke, they scattered, running into a black tent and returning moments later with a glowing safety lantern.

He studied the narrow shaft entry for a long time,

running his hands along the timber support beams, picking larger rocks from the mound of rubble blocking the entrance.

He looked back at Mrs Song. "What's the girl's name?"

"No name," Mrs Song said sadly. "She no speak. We call her Little Five." She gestured at the other four girls and shrugged. "She number five."

Henry nodded and crouched by the open side of the tunnel. "Hey, Little Five. Can you hear me?"

Crickets chirped in the dry grass nearby and insects buzzed around us, but the girl trapped behind the wall of rubble stayed silent.

Henry drew me aside, cupping my elbow and leaning close, his voice low. "Grown men are crushed by shaft collapses all the time. If they survive, they don't last more than a few days. This little one might be in a bad way, Solaine. If she's even alive, which is unlikely. I'll bring the body out if I can, so you need to prepare yourself for whatever I find down there."

I nodded, my throat tight. As he turned away, I caught his sleeve. "Henry, wait." He faced me again, and my fingers dropped down to grasp his hand. "Those things I said last night, I'm sorry."

He gave my fingers a gentle squeeze. "I'm the one who's sorry. You're right to think of your little girl." He glanced at the mine opening, and when he looked back at me, his eyes had turned dark. "Whatever happens, keep looking for her. Someone out there knows the truth."

I swayed closer, wanting to fling my arms around him, beg him not to go into the tunnel, not to risk himself when it might already be too late, that the child might already be dead. I wanted to tell him what I should have told him last night ... that what I felt for him scared me, confused me, made me question everything I believed. That those feelings were real, and they ran deep. So deep I could feel them now, pulsing in the core of my bones, terrified I'd never see him again.

Instead, I nodded and let go of his hand.

"Be careful."

He took the lantern and shovel and climbed slowly into the side of the shaft where the scaffolding had held. He carefully moved aside some larger rocks, widening the opening so he could fit through. Soil sifted from the collapsed side of the roof, and the timber creaked, but the beams held.

Soon, he disappeared down into the darkness.

47

HENRY

I MOVED DEEPER into the tunnel, easing down past the mounded rubble, stopping to scrape away the fallen earth and rubble to widen the tunnel enough for me to squeeze through.

The miners had dug at a diagonal, cutting the mine lower into the earth in the hope of striking a vein of gold-bearing quartz.

The timber scaffold had rotted through in places, splintering where the collapsed side had broken away. I crouched almost double, my boots crunching on fallen rubble as daylight faded behind me. I held the small lantern aloft, letting its light guide me along the stable edge of the shaft. To my right, the pile of earth from the collapse grew deeper, some stones as big as a child's skull.

As I dragged a large rock out of my way, something twitched in the darkness, and my pulse skipped. I leaned forward over the fall of soil to shine my light closer—and a large rat sprang at me.

"Damn!" I shuddered.

"Henry?" Solaine's voice echoed faintly from the entrance. "Did you find her?"

"Not yet," I called back, keeping my voice low. The last thing I needed was to cause another collapse.

I squeezed through a narrow section where the ceiling had sagged, timber groaning overhead. Soil and stones rained down on me, my injured shoulder throbbing as I pushed forward.

A muffled whimper came from the darkness ahead, and my heart began to thump out of kilter. *Thank God, she's alive. But how bad are her injuries ... and can I carry her back through the tunnel without it collapsing on us?*

"Hey, little one," I called, keeping my voice low and steady. "I'm here to help."

The crying stopped abruptly.

I crawled through the tight space, easing under the broken roof beams, the lantern casting wild shadows on the unstable walls. Around the next bend, a small figure sat huddled against the rock face, knees drawn to her chest.

She looked about five or six, trembling, her eyes squeezed shut, her face—what I could see of it behind the tangled mess of dark hair—smeared with dirt and dust. Blood seeped from a long cut that ran the length of her shin, and more blood congealed on a nasty gash on her elbow.

"Little Five?" I reached my hand towards her.

She shrank away, tucking her face down over her chest like a frightened bird. She started crying quietly, almost silently, as if scared to make a sound.

"My name's Henry." I set the lantern down between us. "Mrs Song sent me to fetch you. That's a nasty scrape on your leg. It must hurt."

I shifted closer, gravel crunching under me.

The girl's eyes flew open—round and dark as oil beads in the lantern light. She stared at me, frozen, her terror keeping me at bay.

I went still, frowning as an inkling of memory or dream nudged the back of my mind. Another child, long ago, with bright dark eyes and a wild mop of hair, chirping at me from the past. *Henry, why did you leave us?* My gut churned as I flashed back to how I'd run from her and her family, wanting to save them, but in truth I'd left them to a worse fate—

Get a grip, man.

I smiled encouragingly at the girl. "Can you wriggle your toes for me?"

She shut her eyes, and for a heart-stopping moment, I thought she'd passed out. But then she blinked back at me and shook her head.

I swallowed. Not ideal, but at least she was conscious. "What about your fingers?"

She held up her hands, wiggling her dirt-streaked fingers weakly, blood gleaming on her knuckles. There was dirt stuck in a clump to her elbow, and more blood smeared along her arm.

"I'm going to get you out of here," I told her, inching closer. "I promise. Will you let me pick you up?"

Her lips trembled, but she nodded, her small, round face turning up to me like a little sunflower in the darkness, such trust in her eyes—and pain too. It hurt me to see her smallness, her round face and hollow, frightened eyes.

I'd heard about the mining camp orphans. Kids left behind when parents were killed in mine collapses or accidents, or taken by disease. Some just left behind when the money ran out to feed them.

Smaller children like Little Five often perished quickly from starvation or illness or neglect, their little hearts broken before they'd had a decent taste of life. Before they learned how to survive on their own.

I untied the kerchief from around my neck and shook out the folds, binding it snugly around the wound on her shin. She winced but didn't cry out. I took off my waistcoat and shirt, binding them around her, trapping her injured arm against her chest like a sling.

Her round eyes shone in the lantern light as she pointed to my shoulder.

I glanced down, frowning at the blood glistening through the bandages. I'd grown so used to the throb of it, I barely noticed wrenching it as I'd crawled through the tunnel. I smiled at the girl.

"I'll live. And so will you. Now, let's get you out of here." I scooped her into my arms, shocked by how light she was, her bird bones jutting against my hands. "You're a bit on the lean side," I told her, keeping my tone light. "Does Mrs Song feed you enough?"

She nodded and tried to smile, then shut her eyes again as I turned back towards the entrance. The tunnel seemed even narrower carrying her, and I had to navigate carefully past the worst of the rubble. As I passed another split bearer, something creaked above us. Soil and stones sifted down from the groaning roof struts.

I placed my hand on the girl's head, drawing her closer

under my chin, hunching around her. When the rain of rubble stopped falling on us, I waited a moment and then continued carefully along the tunnel, holding the safety lantern aloft with my free hand.

As daylight appeared ahead of us, the girl flinched.

"You all right, Little Five?"

She tensed against me, eyes wide as she pointed towards the crumbling entryway.

"Yeah," I murmured, the old anger stirring inside me, making me want to find the men who'd frightened her and tear them apart. "The bad men are long gone. The ones you saw yesterday were only traps. Police. You're safe now." I gave her a reassuring smile. "Mrs Song's waiting out there, and the other girls. And a nice lady, Miss Granger. You don't have to be scared—"

The child stiffened in my arms, and she gasped softly. Her small hand reached out and settled on my cheek, and she drew back, staring at my face.

Frowning.

"You saved me," she whispered.

I huffed a breath. "We're not home free just yet. You can thank me once we're safely outside."

"No, before." She patted my cheek, getting my attention, her eyes like black pennies in the fluttering light. "On the street. The horses nearly stamped me to bits. But you saved me."

I stopped in my tracks, my heart stuttering as the pieces began to slide into place. I searched the dirt-smeared little face half-lost behind the dusty mane of hair, her round eyes unblinking in the hazy light.

"Charlotte?"

She nodded, tears welling again. "Is Mama really here?"

My throat jammed shut, and I could only nod. The little girl let out a sob and flung her arms around my neck, her small body trembling as she cried against me. Deep wracking sobs that shuddered through her whole body as she clung desperately, and me unable to hold her tightly enough.

I found my voice. "Seems like five really is your lucky number."

"Yes," she said, her voice muffled.

"Could be it's mine too."

With the sobbing child safe in my arms, I sidestepped a mound of earth and broken timber and trod carefully towards the growing brightness.

Overhead, the roof creaked again.

Something splintered.

Timber squealed, and a deafening crack made me lurch forward, bolting towards the light, hunching my body around the child as the world exploded down on top of us.

48

SOLAINE

THE SOUND of splintering wood came from inside the tunnel, followed by a child's frightened shriek. More of the tunnel began to cave in, and a cloud of dust exploded from the mouth of the shaft, raining down dirt and stones as the cloud billowed around us.

"Henry!" I lurched towards the entrance just as another terrible crack split the air. Mrs Song grabbed my arm, but I shook her off. "Henry—"

The ground beneath my feet shuddered.

Behind me, one of the little orphan girls began to wail in terror.

Through the settling dust, I saw movement in the darkness—a hunched figure staggering towards us, a small girl clutched protectively against his chest. Another crack sounded, and a larger section of the tunnel entrance gave way.

I lunged forward, grabbing Henry's arm and dragging him

the final few feet out into the sunlight as timber and earth crashed down behind us.

We stumbled and fell, Henry twisting protectively around the child, grunting as he hit the ground with his full weight on his injured shoulder. Dust seethed around us, coating my skin, my hair, filling my lungs until I was choking on it.

When I could see again, Henry was sitting up, blood streaking his face from a cut near his eyebrow. A crust of fine powdery dirt clung to the fresh blood seeping through the bandages from his wounded shoulder.

He was smiling—then laughing as he crawled towards me, the girl bundled tightly in his arms, her head buried against his chest. A wild, triumphant smile transformed his dirt-streaked face.

"I got her," he panted, choking on grit, his voice rough. "She's safe, Solaine."

I pushed myself to my knees, my gaze falling to the small bundle in his arms. The girl clung to him, deep coughs racking her little body as her lungs tried to expel the dust. So filthy and thin I could hardly tell she was human, with tangled dark hair and a bloodied leg bound with Henry's kerchief. Henry's shirt was wrapped tightly around her, trapping her small, bleeding arm against her body.

"Take her," Henry said.

Her face was pressed into his chest, and as I reached for her, she stiffened, then slowly turned her head.

Two dark eyes peered at me through a knotted tangle of dusty hair.

Eyes I knew. Eyes I'd seen in my dreams every night for the past four weeks. Eyes that had gazed up at me from the moment she was born.

The eyes widened. "Mama—?"

The world stopped. Everything—the pain in my knees where I'd fallen, the ringing in my ears and the dust in my throat, the heat of the afternoon sun, the weight of fear that had been crushing the life out of me this past month—all of it vanished in that single heartbeat of recognition.

"Charlotte?" I breathed, afraid to hope, afraid to believe.

With a sob that seemed to tear from her soul, my daughter flung her arms around my neck, burying her face against my throat. Her small body shook with the force of her cries, her fingers digging into my shoulders as if she feared I might disappear.

"My baby," I gasped, crushing her to me, my tears spilling unchecked, my heart twisting with a joy so fierce it hurt. "My little wisp. Oh, my darling girl."

I rocked her in my arms, the familiar smell of her beneath the dirt and blood, the perfect fit of her small head beneath my chin. Her small arms locked around me, her body shuddering with sobs. How many times had I held her just like this? How many nights had I cried myself to sleep, aching to hold her this way again?

Through my tears, I looked up at Henry, who was kneeling beside us.

"How is this possible?" I whispered. "Please tell me it's real. Because if I wake and find it all a dream, how will I bear it?"

He shook his head, reaching out, his bloodied hand cupping my cheek. "You're awake, Solaine. It's real. You found her. You found your daughter."

I pulled one hand from around Charlotte to grasp his, our fingers twining together, slick with blood and dirt and tears.

Thank you, I wanted to say, but the words felt as flimsy as the dust settling around us. And anyway, my throat was jammed so tightly I could barely breathe, let alone speak. How could I thank the man who'd just brought me back from the dead? Who'd just returned my world to me. *Again.*

Charlotte lifted her head from my neck, her tear-streaked face turning to Henry. She reached out one small hand, which he took gently in his own.

"You saved me," she said.

"We saved each other, little one," Henry murmured, his eyes meeting mine briefly over her head. He looked back at Charlotte, tucking a hank of matted hair behind her ear, his large hand hovering protectively. "You're back with your mama now, safe and sound."

I held my child tighter, my tears falling into her tangled hair, my heart swelling so full of love and gratitude I thought it would burst. "Charlotte," I whispered, my voice breaking. "Oh, my baby. I'll never let you go again as long as I live."

SHE GRIPPED my hand as we walked down to the river to bathe, and when I stopped on the bank, she clung fretfully to me again, as though afraid I might vanish if she let go.

"It's all right, love," I murmured, smoothing her dusty hair. "I'm not going anywhere. I promise."

The three of us stood on the pebbly shore, Charlotte between me and Henry, her wide gaze on the water.

The sun was already streaking the sky with skeins of pale

pink and orange as it sank towards the west. Soon dusk would settle, bringing the mosquitoes.

I squeezed her hand. "How did you come to be all the way out here, love?"

She shrugged, her small fingers tightening around mine, her lips pinched together.

"You must have been frightened," Henry said after a while. He crouched by the river's edge, flicking a twig into the water. "I would have been."

Charlotte watched the twig as the current carried it downstream, her gaze straying to where Mrs Song and her girls were wading into the water.

The five of them were dusty and worn down after their worried vigil outside the collapsed tunnel. The water was cold, but soon the orphan girls were splashing and chattering. They waded deeper, Mrs Song trailing after them with her bar of soap and words of warning.

"Keep in shallows, Gert. Make Tildy wash behind her ears, Jane. Nellie, stay near your sister …" None of the girls seemed to be listening, which launched Mrs Song into a long tirade in Chinese. Finally, tired of being ignored, she fell silent. Sinking into the water, she floated for a while, then began to wash her hair.

Magpies warbled above us in one of the willowy casuarina trees, its song shrill and musical. Insects skimmed the surface, and a little bird swooped down and caught one.

"How about we wash all that dust off?" I said cheerily, patting Charlotte's hand. "Ready for a swim?"

She nodded. "All right, Mama."

Henry knelt beside us, gently unwrapping the makeshift bandage from Charlotte's shin. The cut beneath was long but not terribly deep, crusted with dirt and dried blood.

"We need to clean this," he said, his voice soft with concern. "It might sting a bit, but it'll feel better afterwards, I promise."

She nodded again, still distracted by the other girls downstream. Gert waved to her, and Charlotte brightened, waving back.

"I'll leave you ladies to it," Henry said, getting to his feet. "Better go and check on those horses." He headed up along the bank a little way, towards where Shadowlark and Mrs Song's little pony, Swanky, were grazing in the grass.

I peeled off Charlotte's dusty outer garments and then my own, and we waded into the stream in our chemises and drawers. Mrs Song had given me a bar of her fragrant soap, and I lathered up a soft rag and gently began wiping the dust and grime from Charlotte's face. When it was clean, I started on her neck, working my way carefully to her sore elbow.

"Gert and Nellie used to come and visit me," Charlotte said suddenly. "In the lady's tent."

I froze for a moment, then continued dabbing the crusty blood off her elbow with my cloth. If I showed too much interest, she might shut down again, so I kept my tone light.

"That was sweet of them."

"They bought me a dumpling once. Wrapped in paper with Chinese writing on it. But the lady took it off me and ate it herself."

"Oh, the greedy thing!"

Charlotte nodded. "I didn't like her."

I waited, but she'd fallen silent, gazing at the other girls splashing further along in the deeper water.

Earlier, Mrs Song told me that Charlotte had come to the camp over three weeks ago, in the company of an older lady and her two grown sons. They had kept Charlotte mostly out of sight in their tent. Charlotte had been confined inside the tent's sweltering darkness, only allowed out for a walk with the woman once a day. They told people the girl was sick with pox and needed to be isolated.

When the masked attackers came in the night and destroyed the camp, killing Mrs Song's cousins, Charlotte had escaped the tent. Jane found her the next morning, hiding under Mrs Song's overturned cart. The older woman and her sons had vanished.

"She took my necklace," Charlotte whispered, her fingers lifting to her throat. "She took Abigail."

I went cold, the soapy cloth stilling on her arm.

"The lady in the tent took Abigail?"

Chalotte nodded, but then fell quiet again. I finished bathing her and then set about washing her hair, rubbing Mrs Song's soap through the long, matted locks.

Henry had been right about Mrs Landy. She was a liar and a thief. She hadn't found Charlotte's charm by the river at all. She'd stolen it and covered her theft with a lie.

I felt certain she'd been in collusion with the men who took Charlotte. I thought back to the day on the bridge. Could Mrs Landy's sons have been among the men who kidnapped her? The more I thought about it, the more likely it seemed.

"Charlotte, can I ask you something about the lady?"

She nodded, still watching the other girls.

I gulped a breath, keeping my voice light. "Was her name Mrs Landy?"

Charlotte shook her head. "Her name was Ma. That's what the men called her. She told me to call her Ma too, but I wouldn't. She got really cross, so I stopped talking."

"Oh, love." I pulled her against me, my voice catching. "I'm so proud of you. I can't think how brave you must have been. I tried so hard to find you, and it broke my heart into bits when I couldn't."

"I know, Mama. But you did find me." Her thin arms wound around me, her face warm as she buried it into my neck. She cried quietly for a while and then pulled back to look at me, wiping her eyes. "And Mr Henry saved me."

I nodded, swallowing tears of my own as I dabbed her cheeks with my cloth. "He's brave, too."

She glanced upstream to where Henry had disappeared. "Mama?"

"Yes, my wisp?"

"Is Mr Henry my pa?"

My eyes filled, and a sound that was midway between a laugh and a sob choked out of me.

"Oh lord, Charlotte. Why do you ask that?"

"He said five's my lucky number. And it is."

The water around us rippled and gleamed in the fading afternoon light, bright laughter and voices drifting up to us. I hugged my sodden child against me, pressing my lips against her hair.

"Can I tell you a secret about Henry?"

I felt her nodding, and then she pulled back to look at me. "What secret?"

"When I was a little girl, a bit older than you, my father brought home a boy who was an orphan just like Gert and

Nellie. For a while, we became best of friends. That little boy was Henry."

Charlotte blinked, her dark eyes wide. "Mr Henry's an orphan?"

I nodded. "He's many things, Charlotte. Some people might call him a bad man because he's made some mistakes. The way Uncle Niall sometimes says mean things about your grandfather. But you know what?"

She shook her head, her chocolate eyes wide as saucers.

"Henry put himself in danger by coming to the camp with me because he knew I'd be scared. And then he went into that collapsing tunnel and brought you back to me. I know he'll never replace your real papa in heaven. But maybe Henry's our guardian angel?"

49

SOLAINE

NIGHT FELL, the campfire crackling in our midst, sparks dancing in the darkness and the rich smells of stewing vegetables and meat wafting around us.

"You found your voice," Mrs Song said to Charlotte as she ladled steaming dumplings onto Charlotte's tin plate. "And you found your mama. I happy for you, Little Five."

Charlotte looked up at the woman, her face solemn, her hair still damp from her bath. "Thank you for looking after me, Mrs Song."

The woman smiled kindly, her dark eyes crinkling at the corners as she added a little extra mutton.

"How that arm feeling now?"

Charlotte held up her bandaged elbow. "Better."

I was sitting beside Charlotte on one of Mrs Song's thick quilts, Henry on a log nearby. The four orphan girls bustled around, helping Mrs Song stoke the fire or wrap chunks of stewed mutton in boiled cabbage leaves, or stir the greens and potatoes. Mrs Song retrieved a second pot from over the embers.

"More dumplings, Mr Henry?"

Henry held out his plate, and Mrs Song ladled generously, the fragrant steam billowing up.

I held out my plate, too. "How do you get the mutton so flavoursome, Mrs Song?" After weeks of rabbits and fish and an occasional possum, the salty and faintly sour, juicy cabbage was a rare treat for us. Even the mutton was astonishingly tasty. "And where on earth did you get cabbages all the way out here?"

Mrs Song tucked her chin into her neck, looking pleased. She pointed through the darkness towards the riverbank. "I grow, of course. Also pumpkin, leek, radish, potato. Ginger and ..." She wriggled her fingers at the oldest girl, Tildy, who piped up.

"Fennel, Mrs Song."

The two younger girls, fair-haired sisters, sat cross-legged by Henry's feet, peering up at him between mouthfuls. The smallest one, Gert, who looked no older than four, reached up her tiny hand and tugged Henry's sleeve.

"Mr Henry?"

He looked down. "What, kid?"

"Are you Little Five's pa?"

Henry coughed sharply and thumped his chest. "Ah ... well, now—" His cheeks flushed pink in the firelight, his gaze sliding over the ground, finally catching on his boots.

Charlotte flicked a leaf at Gert. "He's my guardian angel."

The sisters gaped at each other, then back up at Henry, clearly awestruck.

Henry glanced through his lashes at me, then cast his

head down, bolting through the rest of his food like a starved animal. Then he excused himself and took a bag of oats and some carrots to share between Shadowlark and Swanky.

After dinner, Mrs Song offered to salvage one of the tents for us, but Charlotte went quiet and burrowed fretfully against me, hiding her face.

I thanked the woman who had been so kind to us and taken care of Charlotte. "The firelight is so lovely," I told her. "We'll be all right out here."

"She needs the stars over her tonight," Henry added. "After spending the night in that dark tunnel, the fresh air will do her good."

Once we were alone, we spread out the quilt by the fire and settled on either side of Charlotte, the quiet darkness falling around us. For a while, we listened to Mrs Song's voice drifting from her tent. She was speaking to the girls in her melodic Chinese, her words unravelling what sounded like a story. Soon, she fell quiet, and a peaceful stillness descended.

Charlotte watched us both with bright eyes.

"I'm too happy to sleep, Mama."

"Me too," I said, then looked over her at Henry. He held my gaze a moment, then smiled and settled back, his arms crossed under his head as he gazed up at the sky.

"Charlotte," I said, bringing her silver charm out of my skirt pocket where I'd been keeping it safe. I unwrapped it from the remnant torn from her dress, enclosing it in my fist. I had imagined this moment repeatedly since Mrs Landy delivered it back to me, playing it so often in my mind that it already felt like a memory. "I have something for you."

I opened my fingers, and the silver piglet caught the firelight, gleaming brightly on my palm.

Charlotte gasped. "Abigail!"

"A lady had it, her name was Mrs Landy. I think she's the same lady who kept you in her tent, Charlotte." I swallowed the lump in my throat, grateful to Mrs Landy despite her looseness with the truth. "I told her it was yours and that I was looking for you. She gave me hope that you might be here. And you were."

Charlotte took the charm from my hand and kissed it, hugging it against herself for a few moments before slipping it into her pocket.

She wound her arms around my neck. "I'm so happy, Mama. I missed you."

"I missed you too, my wisp." I squeezed her close, inhaling the scent of her, the familiar feel of her baby-soft skin.

As I held her, I threw the scrap of torn linen into the fire and watched the flames flare brightly for a moment and then consume it, quickly turning it to ash. It had comforted me once, but I didn't need it anymore. Not when I had my little girl safe at last in my arms.

She yawned and settled on the quilt beside me, and was soon asleep.

I couldn't stop looking at her, adjusting the curved collar of her dress, the little capped sleeves. It was one that Tildy had outgrown, the pale yellow fabric printed with miniature dragons glowing faintly in the firelight.

I kept picturing Charlotte back at home, tucked safely in her bed, clean and plump again, her hair shiny. My eyes filled with tears just thinking about it. She murmured in her sleep, her eyes darting behind her lids, as if dreaming of the dark days that now, God-willing, lay behind her.

"It'll take time," Henry whispered, rolling onto his side to look at me. "But she'll be all right, Solaine. I promise."

I nodded absently, still watching Charlotte. "Those men with Mrs Landy," I said, glancing across at him. "Her sons? The more I think about it, the more convinced I am that they're the ones who took Charlotte."

Henry sat up, dragging his fingers through his beard. "They need to pay for what they did," he said gruffly. "For scaring her. For scaring you."

"They will. Uncle Niall will see to it. And I'm sure he'll be able to track down that fourth man you mentioned."

Henry nodded, but I could see the cogs turning. See the tension carving lines beside his mouth and hardening in his eyes.

"Don't you dare think about going after them," I warned. "They'll get their dues when the law catches up with them."

"The way the law caught up with Charlotte?"

He was right, the law had failed us. Failed Charlotte. My old frustration flooded back, but I bit my lips, willing it away.

"You can't blame them for being unable to find her. No one would have thought to search for her at a remote Chinese miners' camp. The Landys were clever to bring her here."

"Maybe they were following orders."

"Maybe. But I have Charlotte back now, and that's what matters. Henry," I added hesitantly, nibbling my lip. "You've done your part, now. You'll need to leave soon, maybe tomorrow. Before the traps return."

"Tomorrow," Henry said quietly, his eyes steady on my face. "Or the next day, when Charlotte feels ready to travel, I'll take you both to Glen Innes and put you on the coach back to Elliotville."

I stared at him in horror.

"Are you out of your mind?" I glanced at Mrs Song's tent, then down at Charlotte, finally glaring over her at Henry, careful to keep my voice low. "The traps are swarming every-where. Mrs Song said they were here yesterday. They might still be on the road. You'll be caught and—" I swallowed. "Don't worry about us. Just take Shadowlark and leave. First thing in the morning. You can be over the border and away to freedom within a few days."

"You heard Charlotte," he drawled, leaning back, his smile slow and vaguely wolfish. "I'm her guardian angel." Firelight flickered over his face, burnishing his dark hair and beard. "Anyway, it's too risky for a woman to be on the roads right now. You've seen first-hand the sort of ruffians lying in wait for unsuspecting travellers. I'll be riding with you to that coach, whether you like it or not."

"Henry, I simply won't allow it. You need to leave tomorrow and head north to the border. You promised to help me find her, and you did. Now you have to go."

He shook his head, frowning. "And leave you stranded, Solaine? Not going to happen. You've a frightened little girl to care for now, and I won't let you do it alone."

"For God's sake, Henry," I hissed, leaning protectively over Charlotte's sleeping form, my hand gently covering her little ear against my outburst. "I've already lost one member of my family to the gallows. I'll be damned if I'll lose another."

Henry stared back at me, his pupils blooming darkly with shock. With other things, too. Longing. Hunger. Hope.

I gasped under my breath, my lips parting as I realised what I'd said.

Family.

My thoughts skittered back to that night we'd spent in the cave, when the thunder crashed outside and the rain fell in a deluge, trapping us in the warm darkness, our faces lit by fireglow. And Henry's words exposing far more about the secret workings of his heart than he'd ever intended me to know. *Maybe fate's not cruel, Miss Granger. Just preparing us for things we've secretly prayed for but never dreamed possible.*

Was that what he secretly dreamed about—a family?

As a child, he'd seen his mother waste away, and then he'd witnessed his father's brutal murder. At fourteen, he fled to save another family from his nightmares. He'd spent years taking out his anger on the world, and as a result, passed most of his adult life in chains surrounded by hardened criminals.

But the look in his eyes, just now. The longing.

The hope.

My jaw trembled as I bent over Charlotte to hide the rawness I was feeling, placing a kiss on her brow and inhaling the clean scent of her hair.

Earlier tonight, over dinner, when Gert asked if Henry was Charlotte's pa, he'd flushed and been unable to answer. Not all men were cut out for fatherhood. I had taken it for granted that a man like Henry Hawke—rough, a loner, drifting through life on the edge of decent society, his heart hardened by years in prison—was one of them.

But what if I was wrong?

You and your family were different, Solaine … You saw me as someone worth caring about. For the first time in my life, I felt awake … Alive. Loved.

Tears stung my eyes, and I sat up, trying to blink them away as I stared up at the night sky.

Fifteen years ago, my father found a shattered young boy by the riverbank and brought him home. My parents had healed him with love, coaxed him out of his shell, made him whole again—or so they thought. But young Henry had been so damaged, so broken by what he'd seen, that his nightmares rose up one night and chased him out of our house, hounding him never to return.

They were still hounding him.

And he was still running.

I inhaled deeply, looking back at him.

"Take Shadowlark," I said. My voice wobbled, my hand protectively cupping the back of Charlotte's head. "The horse was yours before she was mine. Take her and ride out tomorrow. Please, Henry. I'm begging you. Do it for me."

The longing in his eyes vanished, the old hardness returning. His lips clamped shut, his jaw suddenly tight. He nodded once and then flopped back on the ground, tugging his hat down over his eyes.

Within minutes, he was softly snoring.

I almost smiled. Almost.

But my heart was thumping too painfully. Swollen and tender from finding Charlotte alive, from the overwhelming joy of having her back. Yet bruised too, seeing her taller and so gaunt, her eyes huge and fearful, jumping at shadows.

The lady got cross, so I stopped talking.

I didn't want to press Charlotte into saying more about her time with the Landys. How she came to be at the camp, or things she might have overheard while with them. She was too fragile. I hoped she'd volunteer the information when she was ready, but that could take some time.

"Time we don't have."

I glanced at Henry.

Tomorrow he would leave. Within a day or two, he could be at the border, escaping into the wilds of Queensland. He would change his identity, slip into the shadows, find employment somewhere or perhaps even return to terrorising people on the roads.

Once I was back at Elliot House, I knew I'd always be scouring the newspapers for signs of him. Every time I read about a mail coach being bailed up or a travelling merchant losing their payroll to a bushranger, I would think of him.

And remember my time with him.

The way he made me feel, the freedom he'd shown me. The light in his eyes the night he tricked me into almost kissing him. The strength of his arms around me when I'd fallen apart. His rugged beauty in the firelight all those nights by the river.

Most of all, I'd remember him emerging from the tunnel with Charlotte safe in his arms.

I bit my lip and tipped back my head, but this time the tears slipped out and trickled down my cheeks.

Henry Hawke was everything Uncle Niall had warned me against—a criminal, an outlaw, a man who lived outside the boundaries of civilised society.

Yet the law had failed to find Charlotte. And Uncle Niall,

with all his privileges and connections as commissioner, had failed her too. While Henry … Henry had risked everything to save her. Not just by rushing into a collapsing tunnel, but by coming here with me, so I didn't have to face the camp alone. *You heard Charlotte. I'm her guardian angel.*

He was my guardian, too.

More than a guardian. When Charlotte was taken, I had fractured, broken into small, helpless pieces. Over the weeks, Henry had put me back together—but differently from how I'd been before. I was stronger, more capable. I'd learned to snare rabbits, weave fishtraps. Heal a bullet wound with leaves. More than that, I no longer shrank from my father's memory. I was no longer ashamed of him. No longer ashamed of the parts of him I saw in myself.

I barely recognised who I'd become.

And yet, I'd never been more *me*.

Charlotte whimpered, then stirred awake and began to cry, still half-asleep. She reached up to me, and I gathered her close.

"It hurts," she said, plucking at the bandages wrapping her elbow. "Mama, it hurts."

"I know, darling."

She continued to grizzle, and Henry stirred beside us. He sat up and watched her for a moment, then dug into his waistcoat.

"This'll help with the pain, Little Five. Give me your hand."

She reached out obediently, blinking into his face. He placed something on her palm, and when she saw what it was, she smiled.

"Is it Shadowlark?"

He nodded. "Your clever mama carved it for me from a wattle burl. It's my best treasure. Now it's yours."

Her smile turned into a beam, and she snuggled down again, tracing her small fingers over the horse's knotty head, turning this way and that until her lids began to droop. Finally, with the carving clutched to her chest, she closed her eyes and was soon asleep.

I met Henry's gaze, but neither of us spoke. We just watched each other for a moment, and then he settled back on the blanket and shut his eyes.

I snuggled down next to Charlotte, enclosing her protectively in my arms.

I will miss you, Henry Hawke.

More than miss. The moment he rode away from us—tomorrow or the day after—I would start grieving for him. Grieving for his presence in my life, and maybe I'd never stop.

Which made no sense, but when was love ever rational?

Whatever faced us back in Elliotville—my uncle's endless interrogations, his stern disapproval, his suffocating control—I dreaded it all. His gilded cage would be even more confining now, the door locked tight after my reckless escape.

There'd be no hope of buying my horse farm, or of taking control of my inheritance. Uncle Niall would watch me more closely, restrict my movements, and insist it was for my protection. The freedom I'd tasted with Henry would be just a memory.

My only comfort would be knowing that somewhere beyond those restrictive walls, Henry would be out there. Free. Living life on his terms, being who he was without apology. Finally liberated from a life in chains.

Knowing he was out there would help me endure the bleakness of my own captivity.

"But will it, though?" I murmured against Charlotte's hair. Was it even possible to return to that stifling life now that I'd had a taste of freedom?

SOLAINE

By mid-morning the next day, the sun was beating down from a cloudless cobalt sky, making the air crackle with heat.

Mrs Song ushered me into her tent. The dirt floor was freshly swept, and a bundle of thick quilts sat in a pile to one side. Beside them was a rickety cabinet, topped by a tiny altar that held a small wooden deity and a vase of eucalyptus leaves.

Mrs Song opened the cabinet, taking out rolls of clean cloth and a jar with Chinese writing on the label. She helped me dress Charlotte's wounds again, dabbing ointment on them from the jar. As the sun rose higher, the tent became like a furnace, the heavy canvas walls trapping the heat until breathing felt like drawing fire into my lungs.

I thanked Mrs Song and led Charlotte outside to a shady patch under a sprawling river gum, its bark peeling in long strips. We laid our threadbare blanket across the parched earth, disturbing a small black lizard that scurried for cover.

Charlotte plucked restlessly at her bandages, sitting so close to me that the heat of her little body felt scorching. I made her drink frequently from our water bottle, filled fresh from the river this morning. When she refused to drink any more, I drained the bottle myself and laid it beside us in the grass.

A waft of breeze lifted a strand of Charlotte's hair, and I possessively tucked it back behind her ear. Trying to resist the urge to fuss over her, to baby her. *She'll need time*, Henry had cautioned last night. *But she'll be all right, Solaine. I promise.* He was right, Charlotte would recover from her ordeal in time. Once we returned to the normalcy of Elliot House, she'd blossom again. I only hoped Uncle Niall's strict ways wouldn't scare her back into her shell—

"Mama, look." Charlotte pointed towards the riverbank where Henry stood between the two horses.

He was feeding Shadowlark something from his palm, probably a wedge from one of Mrs Song's excellent carrots. Shadowlark took the treat with a whicker of thanks, but as Henry moved towards the little pony, offering in hand, Swanky nipped Henry on the arm and shied away.

"You little devil!" Henry said, rubbing his arm.

Swanky snorted and took off at a gallop, kicking up his small hooves, his shrill whinnies echoing in the still air like laughter.

Henry tossed the carrot wedge after the pony, probably hoping to lure him back, but his aim was so hopeless that the carrot struck the pony's broad rump. Swanky donkey-kicked again, letting out an enraged neigh. Then he charged in a straight line across the valley, finally disappearing into an expanse of long grass.

Charlotte's jaw dropped.

Then she threw back her head and burst out laughing. She laughed until tears seeped from the corners of her eyes, until she was almost breathless, the sound lifting into the blue sky like the pealing song of a kookaburra.

I stared at her, my own lips parting in shock.

Hardly believing my eyes.

Not once did her fingers slip up to cover her mouth. Not once did she drop her chin and try to hide her giggles. Her eyes didn't widen in fear as if she'd done something wrong.

She just laughed.

While I was marvelling, she stopped abruptly, her eyes lighting up.

I tore my gaze off her to see Henry stalking towards us, his worn boots kicking up puffs of ochre dust. He crouched in front of Charlotte, his broad-brimmed hat casting a shadow over his eyes.

"How about a riding lesson, little ladybird?"

"As long as you don't throw a carrot at *me*."

He ruffled her hair. "I was hoping no one saw that."

Charlotte beamed at him. "Mrs Song says Swanky nips all the time."

Henry made a performance of rubbing his arm. "Someone might have warned me. Come on, Little Five. Let's get you up on Shadowlark before that devil decides to come back and finish me off."

Charlotte sprang up laughing again, her small hand disappearing into Henry's big scarred one, his fingers curling protectively around hers. I melted a little, seeing the gentle way he bent towards her despite his impressive height. It seemed impossible that those same hands had once levelled a pistol at an unsuspecting mail coach.

"Watch her arm, all right?" I told him. "I don't want her crying all night again."

"We've a long ride to Glen Innes," Henry said over his shoulder, glancing back. "She needs to feel comfortable on the back of a horse." He tipped his hat at me, smiling crookedly, then he led my daughter down the slope a little way to where Shadowlark was grazing by the river, her black pelt gleaming like polished obsidian.

"Be careful!" I called after them.

Henry looked back. "We will, Miss Granger."

I slumped back against the rough bark, smiling.

Charlotte was alive. She was safe. I wanted to trail after them, stay close to her, but my bones felt suddenly rubbery, as if they were melting. I had been on edge for so long, my nerves humming with fear in the weeks since I lost her, that the sudden relief was like an opiate.

I'd only found her thanks to Henry.

Without him … well. That didn't bear thinking about. Henry had saved her, and in his way, he'd saved me too. Not just *saved* me, but brought me back to life.

My fingers rose to my lips, remembering the soft, hungry feel of his mouth on mine, and I smiled.

He wanted me. I knew that with a certainty that burned hotter than the morning air. He had risked everything—his freedom, his life—to help me. A known bushranger with a price on his head, a convict bolter who could be shot on sight.

And every time I let down my defences enough to let him

in … I heard the creak of a gallows rope, and saw Papa's eyes finding me across the courthouse yard. Felt my uncle's steely fingers burrowing into my shoulders, holding me in place.

Felt my heart shatter into a million fragments that I didn't know how to make whole again.

What if I let myself love Henry, and he died?

What if Charlotte grew to love him, too, only to lose him to the hangman's noose, or under a rain of police bullets, or worse—?

I'd never survive another heartbreak like that.

And I had no intention of inflicting that sort of grief on my child, either. She'd already endured too much in her short life.

Her delighted cry drew my attention down the sunbaked slope. She squealed again as Henry swung her up into the saddle. He showed her how to grip the pommel with both hands and hang on tight, then he walked the big horse slowly along the uneven ground, the reins loose in his hand.

Shadowlark seemed to sense the fragility of her little rider and lifted her legs with exaggerated care, keeping her head high and still, blowing softly through her velvety nostrils as her ears twitched towards Henry's voice.

Henry walked beside Charlotte, rather than leading out ahead of the horse. She kept glancing down at him, wide-eyed, her round face creased in concentration. He said something to her, and she smiled, tucking her chin down. I waited for her fingers to dart up over her smile, but she only beamed wider.

My eyes prickled, and a knot caught in my throat. Another small victory. Another piece of my little wisp returned to me.

More giggles erupted from near the river.

While Henry guided the big horse along the bank, he'd attracted an audience. Mrs Song's four girls had gathered nearby, watching him lead Charlotte around on the horse, clearly awaiting their turn. Their small faces were wide-eyed, their attention fixed on Henry, perhaps remembering their own fathers as they watched him hover protectively beside Charlotte—

Shadowlark's ears suddenly pricked forward, and she made a shrill warning sound, pawing at the ground.

A heartbeat later, Mrs Song's voice cut through the stillness, calling to her orphan girls in urgent Chinese. The girls jerked around, then the two older girls grabbed the younger ones by their hands and began to run towards the trees, their colourful dresses flapping like butterfly wings against the dusty landscape.

I got to my feet, shading my eyes against the glare, my heart beginning to pound.

"Mrs Song?"

She looked back, her face taut with fear, gesturing at the ridge behind me.

"Run, miss … run!"

I turned to see a dust cloud rising over the trees as a group of riders pounded down the valley wall and into the camp, the sun glinting off their weapons. I counted four riders, dust churning around them as their steeds thundered towards us.

"Mama!"

I spun around in time to see Henry gathering Charlotte from the horse, his movements swift but controlled. The little girl was crying, frightened shrieks pulsing from her as she buried her face in Henry's neck and clung to him, clutching his shirt.

He started running towards me, but three of the riders quickly surrounded him, their horses heaving and dusty, muzzles flecked white with foam. Two of the men drew weapons, taking deliberate aim at Henry's head.

I bolted down the slope towards them, my fingers fisted in my skirts, the parched earth uneven beneath my boots, my lungs burning. *They won't shoot while she's in his arms ... dear God, will they?* I drove forward, frantic to reach them, my skirts tangling around my legs, the ground lurching under me.

"Charlotte—!"

Another rider cut me off, his giant stallion almost knocking me down.

"Charlotte!" I screamed again, dodging around in front of the horse, desperate to reach my daughter. Henry's eyes met mine across the distance, and I saw something in them I'd never seen before—raw fear.

He was outlawed. They could shoot him on sight, claim the reward on his head. But his fear wasn't for himself—it was for the vulnerable child in his arms. He hunched forward, his large hand splayed on her small head, shielding her with his body.

Charlotte, my baby. My little wisp.

Would they wrench her away from me, deeming me unfit for letting an outlaw near her? Or would they open fire on Henry, careless of the precious bundle he held?

I almost buckled, my legs turning to rubber, my chest throbbing with the effort to breathe. I hadn't come all this way only to lose her again—or to watch Henry get gunned down for helping us.

As I raced down the slope towards them, the rider pounded after me, his stallion cutting me off again. He slid from his saddle and lunged for me, grunting as he caught my arm in strong fingers, yanking me around to face him.

My fists were already swinging as I turned on him, my only thoughts getting to Charlotte and somehow, impossibly, saving Henry too. Whoever these men were, bushrangers or bounty hunters, they wouldn't get to her so easily. This time, they'd have to kill me—

The man caught my fist in his hand. "For God's sake, Solaine."

I froze in shock and stared at him, blinking against the harsh sunlight—at a face I knew almost as well as my own.

"Uncle Niall?"

51

SOLAINE

"SOLAINE, THANK GOD." My uncle grimaced, as if finding me here was more of an annoyance than a relief. He searched my face, his fingers still gripping my arm. "Did he hurt you?"

"Who, Henry? Of course not!" I tried to pull away, but he held me fast. "Why are you here, Uncle Niall?"

"I might ask you the same thing." His eyes were cold, assessing. "Please tell me you didn't have anything to do with that criminal's escape? Deacon confessed you'd gone to see him ... after I expressly told you not to. Next thing we knew, you'd both vanished."

"I did what I had to do to find Charlotte." I studied his face, suspicion crawling up my spine. "How did you know where she'd be? Cold Mountain Creek is a long way from Elliotville."

"Someone tipped me off." His eyes darted away, taking in the abandoned camp. "A woman I know. She ran into you on the road north of Glen Innes. Said you and another fellow tried to steal her horses."

I frowned. "How do you know Mrs Landy?"

Uncle Niall drew back, eyeing me sharply. "Mrs Landy keeps me informed of the goings on at the Elliotville mine. She's one of my ... informants."

"She's also a convict woman and thief, and she tried to rob me. She told you I'd be at the Chinese camp?"

He nodded, his eyes straying to the group of horsemen on the riverbank surrounding Henry and my daughter, a deep crease carving his brow. "I see we're just in time."

"In time for what?"

"To save you and your daughter from that murderous fiend." His voice rang with triumph as he drew his pistol and started walking me down the slope towards them. I tried to wrench free again, but his strong fingers clawed into my flesh and held me in place. "I see we've caught the mongrel red-handed."

"Uncle, let me go." His fingers were digging into my arm, the tips burrowing clawlike into the bone.

"Not until this mess is sorted."

My old dark dread began to uncoil under my ribs, my chest heaving as a steel band tightened around my lungs. I was struggling to breathe.

"You've got it all wrong, Uncle. Henry helped me find her. He saved her life. Call off your men so I can explain." I twisted out of his grip, but he caught me again, wrenching me around to face him.

"I'm sure that's what he wants you to say," he ground through clenched teeth, his eyes dark with reproach. "But, my foolish young niece, he's not the saviour you make him out to be. He's an escaped convict who kidnapped your child, and then abducted you when you went to plead with him. Unless, of course, you went willingly?"

"Henry didn't take Charlotte. Please listen, Uncle." I was panting, stumbling along on rubbery legs, my gaze fixed on my daughter in Henry's arms. The horses surrounding them seemed restless, and the three men—Deacon among them, I now saw—all had their weapons trained on Henry. "Call them off!" I shouted. "If not for Henry, she'd be dead."

"Hawke's an outlaw, Solaine." Niall shook me so hard my teeth clacked together. "There's nothing more to say. You and the child can ride back with us, but not until we've taken care of things here."

"Taken care of things? You mean—" I gasped, my blood running cold as his meaning drove home. An outlaw like Henry was fair game. Any subject of the crown could shoot him dead without warning to apprehend him. The only thing stopping Niall's men from opening fire on Henry …

Was Charlotte.

I pivoted backwards and drove my free elbow into Uncle Niall's ribs, finally tearing free.

I raced down the slope towards Henry, my skirts tangling around my legs, my boots skating on the rubbly ground.

Henry's eyes found mine—warning me, begging me to stay back—but I couldn't. I reached for Charlotte, desperate to shield her from the guns, but she was crying, her little fists knotted in Henry's shirt, clinging to him like a burr.

So I stood by Henry's side, my shoulder pressed to his.

"Let the child go, Hawke." Niall's pistol tracked past me, steady on Henry's chest. "You're under arrest."

Henry's arms tightened protectively around Charlotte, then he lifted a hand in surrender.

"Put away the guns. I'll come quietly." His voice was calm, but I heard the strain beneath it. "Just lower your weapons, you're scaring the girl. She wants her mama, let me —" He tried to pry Charlotte's fingers loose, to set her on her feet. "Go to your mama, Charlotte."

She shrieked, burrowing more tightly against him, her eyes darting sideways to stare fearfully at Uncle Niall.

I placed my hand reassuringly on her back, letting her know I was near. She was trembling hard, her knobby spine bumping my palm. She'd grown so thin. Been so afraid. Weeks of fear, of feeling abandoned. All I wanted now was to get her to safety, cocoon her in my arms and protect her from any more anguish.

I positioned myself between Henry and my uncle, glaring at the mounted men—Deacon in particular. My father's old friend shifted uncomfortably under my stare, his shotgun loose in his hands, but he stayed in the saddle.

The man beside him raised his rifle higher, sighting down the barrel at Henry, dangerously close to my daughter's bent head.

"Call off the guns, Uncle Niall!" My voice cracked as the band around my ribs tightened. "Let Henry go, and I'll come home quietly. I promise. I'll do whatever you want. Just let him go."

"Hawke's the cause of this mess, Solaine. Let us deal with him as the law allows." Niall's jaw tightened with impatience. "Stop this foolishness and walk away."

"Step away, like he says." Henry's voice was rough beside me. "Solaine, I beg you."

I felt him shift, trying to angle his body to protect both Charlotte and me. He was preparing to surrender, to save us.

"Go," he said quietly. "It's all right."

Instead, I clutched his arm, my fingers tangling in his sleeve as I turned to face my uncle.

"Let us go. The three of us, together. We all go, or none of us do."

Henry's hand found my shoulder, his grip gentle despite the tremor I felt in his fingers. "Solaine, don't—don't give up everything for me. It's not worth it. I'll go with them. It's over."

"It's not over." I looked at him, willing him to understand. "You're worth everything to me. And to Charlotte. We're staying with you. As a family."

Something flickered in his eyes—hope, pain, determination all at once. But I could see him calculating, his gaze darting between me and the mounted men. He was going to do it. He was going to give himself up to save us. If he broke away from us now and tried to run, they'd gun him down.

In seconds, it could all be over.

"I'm sorry I pushed you away before." My throat tightened as I stared into his eyes, my hand slipping loose of his shirt to cup the side of his whiskery face, forcing him to look at me. "We want to come with you. Wherever you go. I thought I could survive anything—even returning to my old life at Elliot House—just knowing you're alive, out there in the world somewhere. But without you ..." My voice dropped to a whisper. "I'm lost."

"I love you," he whispered, pressing his face into my palm. "And I always will, even after my heart stops beating. But I can't let you give everything up like this. You have to think of Charlotte's future. Your future." Before I could stop him, he shoved me behind him and faced the rifles. Charlotte pressed her face into his chest, her small body shaking.

"You be a good girl and go to your mama." Henry's voice broke, his muscles tensed to run, even as he smoothed his scarred hand over Charlotte's trembling shoulders. "Your mama's going to take you home. Go with her now and close your eyes. Don't look back. Promise me?"

Charlotte peered into his face, blinking through her tears. Her fingers unclamped from his shirt, and she swiped them across her damp cheeks. Finally, she nodded.

"All right, Pa."

Henry's face hollowed in shock, and he swallowed hard, gently cupping Charlotte's head and kissing her crown. I slid my arm around Henry's shoulders and brought my palm to rest on his heart, holding him in place beside me.

"Don't run," I breathed beside his ear. "Don't make her watch you die."

Charlotte slithered to the ground and gripped my hand, her fingers tangling in my skirts as she buried her face against my leg. She gripped my hand so tightly I felt her small bones shifting against my palm.

Niall's men glanced at each other, then at my uncle.

"He's her father?" one of them asked.

"Of course not." Niall's snarl carried an edge of panic, the gun twitching in his white-knuckled grip. "The child is confused. Solaine," he barked at me, his face flushed with rage, "for the last time, move out of the way before you and the girl get caught in the fire."

Henry tried to detach from us, but I tangled my fingers in his waistcoat and held him more tightly.

"Don't run, Henry." My whisper was hoarse with pleading and terror. "Don't make Charlotte watch you die ... don't condemn her to a lifetime of nightmares. Please. Old Cap wouldn't want that."

"Solaine—"

"It crushed the life out of me being forced to watch my father die. And it crushed you seeing yours. Please don't sentence our girl to the same fate."

"It's me they want." His voice was even more ragged than mine. "You and Charlotte can have a good life. Better than what I could ever give you. Cover her face, Solaine. Don't let her see."

I shut my eyes and rested my forehead against his shoulder, gripping him more tightly as tears burned through my lids.

"She'll hear. She'll know. She loves you, Henry. I love you, too." I inhaled sharply and stared at him through the blur of my tears. "If you step away from us, I'll watch. That's a promise. And you know it'll destroy me."

His eyes dropped shut for an instant, his face as raw as it had been that night in the cave when he told me about his father.

He was ravaged, torn, I could see it in the shadows hollowing his cheeks and under his eyes. A wild thing caught in a trap, part of him wanting to run to save us, just as he'd run all those years ago from my family.

Only now, another part of him wanted to stand and fight.

"Please," I begged, my voice barely audible. "Don't let it all have been for nothing. Don't make us watch you die."

His eyes opened, his face hardening. "You know what I

am, Solaine. I'd kill for you and the girl. And I'd die for you in a heartbeat. But not while you're both in the crossfire."

Slowly, I nodded. "Pray it won't come to that."

I turned back to my uncle, shoulders squared despite the sickening lurch of my heart.

"I'm not moving, Uncle. Until I have your word that we all leave safely. You can keep my inheritance, everything. I only want my freedom."

The hired men shifted in their saddles. One lowered his rifle slightly.

"Mr Granger, we can't fire at Hawke while there's a woman and child in the way."

Deacon dismounted. The sound of his boots hitting the ground made everyone turn. He stowed his shotgun in the saddle holster, all eyes on him as he strode around behind the horses, passing Niall with a dark glare. Then he stood beside me, his arms crossed as he glowered at my uncle.

"Let them leave, Niall. You heard Miss Sol. Hawke saved Charlotte's life. It's the least we can do."

"For God's sake, Deacon!"

"My loyalty was always to Miss Solaine and her family," Deacon said, shifting closer to me. "Never to you, Niall."

His stance was firm, his hand hovering over the gun holstered on his hip. He glanced at me. "I'm sorry, Miss Sol. When you went missing that night, I felt responsible. I should have followed, even though you asked me not to. After Hawke's escape, I feared the worst. Feared that we'd lost you forever."

"You're here now, Deacon," I said under my breath. "That's what matters."

Uncle Niall let out a frustrated snarl. He tore off his hat, blinking rapidly against the glare as he dragged his forearm across his sweaty face, the sunlight turning strands of his ginger hair to bright copper.

As he jammed the hat back on his head, Henry tensed beside me.

"The fourth man."

I glanced at him. "What?"

Henry's eyes were hard, his face savage as he stared at Niall. "He's the one I saw paying the bushrangers on the old drovers road that day."

My mouth dropped open. "Are you sure?"

Henry nodded. "No question."

"But—" I clamped my jaw and stared at my uncle, the world tilting. Henry must be mistaken. He'd seen the men almost a month ago, only fleetingly. But the murderous look on his face, the hard accusation in his eyes, bore no trace of doubt.

Uncle Niall paid them to take her?

I gasped softly, staring back at my uncle. As I did, the words he'd snarled at me that day in the parlour rushed back. *You need a lesson in gratitude, my girl. So you understand how harsh life can be in the real world. Maybe then you'd truly appreciate what you have here with me.*

Other things, too.

His certainty that Charlotte was gone, that she was probably dead. The speed of his assumption that Henry Hawke was the abductor, so quick to pin the crime on a convict everyone would gladly blame.

"It was you," I said, taking a step towards him. "You paid those bushrangers to take her from me. And the torn remnant from her dress ... you *wanted* me to think they hurt her. That she was—"

"Don't be ridiculous." Niall's voice had gone tight. "Why would I do such a thing?"

"Henry saw you." My hands were shaking. "He saw you on the drovers road, handing over payment. Oh, Uncle ... how could you do that to her? To me?"

Niall's thin shoulders twitched. "You'd take the word of that criminal over your own flesh and blood?"

"After hearing years of lies from you? Yes, Uncle Niall. I absolutely would."

"Then you're more a fool than I thought."

"Do your friends know?" I raised my voice, addressing the mounted men. "Do they know you're the one responsible for Charlotte's kidnapping?"

Niall stiffened, glancing nervously at the others. "You're being ridiculous."

One of the men shifted uncomfortably. "Mr Granger, is this true? You paid to have the child taken?"

"Of course not." The smoothness was back in Niall's voice. "My niece is distraught, confused by this criminal's influence—"

As the first piece of the condemning puzzle settled into place, others began slotting in too.

My grip on Charlotte's hand tightened as I glared at my uncle. "You paid Mrs Landy to bring Charlotte here, didn't you? Planning to hide her at the camp until you were ready to collect her. But why?"

"He wanted to play the hero," Henry said. "Bring her back so he could control you again."

I cast back to that day in the parlour, remembering something he'd said about Mama. *I couldn't save your sweet mother from ruin, Solaine … but thank God I was there to save you. And now your child.*

I drew in a sharp breath. "He's right, Uncle. Isn't he? You knew how broken I'd be if I lost her … and how terribly grateful I'd be if you brought her back. So grateful that I'd happily promise to stay at Elliot House forever. You'd have complete control of my inheritance—"

Deacon growled under his breath. "Is that true, Niall?"

"She's lying," Niall bit out the words. "There's no witness. No proof that any of this ever happened."

Deacon shuffled closer to my side. "Now that I think of it, you seemed pretty certain we'd find Charlotte here. It wasn't just a hunch, was it?"

Niall shifted uncertainly. "Mrs Landy claimed she'd been passing through the camp a week ago, saw a little dark-haired girl that she swore was Charlotte."

"She was more than just passing through, wasn't she, Uncle?" I gathered Charlotte tighter, my heart thundering like a runaway horse. "Your friend Mrs Landy spent nearly two weeks at this camp, with Charlotte practically a prisoner in her tent. When the camp was attacked, Charlotte ran away in terror. Mrs Landy fled, abandoning her here."

One of the men glanced at Uncle Niall.

"The heck, Granger. Is this true?"

"Of course not. My niece is lying."

I stood taller, squaring my shoulders. "If it's a lie, then why did you travel all this way yourself? You could have alerted the police, told them your suspicions. I'm sure if they were to question your good friend Mrs Landy, she'd confess to anything. For the right price."

Niall's jaw worked, and he took a shaky step closer. His hand shook, the muzzle of his gun wavering as he trained it on Henry's face.

"By the time they get to Mrs Landy, it'll be too late. At least, for Hawke. So step away from him, unless you want his blood all over you."

"Easy, Niall." Deacon's voice was quiet but deadly. "Lower your weapon, and walk away. The little girl has already lost one father. You prepared to rob her of another?"

"If it means upholding the law, then yes." Niall's voice trembled in anger. "I most definitely am."

One of the hired men lowered his gun, horror spreading across his face as his gaze snagged on something behind us. I didn't dare glance away, but a moment later, Mrs Song joined us, the two older orphans holding her hands. The littlest girls ran to Henry and wrapped their arms around his legs.

The man swore. "What the devil, Granger ... more children? Did you kidnap them as well?"

"I never—"

"I'm done." He holstered his weapon with a sharp movement, clicking his tongue and jerking on the reins. As he rode away, the other man lowered his rifle. "This isn't right, Granger. You said we were rescuing a kidnapped girl, not ..."

"Not what?" I lifted my chin, catching his eyes. "Not executing a man in front of little children?"

"I didn't sign on for kidnapping kids, Granger." The second man reined his horse around. "We're done here." He nudged his heels into its flanks and rode after the other man. Within moments, only their dust remained.

Niall stood alone, the pistol clutched loosely in his hand.

He ground out a ragged sigh and dropped his arm by his side.

"I never wanted your inheritance, Solaine." His voice had changed, gone bitter and almost resigned. "It was always you. You and the girl. You're all I have left of Lottie. While you're in my care, it feels like she's still with me."

"I'm not my mother, Uncle Niall."

He straightened imperiously, sunlight streaking his bony face. "Oh, but you so nearly are, Solaine. You look like her, and your voice, your mannerisms ... you bring her to life, my dear. And now in Charlotte I'm beginning to see the merest glimmers, too."

I shook my head at the man who had once been my trusted guardian, but now seemed a stranger.

"Mama left the Granger family for a reason, Uncle. She hated being controlled, confined. Kept as a beautiful trophy in a gilded cage. I understand that now. Understand what drove her. Because that same thing drives me too."

"If only she'd stayed." Uncle Niall's gaze sharpened on my face. "She might still be alive today."

I felt Henry tense beside me. Charlotte's weight was warm against my side. All this talk of my mother was doing something strange to my insides. Bringing something to the surface. It wasn't nostalgia or grief—but something infinitely more terrifying.

"You want me, Uncle Niall? You can have me." I kept my voice steady. "Let Henry go, and I'll return to Elliot House with Charlotte. I'll be reserved and quiet, the perfect niece. And I'll never speak of this again."

Uncle Niall froze, his eyes lighting up, his ruddy face

gleaming under the hot sun. He thumbed back his hat brim, his face slackening with relief. "You'll come home?"

"But you'll have to trust me," I continued, my voice hardening. "Every day. Every night. You'll have to trust that I won't poison your tea, won't slit your throat while you sleep. Won't run the moment your back is turned."

I stepped forward, my chin raised.

"Because, despite what you drummed into my head for all those years, Uncle Niall, I am my mother's daughter. And my father's. I'm unpredictable. Reckless. I didn't choose to love Henry, but I do. And I'll never stop trying to get back to him."

The light died in my uncle's eyes. Slowly, bitterly, he holstered his weapon.

"You're right, Solaine. You are just like your mother, after all." His voice was hollow. "I only hope you survive longer than she did."

"My mother loved my father. She was happy with him." I held his gaze. "You lied about that, too, Uncle. But Henry remembered what my family was really like—and he helped me remember them too."

Niall slumped. "Where will you go?"

"As far from you as I can."

I felt Henry's hand find mine, his fingers warm and strong. His other hand moved across to rest gently on Charlotte's head. Together, we turned our backs on Niall and walked towards the camp.

Deacon and Mrs Song fell in beside us, the orphan girls spilling ahead like spring lambs, their bright dresses bobbing, their small boots kicking up dust.

At the edge of the camp, I looked back.

Uncle Niall stood alone on the riverbank, solitary in the harsh midday light, still watching us.

52

HENRY

As we made our way through the wreckage of the miners' camp, a prickle of tension rippled across my shoulders. I glanced back at Niall Granger, standing alone on the riverbank. His horse had wandered off, and he clutched his hat in both hands, gazing after us.

He made me uneasy, staring like that.

I fell back a step, letting Solaine and Charlotte walk ahead. Mrs Song was nearby on the other side of Deacon, her girls spilling ahead like a flock of bright butterflies.

Deacon narrowed his eyes at my face. His lips parted, and for a moment I thought he had something to say, but he just shook his head and kept walking.

Solaine looked over her shoulder and caught my eye, her face flushed and serious. The corners of her lips flicked up, not quite a smile. But it was there in her eyes, the warmth and closeness we'd found together that night beside the river. Radiating from her with even more force now that she'd found her daughter.

I caught up with them again, and Charlotte slipped her hand into mine without looking at me. Natural and without hesitation, as if she did it every day.

A smile ghosted over my lips.

Pa. I stole a glance at the little girl walking solemnly beside me. And then at the woman holding her hand. *She loves you, Henry. I love you, too.* Right then, the pulsing mess in my chest raced so hard, I'd have sworn it was ready to burst straight through my ribcage and fall dead at my feet. *She called me Pa.* I shook my head, looking down at my shoes.

Was it possible that I somehow had a family now?

That I … *belonged?*

The wardens on the island used to say I belonged in chains with all the other dregs, cutting and carting sandstone blocks, digging pits. For all of those desperate years of bitterness, I thought they were right—because the hollow ache of my worthlessness dogged me morning till night and then it haunted my dreams.

But that man was gone. Already dead and buried the moment I'd seen Solaine on the street that first time. In his place walked someone I barely recognised. A man who could hold his head high. A man who mattered to someone.

A man with a family.

We want to come with you, Henry … without you, I'm lost.

It still felt off-kilter, this new skin. But I was looking forward to getting used to it. Working every day to deserve it. To make it truly mine. I was done punishing the world. Done with the past. All that mattered to me now was the future.

The chasm—the gaping hole torn into my soul that long-ago night on the riverbank—was knitting itself back together. I wasn't a loose end anymore. I had a purpose. The things I'd secretly been praying for all my life were no longer an impossible dream.

All right, Pa.

A rush of soft warmth swept through me, and I squared my shoulders, standing taller. Making a silent promise to protect Solaine and Charlotte, come what may, with my life if I had to—

The back of my neck prickled.

Three things happened simultaneously.

Shadowlark made a shrill warning sound, and Mrs Song halfway turned and looked over her shoulder, an almost inaudible gasp catching in her throat. In the silent beat that followed, I heard the unmistakable click of a cylinder locking into full-cock—

I spun on my heel, almost colliding with old Deacon as I slid the gun from his holster and shoved past him.

Niall Granger had trailed after us, his hat gone, his gingery hair gleaming copper in the harsh sunlight. His sunburned cheeks shone wet, and he was shaking so violently that the muzzle of the pistol gripped in his hand was swaying from side to side.

I cocked Deacon's weapon and fired off a single round.

Niall staggered backwards, then dropped to one knee and toppled sideways, his pistol slithering harmlessly to the ground beside him. His left hand clutched his chest, blood quickly soaking the front of his waistcoat.

Solaine whirled around.

She let go of her daughter's hand and took a step, then

started running to where her uncle lay, Deacon close on her heels.

"Uncle Niall!" She fell to the ground beside him. "No, no! Oh Henry, why—?"

I left Charlotte with Mrs Song and the other children and walked over.

Niall lay on his back, both hands clutched to his sternum, his chest rising and falling as the blood bloomed in a bright spurt across his expensive grey waistcoat. His eyes rolled towards me, and he snarled.

"Hawke, you'll hang for this."

I strode closer. "That's for Jim Beaumont," I told him gruffly. "And for making his daughter watch him die."

"Henry." Solaine turned to me, raw fear in her eyes. "What have you done? You promised—"

"I said I'd kill for you, Solaine. In a heartbeat." I nudged the uncle's leg with my foot. "Hear that, Granger? You come near my family again, threaten them in any way, and I'll blow off more than the tip of your finger."

Solaine tore her eyes off me and started fussing over her uncle. She lifted first one hand from his heaving chest and then the other—and gasped.

My bullet had blown the tip of Niall's pointer finger completely away, the small stump at the knuckle dripping blood onto the ground, soaking the side of his waistcoat.

"Oh, Uncle. It's just ... I thought you were—"

Tears spilled down her face. She slumped onto the ground, still holding her uncle's bleeding hand.

Mrs Song appeared with a roll of bandages and silently bound the ruined finger, firmly securing it to the other fingers, her dark eyes darting to Niall's face.

"Hold it near heart," she instructed, then her voice softened. "Bleeding will stop soon. Doctor live in Cold Mountain Creek, only short ride. One, maybe two hour. He fix for you."

Solaine helped Niall to his feet and brushed off his clothes. She retrieved his hat, placing it on his head, and then stood back, swiping at her tears. She used the sleeve of her blouse to mop Niall's face, too.

He went to pull away, but she tugged him back to face her.

"I know you miss my mother," she breathed, her voice only slightly strained. "I know how much you loved her. I'm sorry she broke your heart by leaving home to marry my father. But she truly loved him, Uncle. If only you'd trusted her, forgiven her. Then you wouldn't have completely lost her."

Niall nodded, holding his injured hand up against his heart as Mrs Song had instructed. He suddenly looked old and frail, shaken to the core, his hat askew, his skin chalky beneath a sheen of sweat.

"I am sorry, Solaine. For everything." His bony shoulders trembled as he squinted into her face. "I hope one day you can find it in your heart to—"

"It'll take time, Uncle Niall. God help me, though. After what you did—taking my child away from me, putting her in danger like that. I almost died of fear and grief. Not to mention how close Charlotte came to being crushed to death when the tunnel collapsed on her ..." Her voice broke on the last words, and she glanced across at me, her lips trembling. "If it hadn't been for Henry—"

Our eyes locked, and she stared at me intensely for a moment, as though searching for something, confirmation maybe, in my face. I kept my gaze steady, letting her take whatever she needed, and after a heartbeat, her shoulders seemed to unlock.

She palmed the tears off her cheeks, looking back at Niall. "But I won't hold my grudge forever, Uncle. You can count on it. I won't let anger and prejudice poison my soul the way you let it poison yours."

Niall hung his head and nodded. "I wish you well then, my dear."

Solaine blew out a long, trembling breath, her entire body shuddering, as if she'd been holding it in for decades. "Anyway," she added after a moment. "Without your crime, Henry would be dead. And I'd still be trapped inside your gilded cage, yearning for a life I believed beyond my reach."

53

SOLAINE

"A NEW LIFE," I whispered, taking Henry's hand as we stood at the edge of the camp, the sun burning overhead like a fiery coin. I leaned against his side. "The three of us together. It sounds like a dream."

Henry nodded, gripping my fingers gently, firmly, as if afraid to let them go. He stood rigidly beside me, as if braced for another attack, staring at the far ridge until the dark speck of my uncle finally disappeared into the trees.

Henry watched until the dust settled.

Then he turned away.

"Niall will alert the traps the minute he arrives in Cold Mountain Creek. We might need to prepare for another standoff."

I studied the ridge for a while, then shook my head. "Somehow, I don't think he'll mention us to anyone."

"Oh?"

"He won't risk them discovering his part in the kidnapping. He'd lose his job. Or worse, be publicly disgraced. Besides ..." I gathered the loose strands of my hair and shoved them into my pins. "You shot off the tip of his finger, Henry."

He stared at me, refusing to speak, his eyes hard.

He'd looked at me that same way the night I told him Uncle Niall had forced me to watch my father die. *His fingers were like steel claws, burrowing into my flesh, hurting me ... the next day, my shoulders were black and blue—*

I sighed. "I'm not sure he'll make the connection, though. Uncle Niall is a clever man, and he has his good points—"

"Coulda fooled me."

"Luckily for us, bravery and self-sacrifice are not among them. We won't hear from him again, Henry. You can count on it."

Henry mulled this over for a moment. Then his shoulders relaxed, and the lines of strain in his face softened. He looked at me, his eyes dark and possessive as he drew my knuckles to his lips and kissed them.

"Did you mean what you said?" he asked, nodding back towards the riverbank. "About coming with me?"

I cupped his whiskery face, searching his eyes, the blue irises flecked with shards of silvery grey.

"I meant every word."

"Even the part where you'll never stop trying to get back to me?"

"Yes."

"And that other bit about being lost without me."

"That too."

He narrowed his eyes, rocking back on his heels, smiling

as he squinted up at the sky. "You also mentioned something about not choosing to love me, but you do …"

"Especially that."

He growled softly, and his arms slipped around my waist, tugging me against him. He rested his forehead against mine, his breath stirring the loose tendrils of hair at my temple.

"Tell me again, Miss Granger."

"I love you, Henry."

"God help me, Solaine. I'll never tire of hearing it." His lips brushed my brow, his breath warm on my skin. "I swear, I've loved you from the moment I saw you on the street that day in Elliotville. Looking fragile and mighty, all at once. A lioness. When you smiled, I felt it wrap around my heart and snare me like prey."

I smiled, my breath catching. "You sound like my father. He was a bit of a poet, you know."

"I used to think so, too. But now I understand." The side of his mouth quirked up into a lopsided smile. "He wasn't a poet, my sparrow. He was just a man in love—"

"Mama!"

We broke apart and looked around, my heart nearly flying out of my chest.

Charlotte was waving to us from beside Mrs Song's cart. She and the other girls were loading supplies onto the wagon tray, while Deacon helped Mrs Song lift the heavy harness collar over Swanky's head. The pony shied away, snorting crossly, until Deacon managed to distract him with a carrot wedge.

We joined them on the other edge of the camp.

"Where will you go?" I asked Mrs Song. "Do you have family at another camp?"

She tipped her head towards the girls. "They my only family now, miss. We go west. Maybe other side of Cold Mountain Creek."

"What will you do there?"

"Grow new garden, find work as cook." She seemed thinner after this morning's confrontation, her shoulders hunched, her eyes guarded. "Maybe wash tailings for other miner. Anything to keep my girls together."

Deacon finished attaching the harness pole to the cart and returned, dusting his hands. By the way he was cautiously eyeing Mrs Song, a frown rippling his forehead, I could tell he'd been listening. Closely.

I shaded my eyes and stared west towards the distant hills. "It's very hot and dusty out that way, Mrs Song. You'll struggle to grow much out there from what I've heard."

She patted my arm, smiling kindly. "We be all right, Miss Solaine. I happy Little Five find her mama." She looked at Henry, her smile lighting up her face. "And her pa."

Henry's smile was crooked as he looked at his boots, then he glanced past the cart to where the five girls all huddled together, sifting through some pots that had been smashed in the raid. Charlotte and the smaller girls were sorting brightly coloured shards, while Tildy and Jane had their heads together over a small wooden box they'd found.

Deacon shifted beside me, his shadow rippling over the uneven ground at his feet. He'd always been a man of few words, but I could tell something was brewing.

"Mrs Song," he said carefully, taking off his hat as though preparing to propose marriage. "To be honest, I'm a dreadful cook. I can boil water, but that's the extent of my skills. I don't suppose you'd consider coming to work for me?"

She blinked at him, her dark eyes unreadable, almost fearful.

I blinked, too. "Deacon, do you really mean to return to Elliot House?" I tried to keep my voice steady, but the words trembled with disappointment. "After everything that just happened, you'd—"

"No, Miss Sol. I mean … wherever it is I end up now that I no longer work for your treacherous uncle."

I wilted, a breath escaping. "Then you'll come with us, of course. All of you, including Mrs Song and the girls." I looked at Henry. "Won't they?"

Henry seemed as relieved as I was, his shoulders rippling as he eased out a sigh. "She's right, Mrs Song. It'd break Charlotte's heart to say goodbye to the girls now. She's already been through enough."

"Then it's settled," I said, smiling at Mrs Song. "That is, if you'd like to join us?"

Tears filled her eyes, and when she lifted her sleeve to mop her face, I pulled out my hanky and gave it to her. Her eyes shone as she nodded, her gaze darting to Deacon and then Henry, then me again.

"We like very much."

AN HOUR LATER, we were following a wide dirt track that led up and around the ridge we'd ridden down a few days before.

Insects buzzed around us, and magpies warbled as they

soared and swooped overhead in the warm air.

It seemed like a lifetime had passed since Henry emerged from the rubble of the collapsed mine tunnel with Charlotte in his arms. So much had changed. Before arriving at the camp, I'd felt so alone. Now it seemed I had somehow taken possession of a rather sizeable family.

Charlotte rode in the saddle with me, while Henry walked by our side. Mrs Song's small cart rattled behind us, Mrs Song in the bench seat with Jane, Tildy in the back to supervise Nellie and Gert to make sure no one toppled overboard in their excitement.

As the sun rose higher, the cartwheels rattled and creaked. Swanky snorted dust from his nostrils, his hooves thudding softly on the packed earth. Shadowlark twitched her ears and shook her mane, her head swinging back from time to time to look at Henry.

Deacon rode behind us all, sometimes catching up with Mrs Song for a chat, or answering questions the children tossed back at him, other times playing his harmonica softly as we rode.

"Mama?" Charlotte twisted around to peer up at me, her brown eyes shining from beneath the straw hat Mrs Song had given her.

"Yes, love?"

"Where are we going?"

I released one of the reins, winding my arm around her shoulders. "We're going to find our new home."

Henry glanced up and caught my eye, thumbing back his hat brim so I could see his eyes. What I saw there warmed my bones and made me smile.

Charlotte yawned sleepily. "Not Uncle Niall's?

"No, my wisp. We're going to find our own grand house in the woods, surrounded by paper daisies and rock ferns, nodding orchids and shivery grass."

Her eyes widened. "Like Marigold's house?"

I smiled, remembering our fairytale about the meadow glade and the wicked convict who came along and stole Marigold away. I glanced at Henry, making a mental note to amend our story next time I told it.

Yes," I said, beaming. "Exactly like Marigold's house."

Soon she was asleep, a warm weight in my arms, her hat fallen forward, shading her from the sun.

Henry smiled up at me, tipping his head at Charlotte.

"She called me Pa."

I laughed softly under my breath. Lord, the pride in his face, the wild, joyful light in his eyes. But then my heart twinged as I remembered exactly why it mattered so much to him. *Things we've secretly prayed for but never dreamed possible.*

I flicked him a look from the corner of my eye.

"Don't let it go to your head, Mr Hawke."

"Too late, Miss Granger." He reached up and brushed a bug off Charlotte's hat. "I'm her pa now, and always will be. For as long as I'm alive, and then maybe even from beyond." He dragged off his hat, pushing his fingers through his hair as he looked up at me, the bright sunlight glinting like glass shards in his eyes. "I promise I'll always watch over her, Solaine. Over both of you."

54

SOLAINE

ONE YEAR LATER

THE AFTERNOON SUN blazed over our farm, turning everything it touched to honey and amber. I stood at the horseyard fence, leaning my forearms on the rail, breathing the sweet air as sunlight warmed my skin.

In the yard, Charlotte was perched on Swanky's saddle with her back straight, her little teeth nipping her lip in concentration as she listened to Henry's quiet guidance.

"Hold the reins loose," he said. "Thread them past your littlest finger, then hold it here between your thumb and pointer finger, like this. That's right, you've got it. Now you can gently guide him to go wherever you'd like."

Charlotte had grown confident in the saddle, her face

flushed, her dark hair gleaming like the coat of the pony she rode, her plaits bobbing behind her as Henry led Swanky in a wide circle.

Swanky's ears twitched forward at the happy shrieking that filled the air—Charlotte's giggles mixed with squeals from Gert and Nellie, who sat in the grass nearby making daisy chains. Being among the other horses had calmed the little pony. These days, he hardly ever nipped and had become utterly devoted to Charlotte.

Shadowlark grazed beyond the fence, her flanks gleaming black as polished jet, her tail flicking lazily as she looked up and watched Charlotte's progress around the yard. An equally black foal grazed by her side, teetering on spindly legs.

Shadowlark had filled out since we'd been here, blossoming even more after her foal was born. She was a treasure, helping to settle the older horses when they first arrived, and listening to my rantings whenever I felt the need, her ears twitching and her hairy lips nibbling my fingers. Comforting me, the way she had the night I'd fled from the cedar getters' hut with Henry.

The night Henry had first cracked the shell around my heart and given me hope in the midst of my darkness. *The ones we love sometimes find their way back to us, Miss Granger.*

My attention drifted across the farm we'd built together.

Beautiful breeding mares dotted the near paddock, their coats glossy in the afternoon light. Another paddock stretched into the distance, where a few of our older horses grazed peacefully. Beyond them, the vast sky soared endlessly, breezy clouds skimming the distant forested hills.

It was exactly as I'd once pictured it.

Only better. Infinitely better.

I turned to look back at our farmhouse. It wasn't grand like Elliot House, but it was ours. White-painted boards, a wide verandah, window panes that caught the sun and threw it back in brilliant flashes. Behind the house, Deacon and Mrs Song had built a large garden with vegetables and flowers, and broad pathways meandering through it.

The two older girls were helping Mrs Song dig up turnips and load them into a barrow. When Deacon emerged from the stables and walked towards them, the girls ran up to greet him, their voices carrying in the still air.

Deacon bent and picked a flower from the garden, getting a loud scolding from Mrs Song in Chinese for his trouble, but when he presented it to her with a flourish, she cut off mid-sentence and accepted it with a shy smile.

I smiled too.

In another life, I'd have spent such a day cooped up indoors, attending to my uncle's accounts or helping to plan his busy schedule.

A lot had changed since then.

This morning, I had ridden around the farm perimeter with Henry to check the fences, and then I'd given the children their lessons. After lunch, I vanished into a secluded corner of the garden to capture Mrs Song's exotic ginger flowers with my brushes and paints.

"All right, little ladybird." Henry's voice pulled my attention back. "That's enough for today. You've earned your rest."

He lifted Charlotte from the saddle, and she took off running towards Gert and Nellie, her boots kicking up puffs of dust. The three girls collapsed in a giggling heap, then ran off to the bushland at the back of the house to climb trees.

"Watch out for snakes," I yelled after them.

Henry appeared at my side, his eyes glowing. "The way those girls chatter and shriek all the time, no snake in his right mind will go anywhere near them."

I nudged my elbow into his ribs. "Snakes are highly dangerous and not to be taken lightly," I scolded. "You of all people should know that."

He nuzzled my neck, his fingers dancing over my own ribs, tickling. "You're right, Miss Granger. I should never joke about snakes. What were your words that night I was bitten? *You absolute scoundrel ... I'd rather kiss a toad.*"

I twisted out of his grip, laughing. "Well, I'm Mrs Hawke now, heaven help me. If I recall, you weren't bitten at all. And I stand by my claim. You are a scoundrel."

"But you'd still like to kiss me?"

"Hmm." I turned in his arms and caught his handsome face between my hands, pressing my lips lightly to his. "Always."

"How did I get so lucky?" He pulled me closer against him, his breath warm against my ear. "There I was in chains, a despicable convict doomed to a life of crime. I swam across that harbour, hoping the sharks would get me rather than end up back on the island. From that dark place, freedom seemed as distant as a star. Then I met you—"

"And quickly declared that I was worse punishment than solitary confinement and the cat-o'-nine-tails combined."

He huffed against my neck, his fingers tightening around my waist. "Ah, well. You did shoot at me and steal my horse.

But, love—" His voice turned husky, sending a delicious shiver down my spine as he slid both hands around my waist and drew me closer, his whiskers tickling as his lips brushed my ear. "It was worth it."

"Even the part where you took a bullet for me?"

"Especially that part. Having you fuss over me was like being in heaven."

He trailed off for a moment, and I felt the tension in his body, the weight of words he was gathering.

"The only future I saw for myself back then was grim at best. Being on the run, stealing what I could, knowing one day my luck would run out." He drew back slightly, cupping my face with a tenderness that still made my breath catch. His thumbs traced my cheekbones, his blue eyes searching mine. "But after a few weeks with you, everything changed. I became someone else. Someone better."

I kissed his calloused palm, smiling against his fingers.

"Take a look around, Henry." I pulled out of his clutches and took his hand, hauling him along beside the horse rails.

The wood was warm beneath my trailing fingers, the afternoon heat still trapped in the timber. I waved my free hand at the open spaces surrounding us, at the horses and the gardens and the endless sky.

"This is all ours. All this freedom. All this beautiful space." I turned to face him, still holding his hand. "Without you, though, none of it would have been possible."

He shook his head, a flush rising in the hollows of his cheeks—that shy look he still got sometimes when I praised him, as if he couldn't quite believe he deserved it.

"You'd have had your farm one day, Solaine. It was just a matter of time."

"No, it wasn't." I stepped closer, needing him to understand. "I would have stayed with Uncle Niall. He'd have found some other way to make me stay. He was too clever, and I was too ..." I searched for the right words. "Too afraid of what I'd lose if I fought back. I needed you to help me remember who I was. Remember myself."

Henry's expression softened. "You were always there, Solaine. Maybe buried under the surface sometimes, but always there."

I leaned against the fence, the rough wood pressing into my spine. "When I was most afraid, you gave me courage. When I lost hope, you helped me regain it. This might have once been my dream, but without you, I'd still only be dreaming about it."

I reached out and tangled my fingers in the front of his shirt, feeling his heartbeat quicken beneath my knuckles. I drew him closer, until barely a breath separated us.

"Henry, you've given me the life I've always secretly prayed for but never really believed possible."

His eyes bloomed darkly, the blue turning stormy for a moment. But then a smile—the one that was wolfish and devastating and entirely mine—curved his lips, and my legs turned to jelly.

"Solaine," he murmured hoarsely. He slid one hand to the nape of my neck, his calloused palm cradling my head. His other hand nestled warm against the side of my face. "God help me, I'm so unbecomingly happy right now."

"Me too," I laughed, and then his lips were on mine, crushing and tender all at once, his arms surrounding me completely. I threaded my fingers through his hair, silky and warm from the sun, and drew him even closer, until there was no space left between us at all.

I closed my eyes, letting the sun's bright rays fall warm on my lids as the world around us turned to gold.

ABOUT THE AUTHOR

Anna Romer is an internationally bestselling Australian author of mystery and romance, both historical and contemporary, with elements of paranormal woven in—ghosts, haunted houses, and fairytales. She's also working on a stockpile of dark romantic fantasy novels.

She lives on Australia's beautiful eastern coast, and when she's not writing she's a keen gardener, knitter, bushwalker and conservationist.

If you'd like to join Anna's newsletter for updates and deals, you can sign up at: https://annaromer.com/pages/newsletter

ALSO BY ANNA ROMER

Maeve & the Wolf

The Ghost of Briar Rose

Lyrebird Hill

Under the Midnight Sky

Thornwood House

Beyond the Orchard